# MISFIT'S IKONA

## STORIES OF UNBELONGING AND STRAY HUMANS

### ARAYAN APATRID

# Contents

*To our parents,*

On n'habite pas un pays, on habite une langue.
Une patrie, c'est cela et rien d'autre.
(One doesn't reside in a country, one resides in a language.
A homeland, this is what it is and nothing else.)
Emil Cioran, Aveux et Anathèmes, 1987

Si le monde était un seul état, New York serait sa capitale.
(If the World were a single state, New York would be its capital.)
*Napoléon Bonaparte, early 1950's*

Memento, homo, quia pulvis es, et in pulverem reverteris.
(The ultimate belonging, man? Look no further, to dust you shall return.)
Genesis 3:19, translated by a Jamaican cabby in Brooklyn, 2022

*Dear Reader,*

What you're holding in your hands is a piece of organic writing, cultivated with care and free from editorial pesticides.

Each sentence was nurtured in the wild soil of creativity, far from the monoculture mindset of the traditional publishing industry.

The characters in the story are all free-range, depicted truthfully, without a sensitivity reader chopping off their genuineness.

The narrative is raw and unpasteurized, with no artificial sweeteners or preservatives added.

So please go ahead and savor this farm-to-book experience. After all, authenticity is still legal.

Bon appétit,

*Arayan*

# CESSATION OF BELONGING

Our family ceased to belong over a century ago.

The previous Empire decided to come down on us on two occasions: first when the Crimean War scattered my mother's side like leaves before an unrelenting wind; and then again, a few decades later, in the Caucasus, during the October Revolution, when my father's side was swept into other people's chaos, with their old world shattered in an instant.

My Mom's folks all made it to a safe haven in another Empire not so far away that still had a bit of life left in it. On my Dad's side those who were fortunate enough to escape landed in the very last years of that same Empire and found themselves constitutionally condemned to unhappiness in a nascent republic. The unfortunate ones, well, I thought a lot about them many years later when I was living in Africa, that continent of countless unnamed graves.

We ceased to belong, I was saying, over a century ago and a mere two generations of sedentary existence after our uprooting did not change anything regarding this state of affairs.

We ceased to belong, despite the adoption of a new mother tongue by the very first generation of *regretfully-monoglot-born* offspring. Every single one of them was unable to pronounce a single word in the previous mother tongue and they would then be educated in French to complicate matters even more.

We ceased to belong, despite the reluctant adoption of a *local* family name when some president decided, in the early days of that new republic with a lowercase "r", that *from now on* every citizen had to have a family name.

We ceased to belong and we were blessed, or cursed, depending on the perspective and the circumstances, with an enduring inability for bonding: to a geography, to a national identity or to any other element of *worldview* that was self-proclaimed to be superior to others. We just remained untethered, a thread forever fraying in a world that wrongfully demanded we stitch ourselves into its fabric.

The birth of this contemporary account on *burdensome unbelongings* was triggered by one of those wearing transatlantic calls. You know them calls, transatlantic or not, of the variety that nonchalantly files down one's lust for life. The ones that envelop the subject life in more uncertainty and ambiguity than one needs. One such call was the trigger, one semi-blown fuse on a quayside, one somewhat-expected last straw on the roaming misfit of a camel's overburdened back.

Contemporary as the account may be, it is a nontemporal story. And focus on the meanderings of an individual destiny as it may, it is the story of many endearing stray humans well beyond the narrator. Dare I say, of stray humans superior to the narrator in their wanderings and quests. Therefore, commitment is hereby made to avoid undue navel-gazing beyond the exploration of an array of enduring existential helplessness.

So, the following are stories of people who have been émigrés, migrants, exiles, drifters, immigrants, expats and other uncategorized rootless subjects, with self-perpetuating *de-soiling* processes of varying distances and durations, each carrying the weight of their own unique dislocation. Of people who understood that only by risking everything could they hope to carve out their fair share of life; one that, though perhaps never fully understood or completed, would at least always be their own.

Of people, mainly, who were willing to take many risks, except the risk of letting life pass them by in sedentary comfort and seeing the poem of their life uncompleted at the dusk of their existence.

# RUMMAGE WITHOUT SALE

"What are we supposed to do with the icon?" asks the tired voice on the *oriental* end of that transatlantic call, while I am admiring the seamanship and maneuvering skills of the captain who docks his ferry without touching the fender piles despite the strong lateral current of the East River. Actually, my brother doesn't exactly say it like that; he says *"qu'est-ce qu'on fait avec cette putain d'icône?"*, which would require a less digestible translation. More precisely, he pronounces the last word of that French sentence as an ostentatiously non-French *ikona,* because this is what that object is called in our first mother tongue and how we always referred to it in the family.

That orthodox *ikona* must have fallen off the back of an ecclesiastic truck of quite unorthodox intentions at some point during the last two centuries, at some unknown place within one of the two former Empires where our family tried to live. Neither of these two empires has really led what could be called a tranquil existence, spitting out more than thirty nation-states from their deathbed. Most of those nation-states have highly counterintuitive histories, borders and demographic compositions. Therefore, I sincerely neither know nor can know when and under what circumstances that icon of unfortunate trajectory came into my family's possession. By the way, I also don't want to sound as if I cared a lot about the exact circumstances. Yes, it was part of the paintings and pictures that adorned the walls of our family apartment during my childhood but my main attachment to it is purely on the aesthetic side, not even on the nostalgic and certainly not on the religious side.

I remember the praying hands of Saint Mary, her gaze eternally lifted towards the heavens, and the little silver swords that adorned the icon, three on her left side and four on her right. Each sword was delicately stitched onto the canvas, with the ones on the left side still intact, untouched by time or misfortune. The ones on the right had vanished, they must have fallen off the back of yet another unorthodox truck. I often wondered, as a child does over the most absurd things, if those swords had been melted down or rather sold piece by piece on some shadowy silverware black market. The marks they had left behind were unmistakable: faint outlines pressed onto the fabric, a quiet testament to what was lost on the journey, by the *ikona* and by my family.

Once the apartment of our childhood had shed its souls, my brother took it upon himself to rid the space of its material possessions. He gathered everything of emotional value, though what that truly meant was open to interpretation, and planned to carry it all to the place where he now resides. "This is extremely urgent", he was claiming, before the anticipated earthquake strikes in some uncertain future. What could possibly be so extremely urgent on a geological timescale, I wondered. More than an earthquake, I was rather wary of an unknown calamity of human origin which would strike in some very *certain* future, in line with the regional social dynamics. One can hardly be criticized for always being more afraid of humans than of nature.

Anyway, fact is, my brother lives in Europe and also fact is, our native city is, well, *not that much* in Europe. So, if we send them to Europe, all these objects of sentimental value, paintings, crockery, woodworking tools from before the invention of machine tools, Dad's marine chronometers etc will necessarily go through some customs.

Living deplorably modern lives disconnected from the grandeurs of past centuries, we both were clueless about the book value of those bits and pieces of antiques that the paternal grandparents brought with them from the Caucasus. So, my brother called in an antique dealer to give us a hand regarding export procedures, valuation etc. *Antique dealer*, by the way, is a designation that I profoundly despise in English, for it reduces an honorable savant versed in past epochs and bygone civilizations to a mere *merchant of objects*. Therefore, we will call that person *Monsieur l'Antiquaire*, which feels more suitable to my taste.

When *Monsieur l'Antiquaire* came to visit the apartment and the belongings, despite my preconceived respect for the supposed erudition and education of a person of his chosen profession, he quickly lost the *monsieur* part of his title in my mind. Having forgotten the purpose of the visit that we had explained on the phone, the guy mistook my physically present brother and my videocalled-from-Brooklyn self for some vulgar squanderers of family heritage. Correcting the angle of his bow tie for more fake aplomb, he declared blatantly, "You know, there are so many younger folks like yourselves who want to get rid of that kind of stuff from previous generations that the market is saturated here. You're very unlikely to get any decent money for these."

Wait a sec, who the duck does this ignorant pig think he's categorizing us with by saying *younger folks like yourselves?* And who told him that we wanted to sell anything? We just wanted to learn the value of that stuff for customs and develop an understanding of the procedures.

I'm not going try, over a transatlantic videocall, to explain to an unenlightened china merchant swine with a bow tie how *special* the circumstances of our family were... Nor that everybody's circumstances are unique. Ok Sir, please go home and give us an itemized estimate of the valuation for that semi-desired heritage of ours, put your expert stamp on it so that we can take care of the relevant custom duties. Oh, and please go duck yourself very much, thank you and goodbye.

I cannot help but remember the uncle of a dear childhood friend with the same sort of "furniture problem" that he had solved rather creatively. The uncle, a larger-than-life gentleman of his times, was a great drinker with a thinking problem who would admonish everyone for calling him an alcoholic. "I am not an alcoholic but an *alcohologist*," he would say, having studied the thorny subject of alcohol in great detail over his life. His long relationship with alcohol, which he treated less as an indulgence and more as a subject of intellectual inquiry, shaped much of his personality. He had amassed an extensive collection of stories, theories, and observations about the substance, all of which he readily shared with anyone willing to listen, or unwilling, at times, like any good alcoholic does.

His self-imposed title of "alcohologist" reflected a certain pride, as if his years of consumption as an end user somehow qualified him as an expert in the field. To him, the study of alcohol was not just about drinking; it was about understanding its place in society, its effects on the mind and body, and its role in the complex rituals of life. He had seen and survived every form of intoxication imaginable, from the lighthearted to the destructive, and in his mind, all of it was worth analyzing with the same rigor as any academic discipline.

He had gone to live in Sweden in the late eighties until one recent day when, hearing that his ailing mother had become hospitalized, he had to jump onto the first flight back to see her one last time. On the flight he had *buried* a full bottle of red Johnnie Walker, *full* referring to the one-liter version as opposed to the zero-seven. And without adding much water, I am reliably told.

Arriving in the neighborhood of his childhood, which he could barely recognize after such a long absence, the lurching colossus quietly entered his mom's place in the dark of the night. All these years he had kept the key to the apartment, with an affection comparable to my Sephardic childhood friends' families who have been handing down the key of an improbable house back *home* in Spain for over twenty generations. By the way, I am painfully aware of my obsession with the concepts *home* and *back home* but yet unwilling to see a therapist, thanks.

And that very first night, in the absence of his dear mother, the uncle already started to break down and burn the priceless furniture in the stove of the living room. His choice for the amuse-bouche were the elegant Louis XIV chairs made by a Levantine artisan of the kind that we don't have the luxury of having anymore in our city. As entrée he continued with the closets from the late fifties, made of mahogany, that ultimate symbol status of a tree that grows in far lands where the Empire didn't extend: Each crackle of the flames consuming that dark, fragrant wood felt like the slow undoing of a legacy woven into the fabric of their family history, reducing generations of quiet significance to ash, one splinter at a time. And for dessert, his choice was drawn to the library and all the books it contained, à la Pepe Carvalho, like a true intellectual.

But against all expectations, the poor old lady made it and came out of the hospital a week later. And when she saw the massacre that was perpetrated in her apartment, with the little voice she had left, she cursed him in the eternal manner of that region's mothers: "I would have preferred to give birth to a stone rather than to an animal like you", she said, tears running down her cheeks, helplessly contemplating the outcome of that wanton destruction.

"Don't cry mom", the uncle calmly answered, "I will gladly replace your furniture, you know, Ikea is always a functional option. I like their *averageness*, the way they meaninglessly slip into a space without demanding anything more than assembly instructions and a few hours of patience. I will clean up this mess and buy a few metric tons of that piece of sheet, so that when you will be gone, I won't need to kill myself drunk to summon the courage to set fire to their kind of furniture. Their products seem designed to be burnt anyway, don't they? I see an *invitingly flammable simplicity* in them, as if knowing that someday, in some fit of rage or grief of their master, they'll meet their fate in a pile of ashes without leaving behind any ghosts of significance. This is what you need at home, mom. Ikea is what I want. I had to deal with the mahogany problem while I still had some moral force in me. In a few years I'll be too old and I won't have the heart to set fire to mahogany."

"What are we gonna do with that icon?", asks my brother again from the living room of our childhood, after the haughty and ignorant china merchant and his ducking bow tie have left us in peace. Well, at least we have confirmed that by paying the corresponding custom duties based on expert evaluations we can bring nearly all other objects to safety in his place in Europe, while waiting for our native Hole to further tumble down. Nearly all of them, we can deal with, except the religious artefacts i.e. the *ikona*.

"I don't really know what to do with it", I answer, "My feeling, my geographically very distant feeling, with hopefully still a bit of a functional understanding of The Hole's dynamics is that you just cannot send it to Europe with the rest. You certainly remember the Kalymnos story, don't you?"

"*Putain oui*, Kalymnos", I saw him scratch his head on the screen, "I had nearly forgotten that story. Looks like there really is no way around that subject about "religious artefacts", right?"

The answer is, nope, there really is no way around that bro, you either follow the alcohologist's example and burn that *ikona* or leave it behind in that Hole where we grew up. There is no other option because we are law-abiding citizens and *theft of an icon is one of the worst accusations you can have in Greece*, as a good friend of mine had told me once.

Years ago, when that friend was still serving the French State, she was dispatched on a delicate mission to exfiltrate a fellow countrywoman from the clutches of a cult on the Greek island of Kalymnos. The woman had endured years of abuse under the guise of spiritual servitude, until one day, she decided that her suffering had run its course. The *despot* of the sect, a self-styled local strongman, wasted no time in reporting that woman's disappearance to the authorities, very, but very slightly twisting the narrative as a "theft of icon" rather than the desertion of a pseudo-nun-turned-slave…

The two women, armed with falsified passports and nerves stretched thin, managed to evade arrest at the Athens airport during a tense layover as the authorities had already been informed and they then made it home to France safely. Since that day my friend cannot go back to Greece even for a simple vacation but rest assured that she carries a newfound reverence for orthodox icons…

My brother and I both grew up seeing that icon in our living room. Oh yes, I spent twenty full years with it, which should mean something. But in the meantime, I have lived some other twenty and more years as a wandering misfit, with all the glory of my belongings splendidly misfitting in a bag and a half. And so, the emotional drain of deciding, item by item, what to do with the relics of our never-sufficiently-distant childhood brought me to the point where our beloved icon may as well go duck itself. As long as it doesn't bring one of us to a fully unnecessary court case for international religious artifact smuggling, I'm okay with all kinds of scenarios about the future of anything coming out of our parents' place.

On top of it, as an umpteenth proof that geography is destiny, if we were to send it with the remaining items, that *ikona* would have to enter Europe straight through Greece. Given that those guys are also orthodox and that the two previously referred Empires had quite some extension in their days, both territorially and spiritually, chances are our icon had originally belonged to some church in Greece. So, if the Greek customs were to confiscate it, the *ikona* would just be returning home then… Well, there would be nothing wrong with that in my book.

Through such a return, the destiny of that *ikona* of our childhood would then reach the grace of Franz's epitaph in the Unbearable Lightness of Being: *Après un long égarement, le retour…*

The design intent of that epitaph could be read as "after a long stray period, the return", although the correct word for word translation -if a word for word translation could ever be considered correct- of *égarement* gives something closer to bewilderment and confusion.

Uncommon are the returns without confusion anyway, be it for icons or for stray humans.

# Elementary school
## Determinism

As far as I remember we were just eight years old, maybe nine but certainly not yet ten, sharing a two-person school bench back in The Hole in the elementary school. Unlike the individual chairs with attached desk surfaces used by American kids we saw in the movies, our shared benches were not really grooming the pupils for individualistic destinies. Yet such a destiny is what most of us would end up having, head-on against the norms of the society there.

If I were using any kind of social media, I could now try to find out where my Benchfellow ended up and what he's doing but I have lost track of him after high school when he went somewhere in Europe. Anyway, like many other childhood friends who left The Hole, I have little doubt that he too must have ended up in a *proper place* to lead his life. And the kind of mild curiosity that I sometimes have about what happened to all these distant childhood friends is not reason enough to justify starting a digital presence. I will keep staying out of *them virtual existences* as long as I have a real one.

"I discussed the subject of our possible futures at length with my dad the other day", started Benchfellow, "and he helped me come to my very personal conclusion that there is no determinism at all in this country where we were *led to be* born. I will, therefore, endeavor to lead my life in another country where society functions under clear cause-and-effect relationships, because this is a necessary -although not sufficient- condition for living a fulfilling life in order to reach one's full potential."

That childhood friend of mine always spoke with that kind of disconcertingly mature vocabulary. A proper adult's vocabulary, like, not just eighteen or twenty years old but rather thirty or older, where real adulthood makes its unwelcome appearance. One might think that he spoke that way because we were what some today would obsessively call "privileged children", and to some extent, in a specific sense, I would concur. The *privilege* that I would concede was not based on our parents being able to send us to a private school but rather based on both of us coming from homes with a decent library. This was by far not everybody's case in that private school with a non-negligible amount of eternally-zeroth-generation *nouveaux riches* and in all fairness the school wasn't that expensive for being "private".

Having grown up in a household with a decent library is probably the biggest blessing my brother and I have received in life, especially with the definition of *decent* being limited to the size and variety of the library, not the perceived quality of the contents. We were literally encouraged to read any and everything, which in those years and in that Hole was a blessing and which is nowadays sadly becoming an exception in any country.

Benchfellow's family had a long and unpronounceable family name, despite having come from the Balkans in the last century. *Un nom à coucher dehors*, as the French would say, with the commendable middle finger that nation has always had for political correctness, *a name that would make you sleep rough*. So, to compensate for that long and unpalatable name, anticipating that some names can indeed be *unpalatable*, his parents had given him a monosyllabic first name that could easily be pronounced by speakers of *major* Western languages. "Major languages meaning those spoken by nations who have *really* contributed to humankind's progress, such as English, French or German", Benchfellow clarified, as it was unthinkable for his parents to stoop so low as to have their kid lead his future life in an environment where the vernacular was anything other than one of these three languages.

"What about Italian or Spanish, are they not worthy of this kind of consideration?" I asked, as I had always admired the musicality of the Italian language spoken by my parents' Levantine friends, the last ones who had stayed behind for a while and then left back to their country of origin where they hadn't lived for several generations. "Oh, people from these countries are *Mediterranean subhumans*, like all of us here. What can they have seriously contributed to humankind's progress and evolution? What's the point of moving to those places, *where is progress in such a decision?*" was his confident answer. Rather than his, the answer was probably his parents', and it ricocheted to my ears through the kid's mouth. In those days it wasn't forbidden to label the members of a whole innocent nation as "subhumans", at least not in The Hole. At least not for an eight-year-old kid…

His well-educated, hard-working and highly anxious parents, I was saying, had given him a short, phonetically pleasant name, to compensate for a long family name, i.e. to compensate for their *initial conditions*. "Compensate for", or shall we rather say to *make up* for his initial conditions? By resorting to the concept of "making up" we could leave to some laudable linguistic elasticity the choice between "hiding a perceived defect through the use of cosmetic means" and "counteracting something unwelcome".

Whatever meaning and function are chosen for "making up", his name was merely an emblem of his lifelong struggle ahead about making up for the initial conditions. One cannot but observe that my Benchfellow, that little elementary school kid, had already imbibed a surplus of *inappropriate* wisdom from his parents to be conscious of our initial conditions' burden that kept haunting all of us on our individual journeys.

His parents had a well-defined life plan for Benchfellow. Mine too, without seeming that obsessed about it, had a life plan for us. In broad lines the plan consisted in us going elsewhere *before it was too late* and not only on a geological timescale. Frankly, all parents of our sociocultural circle had the same plan for their kids, consisting vaguely of going to the West, because it was the time when the West still meant something. Or it could at least inspire some aspirations, before the very idea of a better world beyond our borders dissolved into the toxic air of the twenty-first century.

Ever a walking library of aphorisms and quotes, Benchfellow possessed the required level of sarcastic realism to duly consider the effects of lifelong randomness on his parents' deterministic plans. *Man plans, God laughs*, I learned from him, but also *plans are worthless but planning is everything*. We were eight…maybe nine. Isn't this supposed to be an age when we should at most mistake Eisenhower for an ice-cream brand rather than quoting him directly? I sometimes wonder if any European kids of our generation, at the tender age of eight, were spouting off such weighty, half-understood phrases, borrowed from the grown-ups around them, with the same misguided sense of authority and importance that we had?

It is a non-negligible possibility that the wrong set of initial conditions within the right setting leads to accelerated aging, which can then be mispackaged and sold as *maturing*. In that sense one can confidently state that we were pretty mature kids in The Hole, and that ill-advised maturity was the source of our parents' misguided pride.

Accelerated aging or not, when I was sitting on that old wooden bench with that dark blue school uniform, I had no idea what determinism meant, so I had to ask Benchfellow to clarify. "Determinism is about systems and countries are systems, in a way", he lectured, with more baseless self-confidence than a management consultant of unquestionable uselessness freshly graduated from some "prestigious" college. "In a deterministic system, the same causes will lead to the same immediate effects, those same immediate effects leading, in the long term, through secondary effects, to the same outcome, of course when one removes the associated noise. In a deterministic country, when you do a, you will get b, regardless of the day or the place or your *interlocutor*. In this country, when you do a, one day you get b, the next day you get c, another day nothing, or maybe get d or even minus a. Nothing is predictable in this Hole and this unpredictability is what lack of determinism is about. Unlike us unlucky people born here, those born there in the West, those *people who live in civilization,* they know what tomorrow, *their tomorrow,* will be made of. This is proper determinism; all the rest is garbage."

Most of what I retained from that unsolicited lecture at the time was limited to the hypothesis that *determinism was a kind of civilization.* That a well-functioning *civilization* was anything but ours in The Hole, we already *knew.* Wrongly but surely, we knew. We had been bathed in that notion forever. And the fact that we could only use the word determinism in a Western language, as no proper translation existed in our first mother tongue, only came to reinforce this supposed knowledge that we had. The Orient, at least ours, in both time and space, was *unfit for determinism.*

We were eight years old, maybe nine but certainly not yet ten and we were kids with a mission. And in very broad lines that we did not properly understand, that mission consisted of belonging to somewhere else, somewhere deterministic.

We were still too young to know that, deterministically or not, belonging would almost always end up being a burden.

# IT WAS A HOT SUMMER DAY

When we were kids in the nineties, Dad had a shiny black Remington at home. A typewriter, I should clarify, as the Remington family had decided to hedge their bets on both sides of the coin. They were not so sure whether the pen was mightier than the sword, so they specialized in the two most lethal categories of objects ever created by man: guns and typewriters.

Presumably a rifle might have made more sense in our Hole, given the countless directions that life could take, but thankfully, my family has never regretted their pacifist decision to choose the typewriter. In a home with a typewriter, the only other thing needed for a barely literate kid to convert dreams into wastepaper was an atlas of the world, and we had one, given our privileged status of kids-in-a-house-with-a-library. This atlas became my window to the world before I could even read. Its maps were filled with names I could barely pronounce, and the shape of every continent held another promise of adventures.

By the time I was seven and learned to write in the previous mother tongue, I properly started my *wastepaper production* process on the Remington by inventing anti-heroes living improbable adventures on far-flung places that I would find on the atlas. Do I need to state that those would-be chefs-d'oeuvre all came to a premature end after a page and a half due to a combined lack of inspiration and vocabulary? My preferred far-flung place was Mississippi, with its sprawling river and storied past, a name that seemed to carry a certain weight with its soft phonetics, even in the imagination of a child. And the simplicity of my preferred incipit "it was a hot summer day" made my precocious literary ambitions the laughing stock of our family for years to come.

One day, when I was ten and fully literate with a pretty decent vocabulary -therefore *legitimately* without any more interest in writing- I found Dad working on his old Remington that I hadn't touched for over a year. Whisky glass to the left of the Remington, an ashtray with a cheap local cigarette burning away on the right, he was putting the final touches on our family's application letter to the Green Card lottery.

Devoid of any *expectable* melancholy that a potential future uprooting should have unleashed in a normal child of that age, my *froggishly indoctrinated* brain's first reaction upon seeing that letter was to ask why we, products of a *modèle de civilisation supérieur,* would choose to leave for the US instead of France. Maybe more than indoctrination, it was the mental laziness of changing mother tongues again. May the reader find the magnanimity to pardon the ten-year-old child who knew no better, at least it resulted in a more colorful English than if I had moved to the US as a child.

"We do not *need* to leave", was Dad's answer, "but if our desire is to try this, we also *do not need to need* to leave, we have the luxury of being able to leave it to chance". "So, we go for this lottery", he continued, "because I like the randomness of this process, whereas to go to France, the home of that *superior civilizational model* we are the products of… well, for that option we would have to make some conscious, targeted efforts that are not worthy of people in our *condition*. If we get this Green Card thingy, fine; it will be a welcome excuse for some movement and we'll go there. If not, we will continue with our lives here as before".

*The luxury of leaving it to chance...* When age allowed me to understand the value of those moments next to the Remington, I started to think that teaching a child how to nonchalantly embrace randomness might be the ultimate art of fatherhood. In any case, our family did not seem to consider the lottery an important topic for the months to come and had a devil-may-stick-it reaction to it when we finally learned that the gods -or Uncle Sam's lottery balls- hadn't chosen us for that year. Needless to say, we never even considered applying again in the following years; it would have been a fight against randomness, and our family was above that.

A few years later, when personal computers had already become a common household item and our Remington was playing the has-beens in its lonely corner of our own mahogany cupboard right under the whisky collection, I overheard a distant uncle talking to Dad about his recent application to the same lottery for his family. Beyond my family's *decent situation* as Dad had stated, which mentally prevented us even from reapplying to the lottery, let alone making conscious efforts to leave for *other abroads of greener pastures*, this uncle of mine had a much more *enviable situation*. He was a director at a big international bank's local branch and earned big bucks, but he was nevertheless convinced that they had to apply for that lottery, *so that the kids could have a future.* Be it *said while passing*, I lost count of how many parents of how many different sociocultural origins I have since encountered who have cited their kids' future as the main driver for moving somewhere else, from and to the unlikeliest countries.

"When you are the big man of a small place", the uncle was saying, "burst your brass as you may, you will not be able to make it big, whoever you are, because the place is small and small it will remain. This Hole will necessarily drag my kids down or the best it can drag them is horizontal but never up. No single country's trajectory improves faster than an individual destiny, so if you want to save yourself or your family, you are condemned to chase greatness somewhere else, where some people other than your ancestors have already created it", he was continuing, full of undue exhilaration and anticipation for something as utterly uncertain as the Green Card Lottery.

Are genuine enthusiasm and eagerness superior factors in aligning the planets than a blind *in-faith-uation* with and in randomness? Being a technical person, I'm not supposed to give credence to that kind of superstitious nonsense, but in any case, that distant uncle of mine *did* draw the lucky number and got the coveted letter from Uncle Sam. But as few curses in life are greater than a dream coming true, he suddenly realized the unanticipated burden of leaving behind a materially comfortable life, two young kids at primary school, the family's mixed breed cat which was a compulsory accessory for any self-respecting family in our cat-city, not forgetting the fact that his wife did not speak a word of English.

Yogi Berra, the legendary baseball player known for his wisdom with an endearing mix of simplicity and profound paradoxes, had once offered a friend an unexpected bit of advice that became cult stuff when *cult* used to mean something: "When you come to the fork in the road, take it." It was a statement that seemed pretty absurd at first glance, but we all need every now and then the simple reminder that sometimes the best decision is to act, whichever way you go on a bifurcation and trust that the journey will unfold from there.

Alas, having arrived at Yogi Berra's infamous fork in the road, my unfortunate uncle spent painful months *unable to take it*. Despite being barely forty, he would argue with Dad—or rather, with himself in Dad's presence—over a half-empty bottle of whisky: "What am I supposed to do at my age, for Christ's sake? Start over at a gas station or flip burgers like some *faceless immigrant*? That's what they all do when they move to the US. But me? I'm past that age of being nobody."

Does Lady Fortuna truly favor those who are prepared, or is it just another one of those exploitative fables designed to uphold a semblance of social order? Perhaps the myth of preparation is nothing more than a comforting narrative for the powerless, a way to convince the army of underdogs that their fate is in their own hands. In any case, that particular evening of long discussions between Dad and that uncle over the half-empty bottle of whisky, while I was tasked with the mundane tasks related to the replenishment of ice, pistachio and dried fruits, I understood that fortune, destiny and luck all take great pleasure in *snubbing the overprepared*. More specifically, dare I say, the subclass of overprepared who get shaky knees at Yogi Berra's fork.

After much discussion and many weeks of weighing the pros and cons, my uncle finally pulled the plug on the family's emigration project. With a resolute shrug, he chose to stay in The Hole, clinging to the customary embrace of his family, his half-breed cat, and the rest. It was a decision that, in hindsight, seems less like a choice and more like a reluctant surrender to the weight of his own inertia. Nothing fosters inertia like the security of an *enviable social status*.

They finished what remained of that bottle on another occasion, with Dad and a few old friends gathered around, and the uncle moved on, but it wasn't long before his life began to unravel. He lost his job, and that was the beginning of a long descent of spiraling failures, each more crushing than the last, marked by a succession of professional and private misfires that never seemed to stop. One might think that those who have failed offer little to emulate, but it doesn't make them "bad examples", as the best examples are often those not to be followed and, in that sense, I do owe him a moral debt… I am deeply grateful to that distant uncle, not for the lessons he taught me directly, but for the one he unknowingly imparted: thanks to him, I made a mental note to myself to never get shaky knees at Yogi Berra's fork.

Fast-forward to the recent past after I had moved to Brooklyn. The Remington was now part of our family heritage that had landed in the wrong century of digital toys and due to its pretty much meaningless secular existence it was not getting a tenth of the attention that the *ikona* was getting. On my way to JFK for a useless professional trip, I happened to bump into a cab driver who originally hailed from the same Hole as me. Running towards his sixties, but still sharp and *functional like a stapler,* he told me how in nineteen-ducking-eighty-nine the ship on which he was a simple seaman docked at the yards, not far from the Brooklyn Bridge and how he jumped ship. I do happen to live not so far away from those yards and my humble opinion is that it is not humanly possible to despise that despicably touristy postcard setting, so I had a moment of nostalgia for what it must have looked like at that moment. There must be something Portuguese in my soul, as my hardest nostalgias are for experiences I haven't lived, but we will come back to that in Angola.

It followed the regrettably familiar cadence of older migrant stories, ones laced with the weight of regret and silent longing. The tales of how there was no videocalling back then, how he could barely speak to his parents once a week, never seeing their faces again, still unreachable across the pond. The kind of stories where time stretched thin between those fleeting phone calls, with the heart-wrenching realization that he would not have his documents settled before his parents passed away. Then came the familiar narratives of duty-bound sacrifice, where the future generation was the ultimate hope, the carrot at the end of a long, uncertain stick. Them usual migrant tales of better lives, of dreams and illusions, a few fully realized and many fully blown to smithereens. Tales of grit in lieu of fork-standing and fence-sitting, in between resignation to fate and ballsy determination.

Judging by his manners and vocabulary, the ex-seaman was very unlikely to have come from a household with a library or to have possessed in his youth any similar *cultural privilege* that I had. No atlas of a faraway childhood, for example… no such atlas had rocked him towards these American shores, his experience was a pretty much uncharted one. Getting close to JFK, I even committed the sin of thinking that the younger version of this guy was probably *not refined enough* to target New York. That he would have probably jumped ship even at a nondescript harbor call like Altamira, State of Tamaulipas or Mobile, Alabama, as opposed to the great glorious Big Apple. A badly harnessed horse will always end up breaking his shafts, our French teacher Madame Timonier used to say when I was in *terminale* i.e. last year of high school. Maybe she had the intuition that almost all of her class would end up being badly harnessed horses who left The Hole for good.

As I left the car at the airport, I felt the urge to wholeheartedly thank that stranger whom I would never again see in this city of strangers, for the nice conversation and the tales he shared with me. "You have a beautiful life story", I said, "your kids must be proud of their dad, you accomplished so much" and some other banalities that certainly failed to rise to the occasion. One's first words often fail to rise to the occasion when facing strongly lived lives. I was about to continue my prattle, hoping to get a bit more meaningful, when the cabbie answered, without any false modesty:

"It's not about me being special or having accomplished anything exceptional, it is just about New York. It's like standing on the edge of the world and not feeling the pull of it, as if the city doesn't stir something deep inside you. Can this city not stir something deep inside anybody?

If your ship docks in Brooklyn and you don't feel the urge to jump, you are just not normal."

# Spilled blood stains forever

"I don't like the genocide", he serenely stated, scratching his imposing belly with his calloused right hand. He was stroking his long white beard with his left hand where the very tip of the pinky had decided to go missing a few years ago, courtesy of his old lathe, which missed any of the modern-day protective screens and mechanical interlocks. We were enjoying that tiny penetration of spring rays between the buildings in front of his "shop", on that little *street of the dungeon* that was part of the maze that gave birth to the city's oldest industrial market. It was that very same little, tiny little pedestrian street that another *unbelongable gentlesoul* by the name of Anthony Bourdain would stroll through two decades later, during his own long, fateful quest for himself, a brief episode that made me cry when I stumbled upon it in the digital jungle after he had passed away.

*Unbelongable*, I need to address at this stage of the creative process, can be passive and active, with the design intent to qualify a place where a person cannot belong as well as a person who cannot belong to a place. This term serves not only as an adjective to describe disconnection but also as an action in its transitive form, assigning agency to both person and place. In the most ideal of possible grammatical universes, I do conceive the verb *belong* as having both a transitive and an intransitive function.

The *shop* was my preferred refuge during daytime in my teens whenever I was playing hooky. It was the place that allowed me to get soaked in the kind of real-life wisdom that schools have rarely, if ever, provided. The owner called it the *shop* although he didn't sell much, if anything, there. *Workshop* would have been more appropriate, as he mainly used the place to repair some very specific pieces of mechanical equipment. So very specific was the equipment that he repaired and so religiously devoted was his clientele to his black magic art that revealing the type of equipment would be dangerous. It would be akin to revealing that master's identity, even in that sprawling city of large tentacles that is home to some obscure twenty million people. And as a time-tested rule, you would not want to have on your conscience the disclosure of the identity of someone who has *unorthodox* opinions about genocides, past and future, in The Hole.

He had inherited the shop from his late father, who didn't want to leave in the fifties when *objective* reasons to leave The Hole were making themselves unmistakably evident for the family. Despite constantly criticizing his dad from beyond the grave for that *decisional constipation* and eternal yellow light, when his turn came in the eighties, he himself did not want to leave, for reasons beyond comprehension, these lands that had been of his ancestors for as long as civilization existed. Civilization about which, as already stated, my child brain had mistakenly -but *conditionally justifiably*- concluded that it was a foreign notion, something that could not to be found where we lived.

A yellowing photo in the shop, neatly positioned between pressure gauges and old pistons, showed the thirty-seven kids from his elementary school class in their *confessional school,* at some point in the late fifties. He and his future wife, on opposite corners of the picture, as the best future spouses should probably be placed, were the only ones who then *stayed behind.* All remaining thirty-five kids left The Hole as soon as they were no longer kids; most went to France, some to the US, one even to Montevideo, where he founded a family with the granddaughter of people of his own tribe who had emigrated to Buenos Aires after the genocide.

"They all left in search of the most rightful existence, not necessarily the most meaningful and certainly not the most beautiful, but the most rightful existence", he would sum up the stories of his childhood friends.

When his dad was alive, the shop had been a small, cluttered place, filled with bits and pieces of technical equipment: valves, tools, gauges, gears, and various contraptions…mostly things related to ships. It was a humble space, yet it buzzed with the quiet efficiency that came from years of hands-on experience. The customers, a mix of sailors and local tradespeople, would come in for odds and ends, the kind of things you could only find in a shop like his.

Then one day, a few of his good friends came in, looking worn down and frustrated. They had a piece of that specific type of equipment that I couldn't mention, and it had been giving them far too many headaches for way too long for them to continue entrusting their lives to it. He agreed to help them, and he repaired it, they all say *with virtuosity* but he was shy to ask for any money in exchange for that help, fearing he would end up being considered a *repairman*.

"Repairman is as honorable as any other profession", might the Western reader rightfully think and object. Having been a field engineer for many years, I do, on my part, admire the resourcefulness and manual skills of a talented repairman an order of magnitude above the genius of the most brilliant degree-educated engineer you will find. But in The Hole where we grew up, "I will send you to become an apprentice to a repairman" was a kind of boogeyman for kids who didn't perform well at school, the epitome of empty threat by average parents of empty minds.

It must have subconsciously reminded the parents that in our kind of country where people do not *conceive and design* things, they were condemned to barely *repair,* with their small minds incapable of abstraction, what other smart people had conceived. And that process of conception took place in lands where those smart people knew what their tomorrows would be -robustly- made of, tomorrows that would not need to be mended by questionable people of fuzzy geographical origin. All of this has been turned upside down by History, but anyway, such was the line of thinking of average parents in that below-average land back then…

Despite his reluctance to get into that particular trade of a *vulgar repairman*, my friend's reputation spread quickly, and soon enough, one person after another started asking him for help with their faulty equipment. At first, he tried to turn them away, holding onto the idea of keeping away from the mundane world of repair. But as word spread, it became clear that he couldn't avoid it: one guy, then another, and yet another, came seeking his expertise. The requests grew, each one more insistent than the last, until, after the third man walked through the door, he simply couldn't refuse anymore. So, the once-innocent favor turned into a transaction; the guys who had asked for his help became clients, and in turn, he reluctantly transformed into that dreaded, vulgar *repairman* he had always feared becoming.

In theory, there shouldn't be anything wrong with a violin-playing repairman who had studied an array of social sciences, leading to a collection of degrees and who spoke a refined French of past centuries using the sophisticated vocabulary of a Claude Lévi-Strauss. There shouldn't be anything wrong with a *violinist* stuck between two continents and two languages, in which he was alternating elegantly between the most complex sentence structures and the crudest insults of the most creative variety. No, there shouldn't be anything wrong, with the possible exception of, erm, *class betrayal,* for which you would be spiritually hanged in our sociocultural circle…

Thankfully for us kids, class betrayal was a crime he frankly couldn't care less about. So there in his *shop of the last tango,* our Violinist remained, and he continued to repair some specifically broken equipment during the day. Then, in the evening, he would mend some very specifically broken souls, them souls who would come to seek solace in the bottle, transforming the *shop* into a warmer, Mediterranean version of Zola's *Assommoir*.

After having a library in my parents' place, probably the second biggest blessing of my life was being a *regular* in that restricted circle of wise but somewhat heartbroken adults who *hadn't left* The Hole. I mean, some had once left for good but then had *come back for bad* because the return often felt worse than not having left at all; one could say that at least they had the peace of mind of those who had tried. Others had truly never left and were drowning in the bottle the nostalgia of what their lives could have been, thanks to the stories of those who had left. So many years later, when I could understand Fairuz's mother tongue, did I grasp that this monumental lady had summed up their condition to perfection: "*If I return, I'll go mad; if I leave you, I'll suffer*".

The regulars were mostly seamen, divers, builders, and various technical people, a mixture of tradesmen whose lives revolved around hands-on work. And yet, for reasons that remained unclear, a number of university professors had at some point found their way into the *shop*, as somewhat eccentric *guest not-lecturers*. It was a strange and unlikely collection of minds, the kind that didn't seem to belong together in any conventional setting, which was the true charm of the place.

This eclectic crowd was usually completed by a comely soprano, *of some past international renown*, as she was often described with a modest, knowing smile. She would generously fill the air with arias when the mood and the quality of the bottle *du jour* suited her, with a rare but captivating presence, her voice weaving through the shop like a thread of elegance among the high-pressure piping and rows of activated carbon filters. And then there was the charismatic marine biologist, a passionate expert on Lessepsian species, with an almost obsessive dedication to studying the nascent impact of these invasive creatures on our side of the Med. "Nothing good has ever come from the Red Sea", she would sum it up, her knowledge of our seas' delicate ecological balance and the unforeseen consequences of human intervention resonating in the half-empty wine glasses. In The Hole, our glasses have always been half empty.

Many of these folks had seen the wild wide world, be it temporarily, be it in transition. Some had seen it only through the eyes of the others who had navigated the seven seas, when people used to navigate on ships which had names and characters, as opposed to being anonymous slaves to steel monstrosities during precisely optimized stays in ports of call. At the risk of breaking the flow of the text - a risk I will always take with passion - I must state this here: I do despise anything optimized but on top of that I do hate with a passion optimized stays in ports of call, on any continent.

Some of them were dirt poor, some were old money, most were in between. Some liked whisky, some preferred wine, a few even drank without distinction, which constituted the worst offense in Dad's book. They covered all the three different monotheisms, belonging to more confessions than they would care to count and the one thing they shared was the soul-sapping feeling that, as opposed to them there and then in The Hole, somewhere else in the world, some other people, were *living*. No adverb, no *complément d'objet,* no further ado in that sentence, some other people were living, period.

One generally accepted truth of modern times posits that it is very difficult to geographically constrain a group of people who have reached the intimate collective conviction that they are *not living* while somewhere else, some people, are indeed *living*. I must state there are few things I fear more than generally accepted truths of modern times, nevertheless this one may indeed be truly true. And to my present-day self it is even well conceivable that one may prefer to physically cease to live rather than accept defeat in the pursuit of life, that holiest of pursuits regardless of what one believes or not.

However, this present-day self does just not know what to make of all the magnificent counterexamples that were these childhood anti-heroes of mine in the shop. I still see them drown their unnamed sorrows in the bottle around that old stove in the middle of the *shop,* they would always show some genuine joy in sharing and listening to stories from elsewhere. Maybe the *dignity of belonging* was simply what held them behind in The Hole, beyond any more mundane excuses about established lives, jobs, kids' school and such. It must have been the idea that to sever those ties would mean losing a piece of themselves that they couldn't bear to part with, even if it was only an illusion.

"I don't like the genocide", repeated my preferred Violinist, "I don't like this strange moral obligation of taking sides just because I have the same ethnic origin as the victims, of ending up being a double-traitor, regardless of whatever stance I take. My foreign-born nephews think that I'm a traitor for *not caring enough* about the genocide, as if it was really my case. As if it was humanly possible not to care about your own tribe having been slaughtered by the tribe of your present-day neighbors a few hundred kilometers to the East".

"On the other hand, my fellow countrymen -who knows to what degree they are *really fellow*- constantly suspect me of *actually* caring about the genocide. I'm tired of repeating that, whatever may have happened a century ago, our common present in this country depends on all of us being able to not publicly give a rainy day's duck about it. Thankfully my hairy brass is way too old to care about sitting between two chairs on such an existential subject but it still kisses me off every now and then that so many idiots think I must have an expert opinion on the subject and build my identity around it. I just don't like the genocide, isn't it clear enough?".

In that distant Hole of our childhood, the genocide was supposed to be the ultimate elephant in the room and yet everyone talked about it.

Spilled blood, it seems, stains forever.

# Belonging isn't necessarily geographic

My first encounter with the blissful continent of Africa where I was going to spend wonderfully formative years was also in the *shop*, thanks to a community of Senegalese hawkers that Violinist and my Dad had decided to take under their old gentlemen's wings. If it hadn't been for their kindness to all these hawkers, I would have left years later for France without ever having been friends with a person of *truly different background*, as a black person was still a pretty uncommon sight in that racially homogenous society where we grew up. Yes, it was a homogenous society, even if, in that society, we -you, they, whoever- kept hating, ostracizing and occasionally killing each other based on obscure confessional and supposedly genetic grounds. Racially homogenous that society was, because in all fairness, you just cannot tell The Hole's different self-proclaimed tribes from one another but please be so kind as not to tell them this, as everyone needs a reason to exist. Oh, and very often you cannot tell them from a European neither, but again, please be so kind as not to tell this to Europeans: those poor souls with a supposed monopoly on Enlightenment may get offended to be similar to people from a place called The Hole.

So, given that homogeneity of our society, it was unusual, in the nineties, to see a black person in our city. It was maybe not exactly like a native brought from the Indies to Spain by Columbus five centuries ago, but frankly not so far off from it either. Simply put, our long-dead Empire just so happened *not* to be of the overseas colonial variety, which had its implications on the cosmetic composition of its population. And after the Empire, whatever outliers might have been there had been *purified* by the nation-state long before I was born, a shame not just limited to the genocide that Violinist *doesn't like*.

When it came to hospitality, Violinist and his clique were able to have hearts larger than a megalopolis spanning over two continents. So, it was only natural that from the first time when Dad brought a Senegalese watch seller to the shop for a drink, that hawker and his bunch of friends were going to be welcomed there. This would of course include anyone in their bloodline and of course for the generations to come, because the shop was supposed to be such an eternal place.

Dad had just met that first hawker on the street, a mountain of a man who had accepted the invitation to *have a drink* with the understandable hope of escaping from the merciless sun of our humid summers and getting some sort of cold refreshment before going back to meandering in between cars and pedestrians for the rest of the day. The drink story was to be the first one of a rather long list of misunderstandings where they mutually bumped on the limits of their supposedly common vernacular: in Dad's French and in that particular shop's book, *prendre un verre* had never ever meant anything non-alcoholic. The regular crowd of the shop would consider even a beer as *not-alcoholic-enough,* for duck's sake. (We're talking real beers, as at that time the abomination of non-alcoholic beer had not yet been invented, at least not in The Hole.)

"Normally we Mourides aren't supposed to drink alcohol", Mountain stammered, realizing the misunderstanding once they were in the shop. He didn't have much conviction in his voice and he certainly had too much education to refuse, so he grabbed his first cold bottle of beer. Mountain thereby became the ambassador of the shop for what seemed like the whole Senegalese community of our city who kept coming in to blur cultural boundaries anytime they saw the lights on.

At that age I had no idea *what* Mourides were but thanks to my atlas and our subscription to satellite TV with TV5Monde I could already confidently locate Senegal on the map. Or most of the other countries populated by fellow *francophones,* for that matter, from Canada to Cameroon. We were the same bunch watching the same Thalassa episodes on Friday nights from all over the globe, which was as close as cultural kinship would get.

Surprisingly for someone who had navigated so much in his youth, Dad was not into geography and he couldn't really care about who Mourides were. Nor did he wonder what they believed or did not believe in, or if Mountain was a Cryptomartian of Jupiterian origin whose mother tongue was an obscure interstellar dialect that he had inherited from an unidentified grandmother with Saturnian blood. Dad just had enough sense to know that Senegal was quite some distance from our Hole, and he had a simple tenet that the grandparents I hadn't been fortunate enough to meet had inculcated in him: a man who came from faraway lands to honestly pursue his own happiness without encroaching on other people's happiness would always have the seat of honor at our family's dinner table, if that man so desired.

And it doesn't seem to be just a thing from my Dad's family, either. Anyone who's ever been to the Caucasus came back telling me the same thing. These folks, with their unyielding generosity, will keep plying you with food until you can't breathe, and they will be keeping a seat for you at their family table as long as you stay in their city. It's the kind of hospitality that becomes almost a ritual, where no matter how full you are, they will find another dish to shove in front of you, their pride and honor tied to the explosion of your belly.

Don't ask me if all of that is true, though, I have no idea. I haven't been strong or fortunate enough to overcome the weight of the family trauma from the last century to ever set foot on those cursed lands. Perhaps it's better to leave it that way, or perhaps I will convince my brother to go there one day with me: I'm afraid of getting shaky knees if I do it alone, not at Yogi Berra's fork, but in front of History.

Mountain, consequently, ended up becoming a regular guest of the most welcome variety at our family dinner table. He would come in as the light waned into dusk, after having wandered the city the entire day and with a sigh of relief he would unload at the entrance hall the merchandise that he still had left. At the table, he did avoid pork chops as much as contemporary politics, but with that knowledgeable high school dropout we kids could discuss pretty much any subject. He would tell us stories from his continent and give us lectures on why adversity makes men while prosperity makes monsters, according to Victor Hugo, whom he unreservedly agreed with, despite the Mourides' reputation for being industrious tradesmen chasing financial wealth. "We Mourides are industrious with a service mind, not meaninglessly running after prosperity for prosperity's sake. Those who do that are the monsters Monsieur Victor was certainly referring to," Mountain would say, using this wholly *Unfrench* combination of the title *monsieur* with someone's first name, which I since then cherished every time I heard it.

Holding our cutlery properly was a big thing in the family, the kind of soul-formatting mercilessly imposed on the kids, which may have helped me later with the industrial mind-formatting I received in all kinds of safety trainings. *All happy families are alike*, as you rightfully stated in Anna Karenina, *Monsieur Leo*... if not in the way their kids learn to hold their cutlery, at least in the importance they all attribute to the way one holds it. And although I would respectfully refrain from judging the presence or absence of happiness in the family Mountain came from, based on the way he held his cutlery, visibly they did not have the *same version of happiness* that we did in my family… The handle of the fork was almost entirely concealed within his large hand, which wrapped around it as if it were a natural extension of his grip, with only the slightest bit of the utensil still visible.

Like most seventeen-year-olds, I considered all this cutlery-holding and elbows-off-the-table business a serious pain in my neck, so one day I took the liberty of expressing my discontent to Mom, in the intimacy of our kitchen. My simple point was that given how great a guy Mountain clearly is in all respects, one could be a decent person *also* without holding one's cutlery in a given way imposed by self-proclaimed *good society*.

"What we're trying to teach you and your brother doesn't apply to him", Mom fired back, "Mountain holds his cutlery *with his heart* and his heart comes through his eyes. If one day you reach that same level of *humanity*, you too can hold your cutlery whatever way you want or even eat with your hands."

It has since been an objective of mine, certainly unaccomplished, to reach your level of humanity, Mountain, whom I salute from across the pond after all these years, wherever you may be and whatever you may be selling now to make a living.

Those Mourides folks of his could have been some sort of Eastern Mediterraneans in other times, we learned from Mountain, as they open astonishingly long, often *transcontinentally long* credit lines to sellers that they may not even physically meet their entire life. True to the etymology of the word *credit*, they open it simply based on trust, on community, the same way Phoenicians trusted a more than distant cousin in bumduck-Marseille millennia ago to engage in trade, in a world without banks, e-mails or WhatsApp.

Contrary to the Mourides, we were growing up in a country where one was never better betrayed by anyone other than one's own would-be *tribe*, consequently all the kids of my generation were being taught to be suspicious of any and everyone. And yet here was that Mountain guy and his folks who would trust perfect strangers with their money and merchandise based on simply being part of the same confessional tribe of sorts. What a bliss it would be to be able to trust thy neighbor, I remember thinking when he first explained to us their credit system.

Certainly, we all appreciated our long hours of discussions on literature, travel, one's home, and the smell of fresh bread. Certainly, my teenager self did welcome the realization that I may one day reach the level of self-actualization required to hold my cutlery as I please. Dear to me are also the few words of Wolof he taught us that I still remember and the Mourides' specific way of shaking hands that has in the meantime helped my *farceur* brother surprise a few hawkers here and there in the *West*. But beyond and above everything else, what *Mountain* taught us with this unquestioning trust in his folks was that *belonging isn't geographic*. And the great irony of this learning was that in our childhood neighborhood many of our best friends were Sephardic Jews, the very community par excellence that has incarnated *ungeographic belongings* through centuries and yet in my teenager detached blindness I didn't realize the power of that truth until our destiny-seeking Mountain came all the way from Senegal to teach me by his example.

The pity on the matter is that it was still an age when I generally understood what I was taught but I did not necessarily learn it. So, I quickly understood that there were *ungeographic* forms of belonging and then at once I forgot it, needing to understand it again and again in the same existence but throughout different lives…

# They had already
# killed our Dentist

"It's a pretty bold choice to aim for the heart in a suicide attempt, considering there is no guarantee of success. That bullet could easily have ricocheted off his ribs without reaching the heart, you know…", judged the General's Grandson, pensively, puffing on his Cuban cigar, its dubious importation spanning the globe to reach The Hole.

In the nineties one could potentially come by an average cigar in The Hole with a bit of luck and a bit of grit but it was quite something to have a *steady* supply of *good* Cuban cigars… For him this steady supply wasn't mere indulgence; it was part of his identity, a signal of defiance. *A refusal to settle for less*, as a modern-day marketing empty suit would say, that steady supply of cigars was the kind of status symbol Grandson needed.

"I would have gone for the head, the brain is a sure thing", he continued, his macho mustache in the middle of the cigar's halo and deep black eyes hidden behind aviator sunglasses on that winter day, in his dimly lit living room. The walls of the room were lined with polished walnut display cases, each housing several firearms meticulously maintained, every gun with a story he would recount in great detail. Given the extent of his handgun collection, he must have known what he was talking about. One should indeed choose the brain over the heart, I suppose…

"Under different circumstances I could have agreed or at least I could have harbored some doubts," answered Mom, "but he was a medical doctor, a real one from the older generation, he must have been able to properly target the *intercostal space*, and he seems to have reached the heart with the appropriate angle". "A medical doctor, huh", came the counterargument, "he was a dentist, my dear, a dentist. Isn't that a profession that has evolved from barbers, with all due respect for barbers? Worse, it is a profession that was *invented* in a barbershop, I should have said, without much of an evolution thereafter beyond injecting patients with morphine before torturing them."

Quite a frustrated fellow he was, Grandson. Perhaps that frustration was due to paying the price for the improper alliances of his German grandfather's country during the Great War, leaving him stranded where he was never meant to belong. By the way, I always wondered why they called that collective stupidity *La Grande Guerre*, the Great War. Mechanized carnage and mustard gas cannot really have been *that great*, right?

That improper alliance from forgotten times by his never-forgotten grandfather gave him the wrong passport at birth and Grandson was unhappily stuck for life among us, the wrong bunch of *Untermenschen,* quite a frustrating thought indeed. Maybe he was so frustrated because he had once had higher aspirations and ideas of his own worth, as one often has during the younger years, who knows.

I still remember another particular evening, before Dentist had decided to leave us. Mom and Dad were engulfing a bottle of Black Johnnie with the cheap smoke of those tar-laden killing tools in the form of cigarettes coming from the State's factory, in company of Grandson who had dropped by for a drink. The conversation was spicy as usual, tickling many touchy subjects, but overall rather good-natured, until a young Enrico Macias had the bad idea of singing "j'ai quitté mon pays", *I left my country* on the radio.

For the context, in that living room, on that particular evening, all three adults -and necessarily us two kids- came from somewhere else, belonged to nothing and struggled with much. So one might have innocently assumed that a song about unwillingly leaving one's country would strike a chord with all of us... Well, such a thought would have been without taking into consideration Grandson.

"Did I ever ask you to come disturb my peace here, dirty piece of *pied-noir*, you should have stayed where you were ducking the goats", Grandson burst out, in his irascible French of aristocratic intonations inherited from the wrong century. What a rare glimpse into wanton and ridiculous xenophobia it was. What an absurd scene that turned into a blessing for me as I understood how lucky I was growing up in the cosmopolitan open-mindedness of my family. And beyond all the wantonness and meaninglessness of the act, there was a slight technical problem with this statement, just a minor one: his peace *here* wasn't disturbed by a single *pied-noir* because Grandson wasn't living *there*. He had never been *there*, in France, where the pieds-noirs went *back* from Algeria, on the same boat where Enrico Macias improvised his song that brought tears to the eyes of all these adults who were seeing their homeland for the last time. Incidentally, given that the Germans had not kept the nationality for the grandchildren like him at that time, his poor toilet-paper passport, the very same one that we had, did not even allow him to go without a visa *there*, to France where the pied-noirs now lived. Quite a frustrated fellow he was, Grandson and understandably so.

Dentist, on the other hand, wasn't that kind of frustrated guy and if you ask me, he clearly hadn't deserved such an abrupt departure. One might rightfully retort that nobody deserves a suicide, but I believe he especially didn't, particularly at such an advanced age, after years of battling his demons with apparent success.

He had been accused of some obscure crime before the last coup of the last century when he was in his forties, and he had ended up spending many years behind bars until his innocence was *somewhat proven*. When he finally came out of prison, his forties were gone, as were his house and his wife, but that kind gentleman had then been able to reconstitute himself. Or so we believed until his suicide.

Whether he had done what he had been accused of, I obviously do not know and my feeling is that neither did Dad, despite having been one of his closest friends. With the kind of family education Dad had received, he wouldn't even ask a person's *profession* until they talked about it themselves, so I can hardly imagine him asking, "so Doctor, tell me the truth, we're between homies here, did you really kill that guy? And what did you do with the body?"

Anyway, Dentist's innocence or guilt are not the main point, neither is the absence of evidence, in our kind of country anyway. Where no evidence exists, evidence would be created. So they went to his house, brought him to the station and broke him down, time and again, until he confessed. The police then extorted all the money he had, and he spent many dark years behind bars until the judge recognized his retraction of the confessions made under duress.

"Those brutes had tortured him *quite inhumanely*", continued to sentence the cigar-puffing Grandson, who had gone to school with Dentist. Then, extinguishing his cigar in an ashtray akin to a stranger's skin in his creative imagination, Grandson defined *humane* torture according to his very own *humanist* scale as the variety that "first and foremost safeguards the soul" and "furthermore doesn't leave any long-term scars, at least on the visible parts of the body". Visible by whom and in what circumstances, was left to the listener's imagination…

"A prime example of humane torture", he added, "is the nightstick made of a sturdy fabric sewn up in a cylindrical shape and filled with wet sand. When our great glorious policemen beat up a guy with that, he feels the shockwaves down through his marrows, but it doesn't leave any trace. Not even a bruise, because the amorphous sand body distributes the impact pressure evenly on the skin. Torture is unacceptable in any way, shape or form but if it *must* be applied, the wet sand nightstick is the humane form of torture *par excellence*, provided it is administered without any accompanying insults under duress", he finished, "no heme breakdown, no bilirubin increase, no trace". Grandson was an insurance expert of sorts in his day job, without any medical background nor specific expertise on the *heme breakdown process*, one would have thought. At least I would have thought, innocently.

Did we need to learn of Dentist's suicide at such a late age to recognize that a potentiometer connected at the other end of two cables tied to a guy's private parts will always be just anything but a tool to regulate the voltage? Not really. That, as a great many people have already said before us, you leave the prison, but the prison never leaves you? Probably not either. However, I needed another decade to come across a much more elegant description of that soul-crushing experience given by an anonymous Catalan graffitist on the pedestal of one of Franco's last statues that were still in existence on Spanish soil at the time: *once you have been in prison, every single morsel of bread that goes through your throat will bring you back there.*

Our Dentist, once freed, had never ever been able to leave his prison cell or the damp cellar where the police had tortured him, the story was that simple. Once you are tortured, you can't belong anywhere else because the etymologic, *uncommon* sense of the word *torture* dictates that once properly twisted, any tie gets broken, to your former life and former self. Them brutes had already killed Dentist in that damp cellar decades ago, the final act of pulling the trigger was a mere detail that he had the guts to carry out himself. The detail that mattered was his proper consideration and expertise in targeting the intercostal space and not losing face to Grandson in a posthumous manner by failing his suicide.

"It's a pretty bold choice to aim for the heart in a suicide attempt, considering there is no guarantee of success. That bullet could easily have ricocheted off his ribs without reaching the heart, you know…", judged Grandson, pensively. He knew what he was talking about, he really did. After all, Grandson is the guy who ended up with the gun that Dad had reluctantly inherited long before I was born so it would be reassuring for us that he knows about the subject.

A cold little handgun it was, Czech-made, bought in the late forties by our paternal grandfather, according to family legend, from Churchill's bodyguard himself. Why the great English hero of the Free World would vicariously buy a gun from behind the Iron Curtain for his bodyguard was the first question that had gone through my mind when I had learned of the gun's existence on the first of *them wearing transatlantic calls*. I then realized the absurdity of a gun having been in *our* home all my life without my knowledge, followed by the even greater absurdity of simply possessing a gun, reluctantly inherited or not. I firmly believe that homes which have libraries should not have guns but probably this is as wrong as many other firm beliefs.

If two civilized kids with European passports and uncivilized names were to try to smuggle that gun into Europe, it would clearly turn into an even bigger headache than the *ikona*. So, my brother and I decided to get rid of it. And as if all of that was not absurd enough, the gun had no permit or other relevant paperwork existence whatsoever, apparently they too had fallen from the back of an unorthodox, *unstately* truck. Given that none of us had any particular wish to see that *undocumented* son of a gun again, we should have properly gotten rid of it by throwing it to some unsoundable depths of the Med, honestly, but…

But in the part of the Caucasus that our ancestors had to leave, when you lose your adze, you invoke the heavens, not for whomever stumbles upon it to bring it back to you but for them *not to sharpen it from the wrong side.* A wrongly sharpened adze is an *unrecoverable* insult to the tool and to the owner. Dare I say, to the order of the Universe. And to prevent our gun from falling into the wrong ignorant hands, there was no better candidate than Grandson with his large gun collection and other seemingly irrelevant qualities such as his informed opinions about torture on the basis of a detailed understanding of the heme breakdown process. So, in the end my paternal grandfather vicariously bequeathed him with the gun, through us grandchildren whom he had never met. Anything related to that particular gun over seven decades seems to have been done vicariously, after all.

Every now and then the cold steely feeling of that handgun's grip resurfaces in my Brelian *oceanic languors* -in plural, please- as I watch the horizon from the top level of some steel monster in bumducknowhere in the middle of the sea, from Austral Africa to the Gulf of Mexico. I picture that unnecessary piece of my family history among Grandson's large collection of handguns, murmuring to myself, "May Grandson please never choose my granddad's gun when it's his own time to blow out his brains".

And may Dentist's adze, should he ever lose it there beyond the grave, always be sharpened from the correct side by whichever tortured soul ends up finding it.

# Non-deterministic
# Destiny Grinders

"I don't know what the Twin Towers are or were, and I couldn't care less if I knew. Last night, some brasshole stole my passport and my seaman's book. The duckers entered the cabin while I was sleeping on the deck", I said, dismissing the poor urchin who was at the shore end of the gangway.

He meant no harm, he was innocently asking me if I had seen what was just being broadcast live on television, with those planes flown by lunatics hitting the towers one after the other. If everybody has a 9/11 memory, well, mine is mostly one of ignorance...

Two decades later I do feel a tingle of well-deserved shame writing this while sitting in my Brooklyn apartment. However, I guess that at the time of the events it wasn't *illegal* for a nineteen-year-old non-American person toiling away on a diving boat in the Eastern Med to not really know what the Twin Towers were, despite having been subjected to the New York skyline in a million different movies. Take it as yet another new-found limit of cultural imperialism or as another proof of my own attention deficit, but two towers, twin as they may be, in the middle of many others had, alas, not particularly drawn my attention before the events.

Arguably I shouldn't have cared that much about the theft of my papers; the seaman's book was almost useless, unless you worked on a boat under The Hole's flag and those boats were few and far in between. And the passport, well, seen from here it was a pretty meaningless item too, given that it was my passport from The Hole that did not open a single door in life. It was practically made of recycled toilet paper and it still managed somehow to be worth less than the paper it was printed on, yes, I agree.

However, that toilet paper passport was the only one I had at the time and I needed it to cross the big, big sea at the end of the tourist season in the Med. Isn't it a thing for most Western kids nowadays to jump on a gap year after school? I was ahead of my times in the idea but much behind my time regarding the papers required... duck geography, again.

Crossing the big, big sea was a simple dream resulting from the stories about exotic islands and southern seas told and retold by a mythomaniac Cook during a whole season of work, a couple of years before nine-eleven. Those stories, with their ruthless blending of truth and embellishment, slowly carved out a restless longing in me, weaving a siren call for distant, sun-soaked horizons full of uncharted lives. Cook probably had the biggest influence on my decision to look for non-deterministic happinesses after high school on one of them far away tropical islands. They were stuff of the wildest dreams, those islands that *our* long-dead empire of the non-colonial sort, built by gruesome but un-seafaring warriors, had just not been blessed with.

Cook and Soldier were these unlikely coworkers that I had met on that other diving boat, for a previous summer job. Soldier was a master diving instructor who didn't want any money for teaching me how to dive, on *his* own free time after having already spent long hours in the water. Cook was a master dreaming instructor who didn't *pay me* any money for listening to his never-ending stories full of alcohol and full moon parties in the Caribbean, on *my* own free time.

Cook had left The Hole at nineteen on an oil tanker and spent over fifteen years in various island-nations of improbable existence that all sounded like another planet to my teenager self. He was a proper free electron, full of past dodgy dealings in the Dutch Antilles and beyond, weaving through shadowy business ventures, his moves governed by an instinct for survival and an uncanny knack for slipping through the small cracks of the law designed for small criminals. A human grenade with the pin pulled, he used to say he spent years running *boxes of cigarettes* from Venezuela, when Venezuela still existed, both as a country and a dream generator. He used to run "high quality rum" from an island "he forgot the name of" to another one "whose name didn't really matter".

As a side note, the idea that *any* kind of rum can have a significant difference in market value between two Caribbean islands is the very definition of absurd. On top of it, the idea that subject difference can be significant enough to justify a *nocturnal arbitrage opportunity* by a bunch of youngsters on gas-guzzlers that go faster than the local coast guard boats is beyond absurd. So, for any naïve soul who really insists on believing that version of Cook's story, I have a decent bridge to sell between Dumbo and Lower Manhattan, please contact my publisher.

Once he stopped running rum and cigarettes, Cook would proudly say, he had learned to cook while working as a *factotum* at a brothel in Aruba. My teenager self somewhat legitimately wondered why on earth the type of brothel sophisticated enough to have its own cooks existed on the little Caribbean island of Aruba. Beyond that, I had enough knowledge of Latin to know that *totum* meant everything. And I had enough of an ear for the local pronunciation of the letter a in "fac" to blissfully imagine Cook ducking every moving thing in an Aruban brothel, while learning his art of cooking. Anyway, whatever his chef's training curriculum may have been, he claimed that he had come so far as getting a job offer to be Ted Turner's cook at his villa in Mustique. And once having identified the island on the atlas, the same teenager self of mine also wondered why on earth one would call an English island *mosquito* in French… With a wrong spelling on top of it, missing the o before the u.

In a nutshell, whatever definition one might choose to take for life expectancy and other obscure concepts related to statistical fatalities, Cook should have deservedly died at some point *above water* way before I met him on that fateful boat. Soldier, on the other hand, had rigorously been trained to learn how not to die *underwater* and he had then transferred this precious knowledge to his civilian life, making a living underwater. A subsea magician trained in a non-corporate environment to what some corporate bullsheeter would call *exacting standards*, he would carry out the work of three seasoned commercial divers on his own, with great *débrouillardise* and without ever complaining about working conditions. He was never late to work, he never drank and most importantly he never complained about the lacking safety standards. Soldier was the very definition of a valuable employee to any maverick subsea construction company.

And then one day, near-tragic circumstances on a badly-prepared and worse-executed inspection job threw him down current, disconnected from the support vessel. He was out into the open sea, out of sight, slowly fading out of the minds of his colleagues. There, in the infinite emptiness he spent the next seventeen hours adrift, his head bobbing about in between the white horses. Stirred but not shaken, he would joke about the event, blessed as he was with a natural immunity to seasickness.

Seventeen hours can legitimately be qualified as longbrass-time when one is floating even in calm seas, let alone under the winter conditions where the incident happened. Even more so if nobody told you at the beginning of your ordeal that it will be seventeen hours and you are floating out into the unknown. Therefore, any normal person would try to make these hours as comfortable and propitious to survival as possible but Soldier was obviously not *any normal person*.

When they finally fished him back on a fishing vessel passing by, he still had his weight belt on. It's nothing to write home about, an equipment as old as diving, consisting of a miserable rubber strap and a few four-pound blocks of lead, altogether worth a miserable fifty bucks back then and unlikely to be more than two hundred by now. Any diving procedure and any fool's common sense would have required the thirty-pound belt to be jettisoned, if not immediately, latest after the first hour into such an emergency, but Soldier hadn't.

"Business had been going downhill for a while, it was not the right day to dump the company's weight belt", he would say later, stoically. To my admiring ears, he sounded like that famous Galician captain from two centuries ago who found himself in the middle of a raging fire engulfing his ship and menacingly closing in on the gunpowder store. Stopping the seamen who were about to extinguish the fire, the captain had declared, *hoy no es día de mojar la pólvora* - today is no day to drench the gunpowder. I am a simple engineer with a simple old-style worldview, I have great respect for folks who value and defend the equipment that has been entrusted for their use as if it were their own, but... maybe these examples were a bit ducking extreme, huh, just maybe?

Needless to say, given that the subject of our stories is the merciless and ungrateful homo sapiens, no good deed can ever go *underpunished*. It was no surprise then, that Soldier -who had valued the company's fifty bucks' worth of material at the same level as his very own life- was among the first batch to be fired when that company's accounts kept taking on water during the months after his *merry adrifthood event*. Complain he didn't even when he got fired, I guess, because he had told me, no, *taught* me, a few weeks before getting fired, that, "like true love, proper loyalty does not seek to be mutual, it simply is exercised for loyalty's very own sake".

In the following months Cook and I came to understand that while Soldier was good at not dying underwater, this only applied when he was stuck within the clear boundaries of a well-defined operational environment. He knew how to survive hardships and certain risks under the aegis of a mighty army he was no longer part of. The same applied to a caring employer, one he realized too late he had never truly had. Put simply, no two survivors are ever the same and Soldier wasn't the same kind of survivor as Cook. More modern kids would certainly say that he lacked street smarts but they may as well go duck themselves, as he was part of those who taught me the street smarts that kept me alive on the road for the past two decades. "Nothing ends a fight as fast as a knife", I still hear him repeat every time I think about a *bad quarter hour* I spent in Caracas many years later, "I said *fast,* not *cleanly* but we're well past the point in human history where anyone cares about *cleanly.* So, to survive, *thou shalt not find yourself on the wrong end of a knife".*

During his unemployment, the bottle, that perpetual enemy of a certain breed of men, kept bringing him back to that one fateful day in the Balkans, when he was still serving, in the mid-nineties. A sniper had just taken his buddy, about ten feet from where Soldier himself had been standing. One moment the guy was there, the next moment he was gone, "pretty-much like in the movies", with a clean shot to the chest. And what kept haunting Soldier since then was not the whizz of the bullet, the blood spattering on him as his buddy was hit or the other, banally overworked cinematographic details of that life-changing moment; it was mainly the wish to understand the choice of the sniper that he would never meet.

Maybe he owed his survival to a simple technicality, like a matter of angle or a building in between their small unit and the sniper, based on where each of them was standing. But maybe, actually not maybe but rather probably, it wasn't a technicality, because both he and the victim had similar levels of cover towards the area where the bullet came from. So, the sniper, that invisible separator of unknown destinies, had made a conscious choice to kill one of the two guys and spare the other. Or had he made the choice to spare one and kill the other? And why?

On that particular day in the Balkans, I understood way too late, Soldier's destiny ceased to belong to himself and remained stuck at that instant, an instant he wouldn't ever be able to shrug off, wherever he went. He was a proud guy who had been trained to survive by his own merit, which was the whole problem. He hadn't died there but his survival had not resulted *from his own merit* and this had started to kill him slowly inside in these good old times where meritocracy had not yet become an insult. And his despondency then culminated when he didn't anymore have his diving job to prove to himself that as long as he had a last gasp of air, at least underwater, he wouldn't die. The ability to survive is what helps to convince ourselves of our own worth, *in daily practice*.

And one day, as one might expect, he was gone, of course not with a soft-landing, overdosing on pills or something similar. He didn't consider those options as *manly enough*, I guess; I guess but don't judge, what would be the purpose anyway, gone is gone. That day Soldier left with a proper nine mil in his very own head to compensate for the bullet he hadn't been given the choice to take next to his buddy. It brought home how much sorrow and rage could coil into silence, waiting for a release without a properly calibrated pressure relief valve. It left me wondering why so many proud men ended up drowning in the bottle. Oh, and also why the ducking powers-that-be did not confiscate the guns of PTSD'ed ex-soldiers.

On my side Soldier's suicide was followed by two long school years full of the undesired acquisition of some pointless academic knowledge, two years of waiting for the end of high school, *le baccalauréat*. Then came a short summer stint working in the *dream killing industry*, diving with European tourists, day in, day out, on the same barren reef that had been fished to ruin since times immemorial. I already knew the place very well but after that season I had unnecessarily learned by heart the shape of every single rock on that reef down there.

I wasn't really diving, to be honest. I was waiting underwater for the end of the season to cross the Atlantic with one of the only three sailboats that went from our port to the Caribbean for their owners to make some money in the off-season for the Med. I was gonna dance at the full moon parties that Cook talked about so much. I was gonna see colorful reefs full of exotic fish that didn't exist in our seas. I was gonna run rum with the contacts that Cook had promised me and that never materialized... Rum I was gonna run because I was still kid enough to never doubt that Cook had been running anything other than rum and there was per se nothing really wrong with running rum: it was a legal substance, you were just robbing some minuscule would-be state island of some would-be tax income and getting some well-deserved adrenaline rush in the process. Cook was a strange but somewhat good man, he certainly hadn't run any peppermint or milk powder between those islands, right?

For the defense of my naïveté, at age nineteen, after a more or less normal childhood, whatever that may mean, one can be forgiven for not having attained the required life experience and wisdom to fully decipher the extent of nocturnal arbitrage opportunities between Caribbean islands.

Anyway, I couldn't run anything, and I couldn't go anywhere, plain and simple, as simple dreams were pretty simple to kill in The Hole. And dreams stolen by dint of irreplaceable papers are some of the cruelest forms of torture, for duck's sake, it makes my blood boil even now to think about it.

Beyond the passport and the seaman's book, all the thief got was a miserable fifty Deutsche Mark note that was monologuing in my wallet. Not even a cellphone; they used to be luxury items back then. And of course, a large bag of dreams he had unintentionally stolen, as I realized the next day, but I guess dreams are also luxury items when you are born within the wrong borders that some great glorious men defined generations before your birth.

The day that followed the theft was the *nine-twelve*, if I may take the liberty of creating the concept without offending my fellow New Yorkers. And in the Med the charter season kind of goes to the end of September, when these three boats were going to cast off for the Caribbean, the islands, rum-running and full moon parties. One could arguably say, well, from nine-twelve to the end of the month, it gives you almost three weeks to get your stuff settled and renew your papers, plenty of time indeed, isn't it?

"You need to go back to your city of residence to renew a stolen passport, it cannot be done here", began the old policeman behind the counter, a local peasant visibly pleased to observe that my city of residence was a ten-hour drive away.

"You need to put an announcement in the newspaper that you lost your seaman's book and bring that page of the newspaper back to us so that we can write to the authorities in the capital to investigate if the stolen seaman's book has already been used by anyone" continued the receptionist at the Harbormaster's office.

"Then and only then will we be able to issue a new seaman's book for you but no worries, it should take about two months, not much longer", finished the clerk behind the last counter.

He stopped for a moment to check me out, his manners betraying, unexpectedly for a *simple clerk*, a somewhat similar social origin as me, presumably with a family fallen on even harder times than mine. "By the way, if anyone tells you that bribing the Harbormaster can get you a new seaman's book in just a few days, don't waste any of your money or time on it. There is absolutely no way to get it without an investigation by the authorities in the capital, all the rest are lies. And this Harbormaster is both corrupt and inefficient, I assure you the process won't get any faster by paying anyone".

A year or two before that I would have been dumb enough to pay the bribe, nevertheless. But thankfully in the meantime I had had enough of having little chunks of my destiny depend on somebody else's goodwill while waiting for my different diving certificates that had mostly never materialized. And yet, I had spent entire seasons working for those certificates. For junior personnel, the deals in that line of business always consisted of a modest salary, food and lodging on the boat and getting the next level of qualification at the season's end. After a few scams and a few unnecessary fights, I had learned that most employers of non-deterministic countries are shameless hope merchants, with hopes that keep the little guy awake at night, hopes buried below mounds of lies. You know what? I'm not taking this sheet anymore, the Harbormaster can go duck himself and so can Cook's exotic islands.

So, just like that, from beyond the grave, Kafka closed the curtain on the unique weather window for my very own Everest of crossing the Atlantic at age nineteen. And the *uniqueness* of the weather window was not a subject of discussion; I had gotten my *baccalauréat*, I was just going to take one *barely acceptable* year off and come back with stories from across the pond, that eternal dream since the first Spaniards, to then start my degree. There could not be another season of wandering around the year after that one: two successive gap years just weren't within the envelope of what was acceptable for a lifeplan. In short, I had dreamt of trying to marry conventionality with free-electronism, to run with the hare and hunt with the hounds and I had failed. It was the kind of dreamer's experiment bound to fail.

History will certainly pardon me for the very personal conclusion that I then reached through a simplistic generalization from a single data point of failure, which may legitimately be criticized for its lack of statistical representativity, but a *timelessly valid* conclusion it is:

Every non-deterministic country is a destiny grinder.

# Thou shalt not bury your mom according to her wishes

She was strong and successful, a combination which, in our old country, did not result in her being *powerful*, due to an impenetrable absence of geographical coherence in these two attributes that she had: she was strong *in* the West and successful as *seen from* the East, from home, not that I would still want to call that country her home. Let's say she was successful as *seen from the country where she was born*, our common Hole. Or, better said, the country where her ailing mother would end up dying and getting buried. Yes, this is the more appropriate way to talk about the place, given that our common native city did not carry any more meaning for the daughter.

That same city had just seen me come back from the Med with broken dreams about the Caribbean. Crestfallen and disoriented, I was thinking that my stolen passport was probably sold on some distant black market of ill repute in that southern small city of maritime grandeurs that I had to leave behind. One evening in my neighborhood, Strong and I bumped into each other at the deli around the corner, down from my family apartment that is no more. We were good obedient kids sent for groceries by our respective parents. She was well into her thirties, I was almost in my twenties and we were both still unforgivably *kids*.

Kids of badly sin-laden families that we were, I was grabbing a bottle of wine, just for Mom, because Dad would never drink any legally bought drop of alcohol, as that particular state didn't deserve his taxes. Strong was grabbing a pack of smokes for her mom, *despite the stage-four lung cancer*, as she stated with a smile. There comes a moment where any respectable doctor with true empathy for the patient shall sentence "you may eat whatever you please" and Strong's mom had indeed reached that very moment of relief.

Ever the genius, in her previous life among us mere mortals, Strong used to be the older sister of a childhood friend from our neighborhood. She was now a respected scientist in a *prominent* US university and at the time I had scratched my head a bit trying to grasp why a physics major would have any academic thing to do with *ivies*. May the American reader again excuse me for my ignorance of those young years; it's not that the climate in The Hole did not allow ivies to grow on the buildings… it's just that after the Empire collapsed, most ivy-covered buildings were either destroyed or *repurposed* by the republic. After having been cleaned of their ivies, of course.

Strong's parents and ours used to be on dining terms for quite a while when we were younger. My brother used to give math lessons to her youngest brother, lessons that she herself was more than capable of giving but that she would dodge just to avoid generating the usual silly sibling feuds. In exchange for the math lessons, her mom used to ply my brother and me with the kind of tiramisu which to this age makes me think that Proust's famous madeleines could *go get dressed*. I have a hunch that this had to do with the copious amount of Courvoisier that she used to drench the base of the tiramisu with but of course I'm not discarding the quality of the remaining ingredients or her baking skills, it's just a hunch… In short, with these people we were part of a *neighborhood*, when neighborhoods still existed in my native city. "Before the neighborhoods died and my native city followed suit", I should have written.

"That last oncologist's verdict is very clear, my mom has just a few weeks left, at most three months", Strong stated, sipping on the imported bottle of Chianti, a few hours after our encounter at the deli. She then passed the bottle to my brother and lit a meaningful cigarette for her circumstances, looking at the emerald sea of our childhood in the distance. She had been missing that very sea unwillingly since her new adult life had given her no other option than a few restricted summer weekends of sixty-five degrees water temperature at best every year on the US East Coast. Being condemned to swim in the North Atlantic for the rest of an *Ivy-League* life may be the harshest punishment to impose on a kid from the Med, however Strong she may be.

"Mom has been adamant that she doesn't want to end up *under the earth* in this country of ours when her time will come", Strong continued when the bottle was back in her hands, "she doesn't want to be buried according to *their* rite. She's not gonna accept it just because according to the *religion* cell on her ID *that thing* is her religion".

It looks like so far I have forgotten to mention that where we grew up, we had our religion, the one assigned at birth, well, *a religion*, written on the ID, may the reader forgive me for this omission. Not that it's a major subject, I guess… "Some people may wear glasses and some not; the religion of the people you will meet in life shall never have more importance in your judgment of them as humans than if they wore glasses or not… or if they preferred tea over coffee, for that matter" our Mom had told us when we were kids, hence my omission. For some reason people's preference of tea or coffee was not written on their ID but it must have been a simple oversight, right? Mom just cannot have been wrong, people just cannot be *that shallow*, we humans are a superior species, right?

"We cannot bury her anywhere else, like in another cemetery just to escape *their* rite", Strong sipped further on the wine, "because not only did she not want to be buried according to *any* rite but also one cannot be buried in the cemetery of a confession or religion other than the one stated on one's ID. And there still isn't any legal possibility of cremation in this Hole of a place, can you ducking believe it?"

My tender nineteen years were barely getting harassed by the approaching round birthday, which may as well mean that up to then I had faced a rather limited number of reasons, if any, to spend my energy on considerations related to how best one could slide into the next life - burial, cremation or other new-age solutions. Few people I had lost, thankfully few people... Soldier had been buried in the intimacy of a restricted family circle, the understandable kind of family intimacy that is intended to veil the departures that one has had the audacity to decide for oneself. Dentist was my parents' friend, a generation and a half above me, so there was no expectation for us kids to participate in the ceremony and anyway I had school the day they buried him.

"I don't know how they will react if I tell these duckers that my mom did not want to be buried according to *their* rite", Strong wondered when we were uncorking the second, less-drinkable bottle of red, a locally produced bottle. In The Hole, winemaking had a brief and unremarkable history, with the resulting products being either questionable or prohibitively expensive. Therefore, we would always go for one good bottle and keep the less-drinkable ones for after the tipsy-tipping point.

"Can they plainly refuse to bury her, for instance? They should have no such right, my family owns that plot of land in the cemetery, for duck's sake, ownership is still a sacrosanct right in what is left of the rule of law here. Maybe they will refuse to bury her without their rite or they will deceitfully agree to bury her but later pee on her grave in the night. Peeing I could maybe still live with, but what if they pull out the corpse in the night to mistreat it? We have all heard about acts of desecration against the *godless* people, haven't we? Am I gonna literally spend what they call *graveyard shifts* in English as a damned sentinel on her grave until the body decomposes far enough, to be sure that nobody's gonna unearth it?"

One of the competing -less common, but nevertheless competing- theories on the origin of the expression *graveyard shifts,* I was to learn half a life later, is that when the science of medicine was making significant empirical progress in the eighteenth and nineteenth centuries, the experimental needs of medical students and faculties resulted in grave plundering and corpse trafficking in the name of science. As a result, on many occasions the deceased's family would hold watch at the graveyard to prevent any plunder in the first nights after the burial, until the body was of no use anymore to science. Of course, this theory refers to England and some other European countries, because progress was something they made in the West, not in our kind of places. In The Hole or the Empire that was there before, the only reason to open up a grave had *traditionally* been that *simply peeing on it* while the body hadn't yet had time to fully decompose wasn't desecrating that body enough for the hateful peer's taste. The "peer" of this sentence, needless to say, is not the same peer as in a *peer review,* it is pronounced pee-er and not pi:r.

"I've heard that they also don't accept your body to be buried back in this land if you renounce the citizenship", my brother chipped in, in a clumsy attempt to change the subject without charging it too much. He hadn't yet left them, neither the country nor the citizenship, he was a bit less kid than me but still a kid stuck with his initial conditions. "Well, regarding my own burial, whenever it may come, they can go duck themselves", Strong spat the answer, "once my mother is gone, I ain't stepping on this damned soil of theirs ever again and I'm certainly not getting buried here. They can just stick its whole seven hundred and something thousand square kilometers up their stinky brass." A balanced judgment it was, I found, a very balanced and healthy assessment of the situation, free of emotional biases...

As foreseen, Strong's mom died a few weeks after that drinking afternoon and with my brother we went to the burial as two additional pairs of acceptable shoulders to cry on, shoulders that she didn't really need. Her brother was also there but she was the *older brother* so flouting tradition and not giving a duck about her womanhood, she went straight to engage the *emcee* of the unwanted religious ceremony. "My mother never wanted to be buried according to a religious rite, she had no religion, she was a freethinker", Strong informed the emcee, as matter-of-factly as she could, without any provocation, "shall we comply with her last wish so that her soul can truly rest in peace, Sir? *Can* we comply, please?"

Based on our life experience so far in The Hole, we were legitimately suspecting that *people like this emcee* did not need any particular excuse or provocation to behave like despicable brassholes. Truly none of us would have been surprised if he went so far as raising a hand against a woman. We were even considering such behavior second nature for *them people,* proving how many disconnected parallel societies existed within the same country. Therefore, all three of us were keeping a reasonable distance of sufficient closeness to intervene so that we could nip in the bud, by our mere physical presence, any act of disrespect that the *emcee* might be tempted to have towards Strong. In plain English, if that ducker even so slightly started to raise that ugly hand of his, my brother was going to first break that hand and then stick it up its owner's brass. Talk about burying someone *in peace* so that her soul can truly rest in peace...

It turned out we were wrong on that instance. We were as wrong as the *emcee* was clean shaven. Observing the way he was looking into Strong's sad but determined eyes, one would say that he was considering her a *human being and not just a woman,* he had that rare, peaceful, understanding look in his eyes. He had the eyes of someone who had seen enough death and family members to internalize that people may wish to enter into the afterlife differently. "As much as I would like to comply with your and her wishes, madam, I just cannot bury your mother without following the rite, *our* rite," he answered, pensively. "Please have a look at the thousands resting around us in this place, madam, with all respect for your loss, I also have to respect how all these people were buried, they are the eternal community beyond here that your beloved mother is about to join."

The emcee seemed genuine. The emcee seemed honest. The emcee, we had to recognize, was right within his own value system and it was not the emcee's fault that the poor lady was born in a country whose value system did not correspond to her worldview. Or that her circumstances did not allow or require her to leave that country. There was only so much the emcee could do, given the circumstances.

Strong had been -we *all* had been- brought up with way too much decency to be haggling like rug-merchants with a person in a position of authority, even if the source of subject authority, represented by this *emcee fellow,* did not inspire an ounce of respect. Weeks ago, Strong had already shouldered the burden of resignation to her mom's impending death when the doctors had announced to the family that she had stage-four cancer. Then at the cemetery, I could see the on-the-spot development of a new, soul-crushing sense of resignation on her tired face: the damning realization that she wouldn't even be able to comply with her mom's last wish. One should not, if there is any justice on earth, deny a child the possibility of fulfilling her mother's last wish.

After a long moment of silence, she uttered a barely audible, almost emotionless "so she will not be buried according to her wishes" that the emcee acknowledged with a nod. "Alright," she said. "We shouldn't have expected anything else in this place, I know, let's proceed."

So we proceeded… None of us cried there as we were all pensively trying to come to terms with yet another newfound resignation: that to be free at death, one needs to have been free in life. That to be free to mourn your loved ones as you wish, you yourself need to be free. And that this freedom, to us, was a luxury refused at birth. Even if by our own merit and doggedness we would attain that sort of freedom at some point in life in some far-flung place, it could be taken from us in our most intimate moments, in total helplessness, back in The Hole.

We buried her mom according to the rite. Nevertheless, under the disapproving but toothless looks of the *emcee* and his not-clean-shaven wingman, it was Strong herself who lowered her mom's body into the grave, that *privilege* normally reserved for the eldest son of the deceased. Then we all shoveled back the mound where it belonged, waited patiently for intruders to leave and pulled out a flask of decent whisky. After a small sip for each of us, we emptied the generous rest of the flask on her grave to bid farewell and we left the cemetery.

That was the last time I saw Strong. Even to visit her mom's grave, she for sure never came back to her native country. "For sure" as far as I know, whatever that may mean, because at the end our neighborhood ended up not being a neighborhood anymore and we all lost track of each other.

To make a long story short, daughters and sons of this very blessed land surrounded by sea on three sides and by sorrow on all six sides including above and below: did you for a moment dare to think that you would be in possession of your claimed-to-be-own destiny after your death?

# Not responsible for lost or stolen years

Given that I will now take the liberty of a too-tight chronological proximity between two successive chapters, we might as well add the liberty of too tight a *thematic* proximity so we shall stick with mothers and burials. After that one we will put the pedal to the metal, no worries.

It was the week after we had buried Strong's mother, and I was sitting alone at the dining table with Mom. Outside, the late afternoon sun cast long shadows across the room, and the faint hum of the neighborhood seemed to fade into the background. The illustrious, mind-opening Nick Cave from our youth was in town, so my brother had gone to his concert, eager to lose himself in the familiar thrum of the music and the uniquely inspiring lyrics of that genius. Dad, as usual, was busy in his own way, sitting with his friends at some terrace, all comfortably ensconced in the world of their old habits. I could picture that bunch of uglies there, expertly orchestrating the slow dance of time that is the essence of life in the Orient. Dad was very probably conspiring to make the sun set at the precise angle between two ice cubes slowly melting in his whisky glass, in one of the small, deliberate moments that mattered in real life away from unnecessary rush.

He may have been physically absent from the table and the discussion that evening but I have a hunch that they had anyway agreed beforehand on the subject that Mom wanted to discuss with me. The "subject" was not new, it's not as if leaving that Hole to *make our lives* hadn't been the mission, the very *raison d'être* of us kids since the very beginnings.

"Move on", said Mom between *la poire et le fromage*, or rather between the hot goulash and the cold celery dish cooked in ample amounts of olive oil. Since I left The Hole, I may have had two, at most three distinct occasions of sufficient stability in life to have that specific celery dish in my fridge, between Angola and Brooklyn, which is a tragic decline in quality of life. "Move on and don't waste your life here. Move on, my life, move on and let that *on* be somewhere in the West. Move on and don't come back to this Hole, even to bury us don't come back here. Move on, when my time comes, there will certainly be someone else to shovel that soil for me and if need be, I will just wake up, bury myself and die back. You move on, my life, please, you move on."

"I don't know for your dad", she continued, deep into the technicalities of the burial process, "but me, I will make them bury me vertically, not lying down comfortably, so that even the ground cannot pretend to support me during my eternal rest. I have stayed upright in life, I will stay upright in death coz I don't want the ground to have any rights on me, I need nobody's and nothing's support."

"You know it has now been four generations that my family has left Crimea and since then we haven't counted on anybody. So, it's only fair that I don't want my children to have to count on anybody for whatever they will need to cope with, against whatever this miserable place can throw at them. You should not stay here where you *cannot become*. Move on."

At this stage of the account *one* could, many other *ones* could, under many other circumstances, infuse this narrative with some dramatic flair, as it now seems to be standard procedure within the contemporary candy-ass approach to storytelling that prevails in the Occident. *Oh my dear, you had to leave your country at the tender age of twenty, on grounds of freedom of conscience, how unfortunate, blah blah.* Over the last two decades in the West I have come across a great many people of, I'm sorry to state, quite limited intellect with high opinions of their understanding of the world, who were dying to *distort* all my limbs to force my body and soul into their preferred mold of some victimhood And believe it or not, some of them folks were lobotomized enough to actually pronounce "tender age" and "twenty" in the same sentence.

If the subject is tenderness of age, well, at age twenty, the paternal grandfather whom we could never meet had already endured three years behind thick and corroded bars in the remnants of the first Empire. Not that it was his choice or an expected kind of bump in the road. It's just that a few months after his family had to leave the place and start a new life in our Hole due to the October Revolution, they had chosen him, as the oldest male child, to be sent back to where they had come from. It was the very country where that great humanist Stalin had come from, if his cursed name must be mentioned to create geographical context.

On a mission he was, Grandpa, hoping to recover some *bits and pieces* that the family had been obliged to leave behind when they left hurriedly during the Revolution. On a mission he was, as if a seventeen-year-old kid was going to *stick in the back pocket of his pants* the houses and apartments they had left behind. And all the goods and chattels contained therein, right? It was not a successful mission, one must say, in all fairness, as they put him in jail the next day after he arrived, the kind of jail no Hollywood movie will ever do justice…

When Grandpa could finally return to The Hole after these three horrible years, a haggard ex-prisoner with no sentence ever pronounced against him, he was genuinely grateful to be alive as well as at a loss to understand why they hadn't killed him. Killing him would have cost them nothing in that land of eternal unaccountability. Tenderness, maybe; who knows? After all tenderness is what this passage was supposed to be about.

So, out of regard for what my own blood had to endure a mere two generations ago, this account shall refrain from giving in to that lame schmaltz about me leaving my native country in search of freedom, be it freedom of conscience or any other type. And actually this we shall do, not only out of respect for my grandpa but also because I *did not have to leave at any cost*. It was a conscious choice, the very luxury that billions of fellow humans just cannot share… Oh, for sure, money was a bit of a problem and visas the other, but I was a young, able-bodied person, intellectually *equipped to the teeth*, or at least so I believed. And I was finally putting into action the mission which my brother and I had both been subconsciously prepared for all our life by our parents. In all fairness, nobody was running after me with a machete to chase me away from home.

I may, at that time, not have fully grasped the most relevant reasons behind that choice, I may have simply made the jump *thanks to* some lack of ties to where I was living, but all these points don't really matter anymore. What really matters is that after that dinner with Mom, in and through the years that followed, I singlehandedly wrenched my freedom away from that destiny-grinder of a Hole, and as a consequence I now have the option of getting myself buried vertically if I so desire. Or at any oblique angle of my preference, for that matter; I'm currently considering thirty degrees as it has a nice cosine, thank you very much.

Recently, a-few-months-ago-recently, a fellow New Yorker actually hit the mark on why, deep down, we had both left them non-deterministic destiny-grinder countries where we were born, on opposite sides of the pond. Needless to say, the fellow New Yorker was as much of a *real* New Yorker as I am; he was born abroad, like half the population of this city. In his particular case, the birthplace was that Spanish-speaking bumducknowhere of modern Venezuela, managed by an ignorant bus driver. It was a country turned into a tropical nuthouse that has been shredding thirty-seven metric tons of innocent dreams per inhabitant per year over the past decade, without blinking an eye.

My fellow New Yorker's Spanish had those heavily guttural ways of people from the Western part of his country, from that beautiful city by the murky lake, where I had to spend a few months of a previous life, *schlepped* by semi-professional circumstances. Guttural is probably not the right adjective, not doing justice to what any acting teacher would qualify as a *placement even lower than the lungs*, bordering on ventriloquism. His voice emerged from somewhere so deep in the chest, vibrating with such raw power that it seemed to echo in the bones rather than the ears. And rather than being punctuated, his sentences were *riddled* with heavy shots of nine-mil *vergación* sown in between every other word. The closest translation of *vergación* is probably "duck it" but no offense, it's just a common exclamation in that very specific Maracucho dialect.

"Tomorrow-sellers are what they are, *vergación*, these freaking smugglers, they sell you tomorrows that have never existed. They keep telling you their lies of 'day after tomorrow'... *day after tomorrow we will cross the border* they say, and there you are like, *vergación*, still in the ducking Darién Gap, with miles and miles of misery between you and a decent existence up north", he was ranting and raving... "Just like the employers back home, vergación, liars with empty promises and sheetloads of excuses for why they will *only be able to pay you next week*".

Vergación had ended up in New York without any particularly favorable set of *initial conditions* pulling the strings for him. He was a young graduate when the bus driver's spiritual father, the Chief Thief, had stolen their country back in the day, but Vergación hadn't been much concerned with the events at the beginning. That is the nature of really bad changes; they rarely cause concern at the beginning. In all honesty, Vergación's part of the world can't really be called an example of stability either, so he was thinking, "Well, business as usual, this too shall pass, there will be another set of thieves taking over the place, who cares". They were all used to conventional thieves, anyway. Most thieves tend to steal within the operational normalcy of an *acceptable bandwidth* of some sweet spot, he thought. They will let the common folks, the backbone of any economy, continue to make *enough of a living* so that life can go on without the country either sinking or floating, he imagined. And this kind of turned out to be true in the beginnings, the very beginnings…

But then the Chief Thief and his self-righteous assassins became emboldened, *envalontenados,* by impunity and they removed all checks and balances, one by one. With the complicity of many first-world useful idiots, needless to say. Everybody likes a revolution that makes somebody else poor, just not in my backyard, please.

The dirtbags then decided to widen that *acceptable bandwidth* of theft and started to pare down the middle class to the bone, with their colorful and wide spectrum of injustices ranging from confiscations to wanton assassinations. The broader the scope of their predation, the more they preyed on the people, gnawing slowly toward the edges of survival. But maybe the guys were too slow or maybe the bone was situated a bit too deep in the flesh. In any case, the problem was that the crash didn't come immediately, it took a few more boiling-frog years with Vergación thinking, "Well, this has been going on for an unusual length of time but it should pass, at some point this too *should* well pass, right?"

Fact is, it never passed, as we all know by now. So at some point, by force of circumstances Vergación snapped and left his country, like many other millions who had already gone into exile. He ended up crossing all of Central America, part on foot, part on the hackneyed, shabby, yellow, old converted American school buses with sleepy peasants and clucking chickens and mostly on whatever means of transport the local smugglers put him on. Sometimes the roads were little more than tracks through the jungle, where the cars seemed to crawl along, their engines sputtering under the weight of time and distance. At other times, he found himself crammed into the back of a rickety truck, elbows tight against the sweaty bodies of strangers, their faces marked by the same exhaustion, as the hot, humid air swirled in a suffocating haze. The landscape outside seemed endless, with its sparse villages, rolling hills, and deep riverbeds, all flickering in the heat waves as the journey stretched on and on.

After eight borders, once he was finally north of the river, safe and sound, Vergación found the first acceptable roof over his head and the first job, regardless of whether it was acceptable or not. And he started to work, to work his brass off. This he did, of course to survive and to put food on the table, but "before anything else, to recover my dignity", he would say, to feel worth something. And he worked, worked and worked to *thank the benevolence of the circumstances* and the regular paycheck that would exactly correspond to the hours he had put in, nobody stealing his hours and efforts anymore. At every paycheck, he would admire the validity of a signed contract, appreciate the value of the given word, and feel deep gratitude for all these basic assumptions of the non-grinder countries.

Being brought up in the Catholic faith and having been surrounded throughout his childhood by Virgin Mary statues, Vergación had seamlessly taken on the Lady Liberty as the new saint of devotion in that second life of his, with his newfound freedom, which I realized one day when we were strolling down Brooklyn Heights. Turning around a corner, as we had just gained a line of sight to the vast sea and beyond, I saw him cross himself, and I instinctively started looking around to identify a church we might have passed by. The Danish Seamen's Church was already a full block behind us, and I knew the neighborhood well enough to recognize that there shouldn't be another church right there. I was a bit surprised but didn't want to say anything, as we were taught in our childhood not to stick our noses into other people's saints and temples. Seeing my slight confusion, however, Vergación felt he had to clarify the situation. "It's Lady Liberty," he pointed out to the sea, "I always cross myself when I see her. A *proper Catholic* might say that it's an act of blasphemy or could dismiss it as just a meaningless superstition, but I've been doing this since I came to New York. And what I believe in is nobody else's business, right? I just can't imagine that anybody who has come to this city from somewhere else can look at Her with indifference, there surely are as many admiring ways of looking at her as there are uprooted folks in this city. And mine involves crossing myself, nothing more."

Backtracking from this Lady Liberty sidetrack… I was saying, Vergación hit the mark on why, deep down, we had all left them non-deterministic destiny-grinder countries where we had been lucky or unlucky enough to be born. Later that day, as we were finishing our last pints in a cozy bar on Atlantic Avenue, his big brown eyes locked on the usual "not responsible for lost or stolen items" sign in the establishment. It hung in a well-lit part of the bar, perched high on a wood-paneled wall, with letters so bold they seemed almost accusatory. The sign was crafted to ensure that no reasonable patron could pretend not to have noticed it, as its message was visible from every corner of the bar.

"This sign," Vergación said after emptying his pint, his hand lingering on the glass as if weighing its emptiness, "this very sign, they need to hang it high at the border of my country, in bold letters, visible from miles away." He sighed, his voice carrying the weight of unspoken memories. "But hanging it there wouldn't be enough. No, they'd have to whisper it too, softly, into the ear of every newborn baby, right from their first breath, before they've even had a chance to open their eyes to the world they're about to inherit."

He paused, his gaze fixed somewhere beyond the dim bar, where the hum of distant conversations blended with the clink of glasses. "Whisper it gently, like a lullaby, but with the force of a warning:

"Kiddo, our country is not responsible for lost or stolen years."

# Suffering History

"Move on and let that *on* be somewhere in the West", Mom had instructed me and what the West meant for my young and ignorant twenty-year old self was necessarily France, that distant lighthouse, shining brightly through the fog surrounding our existence in The Hole. The obviousness of that choice was not only due to the fake mother tongue in which we had been educated since our childhood: France, not the country as such but most importantly the Republic it incarnated, was an ideal. It was the *superior civilizational model* that shaped our thinking and the mental model that we had been following all our lives.

We did not have any particular reason to follow that model, as both countries did not have such a significant historical connection… Some mutual commercial privileges, a few treaties here and there that had opened a few markets but not many hearts. We hadn't *gone to a single war* together, for duck's sake… But it was the Republic *who* had agreed in the nineteenth century with the then-ruler of the land to found my school and they had since regularly sent teachers to The Hole, so I was grateful.

Oh they weren't all perfect, the teachers, *loin s'en faut*, and the correct translation of "far from it" should be *tant s'en faut* but let's not grammatically overcomplicate the modern Frenchmen's already miserable lives. So I should actually be proud of myself for having decided to study in France *despite* my high school experiences with them. A good many of those folks carried the proprietary air of those who had come to civilize the *inferior* races that we were... Those were mostly the *bon pour l'Orient* variety, "good for the Orient", opinionated spoiled brats with a state contract for life and armed, in their little mind, with all the rights bestowed by their contract and status but rarely with the corresponding obligations. A given set of obligations that correspond to a given set of rights is for *inferior* people, not for French civil servants.

One of my general principles in life is that one should never behave arrogantly with fellow humans, unless dealing with arrogant people, in which case one should be without the slightest mercy... One day during our last year of high school, one of them *bon pour l'Orient* duckers, namely the physics teacher whose name I forgot, was getting on my nerves with some arrogant observations about why I should pay attention to whatever he was trying to explain to us. The word "civilized" showed the tip of its nasty nose somewhere in the sentence. Oh how I hate that word... So I took the liberty of posing a question in front of the whole class: "With all due respect, Sir, my family descends from two Empires, which makes me seriously wonder who the duck you think you are to *civilize* me, coming from your provincial sheethole of Limoges?"

Sure, this was no way to talk to a guest in our country...because in The Hole's culture even if the guest doesn't behave, you as the host are supposed to behave. And this certainly was no way to talk to a teacher. I was just another rebellious teenager and whatever the matter had been, it must have been so unimportant that today I don't remember anything specific about it. What I remember, though, is the answer, the memorable, the rememberable answer.

It could be said that the answer was treacherous, clearly ill-intentioned or borderline *straw manning* because it was moving a childishly ad hominem attack into an unrelated general territory. But correct it was, correct to the bone, that answer: "Whatever once-glorious and bygone empires your honorable family may be descending from", the physics teacher started… "fact is, the sad fact is, the crème de la crème of *my* nation gets educated at the Lycée Henry-IV by their fellow countrymen, whereas the French State sent *me,* a foreigner, here, to educate the crème de la crème of *your* nation, at your state's request. So maybe, beyond this land's traditional hospitality, I should legitimately be in a position to expect at least that you behave as a deserving member of that supposed intellectual crème de la crème of your nation, don't you think so?"

Correct it was, the answer, correct to the bone. Now, two years later, after the dinner discussion with Mom, I realize it was correct to the marrow, as I was the one going abroad to study in that teacher's country. If one day, ever, one of that ducker's grandchildren comes to The Hole where I was born, to study in a language different from his own mother tongue of French or in that *reluctantly accepted lingua franca* called English, then we may reopen this discussion, most likely from beyond the grave for both the physics teacher and myself. But in the meantime, I had come to understand something crucial. You might be an average fellow from a below-average provincial hole in France, a place where they once shelved incompetent generals during the First World War. (The city of Limoges, after all, contributed the verb *limoger* to the French language.) I might be descending from two glorious empires, the first one may have gifted humankind with the most prolific literature ever, the other one may have invented true cosmopolitanism two centuries before the West. And even your great Napoléon Bonaparte, without ever setting foot in my native city, may have been flabbergasted by it… It doesn't matter, I am to defer to the superiority of your model given the circumstances and rightly so, period.

One sleazy philosophy teacher was constantly running after twelfth grade girls, probably thinking that it was legal to horizontalize one's students, given that they were already eighteen. A cheap, lowbrow orientalist with a bloated ego, that French charlatan had changed his religion after marrying a woman from another, *more rigorous* religion and he was talking all the time about his new-found *faith*. One could potentially judge that he did a good job as a teacher, in an indirect way, by unintentionally teaching us youngsters to be wary of people who need to convince others about how great their new-found religion is. Or to be wary of forty-something year old married sleazebags who run after eighteen-year-old kids that they are supposed to educate rather than get into their bed. At some point, fed up with all his insistence, one of our good friends decided to *try* the guy, wanting just to get it over with. "Not only are his classes extremely boring but sexually speaking, he is nothing to write home about", she had sentenced after the disappointing experience. I guess one should avoid sleeping with people whose classes are boring.

Another philosophy teacher we had, an old and opinionated heavy drinker with an imposing moustache, was dating a young illiterate construction worker from the East of The Hole. "Dating" is maybe a bit of an exaggeration for what was mostly a transactional relationship. It looked like the guy was staying in the teacher's place in a kind of sex-for-bed *barter agreement* and nothing else. I'm not being judgmental, it's just that I fail to see what they may have been talking about given the absence of a common language and I don't really know if a relationship without any talking qualifies as "dating". Unless, of course, one of the parties has a speech or hearing impediment, which wasn't the case for those gentlemen.

The way I talk about our philosophy teachers, it may sound like all they were doing in The Hole was sleep around with random people including their students. It wasn't the case: they always found some spare time to give us classes on Platon and Kant. It may sound like I am self-righteously questioning everybody's right to sleep with whomever they please. Well, it honestly isn't the case either. I'm all for freedom as long as it doesn't encroach on other people's freedom. It is just that I take the liberty of questioning the capacity of an *agrégé de philosophie* who spends his whole evening with an illiterate guy with whom he doesn't share any common conversational language to then, first thing in the morning, properly explain the Allegory of the Cave to some kids *at the crème de la crème de mes couilles* bilingual school of the *Elite de la Nation* blah blah. Just that very point I am trying to understand, nothing more, and I think what I have is a legitimate type of questioning.

When he was eighteen, on his first day at La Sorbonne, the not-yet-famous-but-clearly-gifted professional sailor Olivier de Kersauson noticed something odd in the uninviting lecture hall. As the economics professor paced back and forth at the front of the blackboard, gesturing emphatically about obscure matters related to market forces or fiscal policies, Kersauson's ocean-blue eyes caught sight of a hole in the sole of the old man's shoe. It wasn't a large hole, but it was there, a quiet emblem of wear and disregard. Many would have dismissed such a detail, perhaps many more would even see it as a charming sign of academic absentmindedness. But not Kerso. To him, it was more than just a trivial flaw; it was a signal. If the man tasked with teaching him the ins and outs of *money* couldn't even manage to secure a decent pair of shoes at that age, then surely something was seriously rotten in the system.

Kerso wasn't exactly brimming with enthusiasm for academia to begin with, and this realization was the final tie-down strap around the coffin. Paris, with its endless grey streets, felt suffocating, too far removed from the wild, open sea that called to him. He sat there for a moment longer, letting the professor's words fade into the background, then quietly gathered his belongings. Without a second glance, leaving behind the musty corridors of higher education for the briny air and endless horizons of a sailor's life where a hole in the equipment was in the *right order of things,* he walked out of the classroom. And rightfully so.

To give praise where praise is due, at my high school we were blessed with a succession of excellent math teachers who armed me for life, because, in case you didn't know it, the French obviously *invented* math, like most other things that had a major contribution to the progress of civilization. Furthermore, our biology teacher and chemistry teacher both had irreplaceable contributions to my personal path to civilization, through their technical support of my nascent winemaking endeavors.

Modern kids obviously find every kind of winemaking technique -or bomb-making instructions, if they are so inclined- on the net. Thankfully, when we were that age, if a subject matter of interest wasn't in our parents' or the school's library, we actually had to go *talk to people* to learn about it. And wine is quite simply a matter of biology for making it and of chemistry for conserving it. So, thanks to these two teachers I was able to produce *quite* a few *chaptalized* bottles of questionable taste but strong alcohol content, which was perfectly suited to the needs and comprehension abilities of youth.

These bottles waited a long many years for my return home until one day Dad decided not to extend their pain any longer. Fully home-made, it was alcohol without any associated taxes paid to the state, which made it legitimate in my Dad's book. So he *buried* them with the usual band of uglies over long evenings of existential discussions at Violinist's shop.

Chaptalization, by the way, is the centuries-old technique of adding sugar to the grape must in order to enhance the fermentation process and the corresponding alcohol output. This method is often used in cooler wine-growing regions to ensure that the fermentation reaches its full potential, especially in years with less-than-ideal weather conditions. Centuries-old as the technique is and despite the Roman roots it might claim, obviously it had to be *invented* -a bit like math- by a Frenchman with an overload of grave-sounding first names, *Monsieur* Jean-Antoine-Claude Chaptal who baptized the process.

There is an apocryphal quote from Nietzsche that I, strangely, only found in the Spanish language, without an even remotely similar fact-checked statement of this in his native German or in translations to other tongues. *History*, goes the quote, *there are nations born to write it, there are nations born to suffer it.* And apocryphal as it is, I would love to invite whoever coined that quote for a few glasses of preferably *unchaptalized* wine. Maybe it will also have to be another encounter from beyond the grave, as I suspect the originator was the late Señor Manuel Vazquez-Montalban, that prolific creator of universes and expander of horizons.

No matter who was behind that timeless gem of wisdom, some nations seemed indeed born to write history and others born to suffer it. And although it was rather clear who the *sufferers* were, my twenty-year-old self, in that blissful ignorance of youth, was still under the illusion that France was among the *writers*.

From where I stand today in Brooklyn, it turns out I had bet on the seriously wrong civilizational horse and I came to the very late conclusion that France, all in all, should be reduced to a mere parenthesis in my life. It was a stage, a backdrop that framed my aspirations, unfortunately for quite some time, before I understood how misplaced those aspirations and the associated illusions were. But on that distant day of the sixth of September two thousand and two, as I boarded the plane leaving The Hole for France, I wasn't just getting ready to cross borders; I was shedding a skin, stepping into a new self. All I knew and felt was that the day had just become my chosen birthday.

# ALL FATHERS SHOULD BE ABLE TO TALK WITH THEIR KIDS

"The kid will be turning six next week and there is not a single thing I can tell him, nor he to me", sobbed the despondent voice of a lonely father talking on his old cellphone next to me while I was waiting for my tramway. "I missed that cursed train of bringing him up bilingually", he continued, almost crying. "We divorced too early and now he's on the path to becoming just another German kid, without any shared language between us two. How I hate my life, for God's sake, how I hate my life without being able to talk to my only son."

That Father must have been in his early forties, an *average foreigner* as they come, without anything particularly appealing about the way he dressed or looked. The way he spoke my first mother tongue, for that matter, was particularly unappealing to me. His merciless butchering of all our long vowels into their quarter lengths and his relentless transforming of all the open vowels into closed ones, with all the *wrong* intonations on top of that, was drowning out the music I was hopelessly trying to listen to. And he was the kind of guy who would get a fresh shave in the morning and who would then get unfairly scolded by his boss in the afternoon for not having shaved since the day before. He had that *horse-thief kind of pilosity*, as Mom would say.

Being clean-shaven used to be something important back in The Hole. It was certainly the case in many other places during the last century, the one where disciplined armies of clean-shaven guys won wars that were considered legitimate and ended up subduing the bad guys. Or at least that's what we were told in history class.

Anyway, combining the *wrong* intonations and short vowels with his hairy looks, Father was clearly from the East of The Hole. And I hate to break it to you, but no self-respecting person of my native city will stoop so low as to consider someone from the East, from *that far East* as this guy was, as a peer to address any word to. It would just mean some sort of social death to be seen talking to *someone like that.*

By the time of that eavesdropping event, I had been studying in France for over a year, in that picturesque border city exuding an old-world charm, with the Germans just across the river. From day one in my new life, as a precautionary measure I had started shunning them people who came from our Hole, even the western part of it. I had deliberately walked past anyone talking our language without showing any sign of understanding, let alone interest. Arguably the whole history of different populations on this Earth has rarely been one of exporting their best and brightest to mingle with other populations. In the specific case of my Hole, well, I can confidently state that it has almost never been the case, so there was some statistical coherence to my shunning approach.

Admittedly, with this statistical generalization in this foreign land I was depriving myself of the rare gem that could be a kindred spirit to chat and grab a few beers with. However, thanks to -or perhaps because of- my bicultural upbringing, France didn't feel foreign enough for me to be willing to engage with a number of *undesirables* from the other nation just in the vague hope of finding that rare gem.

Father and I may both have been born within the same borders but those borders were drawn way before I was born. I didn't see then and I still don't see now, why the drawing of some imaginary lines a century ago by unimaginative civil servants, who rarely served anything other than their own interest, should define who would and should my *fellow* countryman be now. Them *reputedly fellow* countrymen of mine, I don't share their sense of belonging, nor their worldview, nor their religion, so why should I make the effort of talking to them once I left The Hole?

There was a logically acceptable argument that I was oversimplifying the matter by generalizing so much, because the worldview of those thousands of different people certainly isn't a *monolithic block*. Well, against that argument I was ready to state that I almost certainly didn't share *any single one* of the many *possible* worldviews of those who had decided to come to France, or to Germany across the river, for that matter. Why waste even an iota of energy in talking to this guy? My tramway will come soon, and I will move on. I do wish all the best to that Father in his future life, including a swift normalization of his relation with his only son. We all have our struggles in our present life. I have barely enough money in the bank for another five months. My studies leave me almost no time for side hustling. Let's move on, thank you very much.

Moustaki saved the day, Georges Moustaki, born Giuseppe Mustacchi in a Mediterranean port city that still brings tears to the eyes of my best Corsican friend's mother. Moustaki saved the day, one could say, if day there was to be saved in such an existential matter. While Father continued sobbing about the German mother of his kid and their lack of a common language, Moustaki, the real fellow countryman without common borders of my heart, was singing *je suis un retard, une absence* in my Walkman. *Absence* is an easy one to translate but *retard*, beyond obviously not having the same meaning as the English *false friend* of the same spelling, is not really the same as *delay,* and the nuance is significant. *Retard* should more appropriately be translated as *lateness*, although to my taste this does not convey the whole picture either, not in that sentence. Thankfully they haven't yet been able to homogenize the world enough to make everything *translatable.*

Anyway, our beloved late Georges was singing *I'm a lateness, an absence* and having been blessed to grow up with Dad, I felt for that Father becoming a *lateness* in his little kid's life. Some unknown kind soul inside me felt the urge to intervene as soon as Father hung up, surprising myself in the process before the self could shut that voice up. "*Brother*, would you like me to give you a few classes of German[1] so that you can communicate with your son? Don't grow apart from your kid for something that simple, come on, I can give you a hand."

"I'm a man of limited means," answered Father.

A single short sentence can well carry the weight of an entire paragraph and beyond, hence my leaving it alone above. I viscerally despise corny formulations but to the best of my human judgment, without any demagoguery, this is one of the *heaviest* sentences to come out of any father's mouth on this earth.

No *man of limited means* should be left unable to speak to his own son, whatever the extent of his material limitations, for duck's sake. "I'm a student of *not so limited time*", came my answer, which was a blatant lie as anybody preparing for a French *Ecole d'Ingénieur* can testify but duck it. "I really have a lot of time so don't worry about it, you don't need to pay for the classes."

This is how, in all improbability, I ended up finding the not-really-fellow countryman with whom to grab a few beers every now and then, accompanied by some pen and paper to help him make sense of the manifest burdensomeness that characterizes Goethe's language. He was in his forties and I remember having then taken the inner liberty of finding *that kind of age* old, seriously old, like, *one-foot-already-in-the-tomb-old*. He had come to France at my then-age, in the usual

---

1 I am indeed fluent in German, having spent an exchange year in Germany during high school, which is a sideline of my life that I prefer not to emphasize. If France's role in this book is be reduced to a mere parenthesis, as previously mentioned, then Germany's intended place, both in this book and in my life, is to be even less: an *absence of parenthesis*, this mere footnote, the only one of the book, with all due respect and love for the few Germans whose presence in my current life is a source of joy.

mix of half asylum seeker and half guestworker, or *Gastarbeiter* as they say across the Rhine.

After finding his way around in France, Father had decided not to be part of the local community of his *fellow countrymen* and had started to shun them in order to give himself the best chances of integration in France. He could not have anticipated that, for the French, integration in France is on paper mostly welcome but in practice rather *unaccepted* and, in the rare instances where it is indeed achieved, it becomes highly unpalatable for most locals. Anyway, once he told me about his self-imposed integration approach, I started taking a particular liking to that guy from the East. Randomness seems to have enjoyed the opportunity to put us two outsiders *devoid of belongability* in the same tramway station that day, with a random shuffle to Moustaki's song at the right moment.

In the following months I discovered that integration, even pushed to a stage of biculturalism way beyond what could have been expected from a person of his *humble* background, did not result in a proper shift of his life's mental epicenter to France, let alone a clear-cut uprooting. He had been living abroad for twenty odd years and yet he was still following the *forum*, that last oasis of free speech on the net, on a daily basis, to understand what was going on in The Hole, *back home*, in his own words. Using the concept of *back home* already covers where one's priorities lay, which made me pretty sad for the guy, as he had more to recover from life than just his son's mother tongue.

"That *pool media* is all sold to this corrupt government," he would rumble over the next beer and despite having left the country much later than him, I had no idea who had pooled money to buy what channels and newspapers and why *pool media* was a concept. The bitterness in his voice rising with every word, he would continue "but I'm pretty sure they have come to a dead end this time. The cracks are showing, and you can only paper over them for so long. The opposition will win the next elections, people are fed up with that one-man regime. There's a fire building slowly, a determination that wasn't there before. People are hungry, no government has ever withstood the noise of an empty pot."

I didn't care much about the political validity of these musings and observations, I just felt sorry for Father's *almost-completed* integration and wondered if it was going to be my fate at some point if I were to stay in that country for that long. Here was a naturalized French citizen and hence the proud father of a little *somewhat French-German kid*. He was working in France, living in France and was subject to substantial French taxes but he knew his former country's politicians better than his now-own country's politicians. He had not even been able to go back to The Hole for over two decades due to the political asylum story and yet his life continued to evolve there, *in absentia*. So, he would prattle, beer over beer, German lesson after German lesson, about people and policies that were already thousands of miles away from his own daily realities and my own mental map. He would dissect other people's elections that I already couldn't give a sheet about and that he should definitely not care about either.

One thing I must give him though, from a different perspective, is that his acquired illusion about elections could be considered as the best proof of his *unmistakable* integration in a Western country but in the bad sense of the word. Have any elections ever changed anything for any society mostly consisting of simps that have been left uneducated on purpose, for duck's sake? There are not many things modern that I find more despicable than the Western media's *expectation-mongering* about this silver-bullet solution called *elections* in them distant, dysfunctional, disheartening countries. Elections never changed anything. Elections you can rig. Voters you can buy. And like any merchandise sold in bulk they tend to be cheaper per capita. And, surprise surprise, a lot of times you don't even need to cheat to win elections, in particular if you have *properly designed* your constituents. "What are you gonna do", a former president of our Hole had once declared, "are you gonna import voters?" Which the opposite camp eventually did after he passed away…

Call me an enemy of modern democracies -which I'm not- but there is one freedom that I acquired at great personal cost over the years and I will not relinquish it anytime soon. With all due respect for the choices and constraints of those who vote with their hands due to constraints of geographical mobility, I have voted with my feet all my adult life and I see no reason to change my approach.

Father had a remarkably structured understanding of the French language and grammar for someone who had acquired it at an adult age and without any formal learning. This made our life easy for his German classes as I could build it on his existing French, which is a language of the same Indo-European family, just with a different word order. It would have been much messier to try to build on our common mother tongue, as it came from a different language family and has a grammar structure that is totally unrelated to any European language. There was a reason why The Hole would never become European, I guess. Geography is certainly destiny but language seems to have nothing to envy of geography in this regard.

We were able to make decent progress on Father's German, which even translated into some sort of unexpected progress with his German ex-wife who began letting him see their kid more often, building a better father-son relationship. Over time, these small steps began to accumulate, subtly shifting the dynamics that had been strained for so long. It wasn't a complete reconciliation, but it was a tangible improvement, and they all seemed to move in a direction that felt healthier for the kid's future. I ended up meeting that kid one day for ice-cream on the other side of the river, in that little town where all of us students would bike from France to buy cheaper groceries.

Unrelated sidenote, I just hope they have by now shut down that malt factory on the way; what a pain it was to be biking back uphill next to that unbearable smell invading one's lungs with thirty pounds of groceries in a backpack.

He was a wiry little thing, the kid, with a habit of tilting his head slightly when he listened, as if trying to catch the world's secrets from a better angle. Despite Father having dark brown eyes and being *swarthy* like most people from the East of The Hole, the kid had captivating blue eyes that had ricocheted from four thousand kilometers away, over eight centuries. They were the legacy of a European crusader who had sown them along the road during the Third Crusade, with some mayhem and wanton destruction.

That shopworn image of Father eating vanilla ice-cream with his beautiful child in that little German town is mostly what is left from them in my memory, as I moved on with my life once his German had reached an acceptable level that allowed him to build on without my help. Also, I moved far away from that river and ended up in greener, *thankfully-non-French* pastures. These were the days before uber-digitalization, so once I stopped having a French phone number, Father became part of those destinies that happened to have crossed my path at some point and that I ended up sowing somewhere along the road during my own *peaceful* crusade, without any expectation of further news. He became one of these destinies that, if I were to meet again somewhere by accident, would bring me to discreet tears that attentive strangers could interpret as nostalgia of good times past. Attentive strangers don't often realize that in such encounters we mostly cry not for the memories but for our own youth that has passed; homecoming tears are just a navel-gazing story.

Every now and then, when I try to convince myself that I had significant positive contributions to some people's lives, that kid is part of the first few that come to my mind. I see his face, that mix of mischief and hope, and I tell myself that maybe, just maybe, our German classes with his father made a difference for him. I like to think of him growing up with some semblance of fatherly presence, with a voice of guidance when he needed it, with someone who has failed enough times to give him advice on *what not to do* while navigating the storms of life. I like imagining that kid *somewhat accompanied* in life, with a father he can talk to, which is already an achievement in itself, though never sufficient.

Never sufficient, because *one never heals from one's childhood*, as Jean Ferrat used to sing.

# Of meaningful metrics of life in a favela

I ended up spending six rather long years living in Europe, first in France, then in Spain, a stretch of time that seemed both fleeting for the pleasures and endless for the ambitions.

In the end, these six years can cynically be condensed into three pieces of paper that prospective employers want to see, what they call degrees, of the engineering variety in my case. On the uncynical side one could well state that I had all the formative and pleasurable experiences of being a student in Europe, drinking more than one should, backpacking with Interrail and enjoying the treat of encountering several cultures within a few hours' drive, that tremendous cultural luxury that most other continents simply do not offer.

Nevertheless, deep inside, that *Eldorado under assault* and I rarely meshed, which gave me itchy feet. Despite most of my memories from those days being rather positive, all I saw over the future of the continent were ominous clouds and I had no desire to stay there one more day than strictly necessary. What had once seemed like a geography full of opportunities now felt heavy with the weight of uncertainty, and as I walked through its streets, I felt the sharp sting of *inevitability* in the air.

How dare you, you little snob from The Hole, how dare you not dream of settling down in that continent of dreams with its grand old cities and cobblestone streets? The place where history and art seep from every crack in the ancient walls, where revolutions were forged and kings dethroned, where every corner seems to hold a story and every shadow a whisper from the past? How dare you think yourself above the allure of Paris's lights, Rome's ruins, Berlin's energy, or the misty, poetic streets of Lisbon? Europe, where philosophers and poets crafted the very ideas that shaped our world, where cathedrals and museums hold treasures beyond imagination, and where the very air is thick with the weight of centuries...

Does it sound repulsive enough, akin to some cheapbrass *in-flight-magazine* stuff or does the honorable reader want more?

How dare you turn your back on the place that is today, for so many, the ultimate destination of secure lives with social welfare and sweet idleness, what they call *farniente* down South, how dare you? You should be willing to sell what is left of your soul for such an easy life, to obtain one of those doors-and-gates-opening passports. Oh well, maybe you did sell it or maybe you just don't have much soul left, who knows. But how dare you snub our continent, you little snob from The Hole, who do you think you are?

With all due respect, for me that non-melting pot of a continent had already been bathing in too much *social granularity* since its birth, with its already too many nations, cultures and people. And then came the *others,* a multitude of others, from all over the world, in search of sweet farniente or whatever else. Given that the entire world is an order of magnitude bigger than Europe, the *others* came with an order of magnitude more granularity among themselves, their intentions and their values compared to the *locals,* which is in the natural order of things; there's no need to take offense. Meanwhile, as if this wasn't enough, someone decided that this entire crowd should now have a common destiny as a Union, no kidding. I cannot be the only confused external observer who keeps scratching their head about the potentiality of common destinies between a Finn, a Hungarian and a Spaniard, before even extending it to *all the others,* can I?

After having thrown out my paternal grandparents, the Soviets had gone through that same meaningless illusion, and this had happened long before that Europe of bureaucrats ever attempted it. The result of their grand experiment was there for all to see, after having spectacularly crumbled under the weight of its own contradictions. They believed they could reshape society, strip people of their roots and somehow mold a new, *pure* common identity, top down. If you think you can separate your mother tongue and what your mother cooked when you were a kid -the dishes that marked celebrations, grief, and those *ordinary* Sundays- from the core of who you are and whom you might embrace as your own, History shows that you may be in for a nasty surprise. Such efforts to erase those fundamental connections rarely hold, more often they leave behind a sense of loss and alienation that keeps festering. At least, this is a gut feeling shared by most of humanity, an unspoken understanding that there are certain things, certain ties, that cannot be entirely cut without leaving a wound that never fully heals. But don't take my word for it, dear empty suits of Brussels, keep trying, keep *regulating*, I know you love it. Keep stealing people's oxygen, dear parasites, I just do not intend to be part of that experiment. Remember my principle of voting with the feet.

At the end of my time in the Old World, a number of *normal* people around me had already started to find it harder and harder to make a normal place for their normal selves in that strange mix. Many brilliant French friends I studied with left for greener pastures, after their studies that had cost the taxpayer half a minimum wage per month. In them greener pastures, most of them turned out to be happier, safer and better paid compared to back home in France, which was a difficult combination to beat so they stayed. So why should some nondescript foot soldier from The Hole cover the combat posts that natives have abandoned, for duck's sake?

Europe had been suffocating the best part of my soul insidiously for the best part of the last few years. I had less than one year to go before the third and last piece of paper "needed" to certify that I could be professionally useful to someone in exchange for compensation, when the mind-opening prompt came. It was in the form of a German copy of *Brazil, Country of the Future* by Stefan Zweig, in a second-hand bookshop of a no-name Catalan city off the beaten tourist path.

That worn out book in its original German version had gone astray from its more *expectable* trajectories up North to end up in that Catalan bookshop. In the final analysis this was not very different from my own trajectory. That book ultimately led to me becoming the first one in my family to cross the Atlantic, which to this day makes me feel blessed, rather than proud. I crossed the Ocean on the *shoulders of the giants* that our grandparents had been and thanks to the moral toolkit and vision that our parents had given us.

The reasons behind my crossing were so much more *benign* than those of Stefan Zweig's that it would be utterly indecent and out of proportion to make any comparisons. However, drawing innocent parallels should be morally allowed, even if our parallels would be diverging ones. That Viennese gentleman to whom I owe my crossing had gone to Brazil in old age, for a *tired ending*, with Europe burning down behind him. On the contrary, I was landing in Rio with the vigor of my youth, for a fresh start and with Europe herself not yet aware that it was burning down behind me.

Maybe I'm being too harsh on the Old World after all these years, after time has warped my memories, smoothing some edges while undeniably sharpening others. Maybe, it's simply the case that, as is in my genes, whenever I see a bridge, I feel an irrepressible urge to burn it and that time it was no different. Whatever the real reasons behind my departure, I found myself in Rio de Janeiro, caught between the glimmering sea and the wild embrace of the mountains. It was in this city, this fabled end-of-the-road destination for so many adventurers and swashbucklers who had outlived their prime and outgrown their time, that I had a first taste of the Americas. And for that, I feel a profound, almost posthumous gratitude to Herr Zweig, that chronicler of exile and nostalgia, for bringing me there in spirit before I ever set foot on this soil.

It's also in Rio that I met the night shift receptionist of a slightly above-average hotel who was moonlighting to put some guava jam on his extended family's semi-stale bread by poaching all kinds of sea creatures after his nocturnal day job. It was only fitting that I, an engineer with the infamous *three pieces of paper* in the luggage, would partner with that humble high-school dropout to go spearfishing and add some *butter to my spinach*. It was fitting, certainly because spearfishing was a job in which I was competent, a competence won in merciless waters that had far fewer fish than Brazil. But primarily, it was fitting because my own *day job* did not pay that well, despite the three papers and the rest on the CV.

I had just accepted the first engineering job under a local contract that had come up with an employer willing to sponsor me for the visa, so the salary was not great, but at the end of the day isn't it all a matter of expectations? Fresh starts tend to be great equalizers in most places and this is especially true in Rio, that fertile ground, that potting soil of absurd dreams. As a consequence, I was just glad to be there, having found a decent fishing buddy and spearing exotic things that I had never seen in the Med. The ones that I had speared *elegantly enough* were sold to a second-rate restaurant. The ones where I had hurt the filet in an *uncamouflageable* way would end up being my own source of protein. What a primitive sweetness those distant days held!

In my many years of spearfishing, I have rarely seen someone move as gracefully underwater as Receptionist but most importantly I have never, ever seen such a corpulent -not to say obese- guy freedive to half of the half of the depths that he was reaching without any visible effort. He was using those cheap, short, worn-out fins locally made of the lowest possible quality plastic and he was sliding with a rare combination of speed and elegance underwater. "You sporty people have no notion of sparing your energy, you behave as if it had no limits", was his answer to my astonishment about his freediving capabilities, "you are so used to *being able* that you all keep prancing around through life with impunity, above or underwater, without thinking twice about how much more effort the same moves would require *for us fatties*. When I'm not in the water, I always look for a valid reason to put one foot in front of the other under this heat and with this humidity, so I just apply the same principle of energy conservation underwater. I won't make any unnecessary movement or even have an unnecessary thought that would make me spend any extra oxygen, this is the basic secret of my *barrigão* going down past fifteen meters and catching all this fish."

Receptionist came to Rio from a small village close to Campina Grande, in the Northeast, one of the poorest regions of Brazil. He and his wife had been living in Rio for most of their adult lives. Despite having come there separately, they had naturally met in the same place where they lived and where many residents were actually first- or second-generation Northeasterners. By "the same place" I mean the same hood or, as the modern reader will certainly know, the same *favela*, a concept frowned upon by Receptionist. "We live *no morro*" -literally on the hill- he said when they invited me for a BBQ one week-end, "and I call it neither *favela* nor *comunidade*", he continued, "one stinks too far to the right, the other too far to the left". Not much seemed to stink to the middle in Brazil in those days, as it looked like a precursory social lab of our overly polarized modern societies.

Before going to their home for the first time, I already knew that Receptionist was *etymologically* right with his use of *morro*, as I had gulped down a few thousand pages on Brazil since my stumbling upon *Brazil, Country of the Future* while in Catalonia. So, I had already come across the story of the demobilized soldiers in the nineteenth century returning from a meaningless internal war where they had been stationed on a hill, *morro,* on which the favela trees were abundant. But once I went up to their home, I understood how *physically* right Receptionist was, because living *no morro* consists mostly of a fight against gravity, for duck's sake, it is a continuous up-*morro* battle.

In many, many places on Earth people tend to think of places up the hill as luxurious dwellings with nice views, like in that distant Acapulco of the seventies that the first generation of jetsetters had invaded, that playground for the rich and famous with its sun-soaked beaches under rolling hills. Truth is, living up the hill is only luxury when some sort of celestial power -slaves, electricity, fossil fuels, whatever- transports the goods, commodities and services one needs up there. Needless to say, this wasn't the case in Receptionist's *morro* so I could see firsthand how he indeed had to be a master of saving his own energy, *contrary to them sporty people,* fighting these vicious uphill slopes, one step at a time, drenched in sweat.

"Don't your people in the *first world* have any local problems to deal with?" asked Receptionist's wife one day when she had already gotten to know her husband's spearfishing partner much better over time. *Much better* but not good enough to know that I wasn't from the first world. I rather came from some Hole, having barely ricocheted off some countries claiming to be first world, first class, first something. Whatever, she didn't need to be able to point to The Hole or to any other country on the map. She was a *locally* very smart woman who was more versed in the art of *jeitinho,* somewhat translatable as resourcefulness, than most people in those first world countries she couldn't find on a map. A knowledge of geography does not necessarily increase any chances of survival or make you a more well-rounded human being if you don't have universalist aspirations. And universalist aspirations thankfully still come after survival on a human scale of needs.

"I'm asking this, because" she continued without waiting for my answer, "to me it looks like they must be bored stiff, all these kids from your perfect places who come here to *help us*. They come to help us without first asking if we need it, obviously. In the meantime, we have come to have more first world NGOs per inhabitant in our *morros* than they have bakeries down the slope in Rio's Zona Sul, *on the asfalto.* Don't you think it's a bit over the top? Needless to say, the rate of teenage pregnancy *up here* is probably ten or fifteen times higher than *down there."*

What a pleasure it was, having conversations with that squat *nordestina* lady, a primary school dropout who cooks *moquecas* and *acarajés* for a living. How refreshing it was to rub neurons with her raw, brute intelligence after a day in the office with formally smart, degree-educated kids who mostly didn't know sheet about real life. Apart from some marketing cosmetics such as college degrees and some rhetorical skills -i.e. ruthless bullsheeting capabilities- the main difference between her and a spiffy team of snotty analysts from DuckKinsey is just that the latter are paid several hundred dollars per hour to invent the same metrics *per inhabitant,* dipped in different kind of Excel sauces. Clearly none of them sauces is worth an ounce of her *moqueca.*

"It is as you say" was all I could answer, "those kids from *reputedly perfect* universes lack a sense of mission in those distant first-world societies where they grow up. Often they lack affection or family values, and they struggle to belong, so they look for meaning somewhere else. A lot of times that somewhere else turns out to be *somewhere poor* under a different sun, as it tends to make them uneasy facing poverty in their home country, where it clearly also exists. Poverty at home just isn't exotic and they prefer not facing their own societies' injustices, I guess"

"And the demise *of* your very civilization will come *of* this lack *of* sense *of* mission *of* theirs, *of Sendungsbewusstsein* as we say in Goethe's language ", answered the squat *favelada* in the parallel universe of my imagination where she was a German-speaker, with a powerful chain of the beloved German proposition *von*.

# THE COUNTRY OF THE FUTURE, FOREVER

Happiness, a lot of happiness -countless moments of great happinesses, in that ungrammatical plural form- captures well the essence of those carioca years that I'm still deeply nostalgic about. Life in Rio had a kind of exuberance, a vibrancy that colored even the simplest moments with a sense of joy. The anonymous laughter on a sunlit street corner, the warm nights under swaying palms, the easy friendships forged over a shared drink or a dance, each of these memories now lingers like a sweet echo, in a way that I think about very few places. Those years were filled with a happiness that was *unpretentious,* which almost makes me feel the heat of those days on my skin sitting in the Brooklyn winter here.

But nostalgia, for all its power, doesn't factor into the unpredictable, Brownian motion of stray human lives; it's nothing more than a longing that will keep tugging at the heart without steering the direction. So, despite how those days still shimmer in my mind, I never went back, as I went on carrying pieces of the past that other places had also contributed to on my trajectory. My nostalgia for Rio remained just a quiet ache, a wistful smile, while the world continued to spin and I drifted with it.

As an *aparté* regarding Brazil, we were recently evaluating an opportunity for a possible *incursion* into the country, and my business partner from Brooklyn burst out "fuhgeddaboudit, no way to do business there, Brazil is a black hole… I never understood that place even when I was living there, we're not going there!", which still makes me laugh. A passing nostalgia it is then, what I have, given that a black hole pulls everything within its reach like a ravenous god of the cosmos. A dark maw where even light falters and falls, swallowed by its insatiable gravity, as time and space themselves bend and vanish into nothingness. At times Brazil was a great nothingness.

I'm not against returning to a place and I'm not for drifting on *for the drift's sake* so going back to Brazil could have been a pleasant comeback after many years. However, from the perspective of our line of work, my business partner's judgment was right. Right it was, and also surprisingly generalizable to many other aspects of Brazilian life: an eternally non-aligned country naturally develops its own ways of doing things and for an outsider used to other ways and manners, such a country becomes some sort of a black hole as it, in its own way, decided not to belong to the *concert of the nations*. "Brazil is a black hole" has since taken its place in my proud list of useless nuggets of wisdom. That particular list is legitimately proud, as *usefulness* mostly deprives nuggets of their wisdom, but I digress.

Back in those carioca years I was neither yet able to identify Brazil's particular kind of black-holeness nor had I been much interested in understanding the limitations that this *left-aside-from-the-world-ness* imposed on the pursuit of a more well-rounded type of happiness. My experience of life had not yet instilled in me that specific urge for the presence of *connective erudition* in my immediate social vicinity, I was able to live surrounded by any given level of ignorance. So I was content with the exquisite bubble in which we were living the day with a bunch of bubbly friends and acquaintances, away from the World, away from where *things happened,* important or not. That country may well be the most geographically accessible yet encapsulated place on Earth.

The conclusion that superficiality indeed is not deadly is a meaningless -and borderline harmful- takeaway that I kept from them happy years in Rio. I spent a superficially marvelous time between a cheaply paid operational job that I nevertheless loved, the compulsory carioca beach-bumming and the spearfishing sessions with Receptionist on the *Cagarras* islands, where the visibility of the water and the catch of the day were never predictable.

Beauty, that prerequisite for happiness, or at least that extra benefit which almost never hurts, was so dominantly present in its various forms in Rio that it singlehandedly erased all the various forms of unhappiness and ugliness, endowing us with wonderfully numbing visual filters.

In the beginning was the natural beauty of Rio, the exceptionality of the place that must have stunned even the most *unelevated* soul among the expendables that the explorers Cabral and de Lemos had schlepped across the pond in fifteen-oh-two: the lush combination of all conceivable shades of green and blue within eyesight, the views up to the hills or down from the hills, both beautiful in their own ways and the eternal Ocean, eager to embrace, comfort and reinvigorate us five centuries later while we were looking for the next *robalo* to spear.

Rio's landscape truly was one that defied logic, a perfect composition of nature that could not have been designed more harmoniously by a human hand. The hills rose dramatically almost from the sea, as if sculpted by some forgotten god, with forests clinging to their steep sides and pouring down like velvet-green cascades. It was not just the kind of sight that stopped you in your tracks, it was *aptly* sabotaging most human endeavors of urban and social organization by sticking hills in the middle of any conceivable urban fabric.

Then, the man-made beauty of that once imperial capital kept jumping on me at the least expected moments, around the least expected corners of the city, where yet another building destined to fight the tropics would emerge out of the blue. Rio is the first place where I saw old and older buildings whose design intent, whose very *raison d'être,* seemed to be to wrestle with heat, humidity and bugs, to stand tall against the tyranny of the tropical climate. Those buildings didn't try to hide from nature. Instead they both embraced it and fought it, in admirable imitation of the most perfect marriages. The wide verandas, the high ceilings, the thick walls, and the cool, shaded courtyards all spoke of an architectural wisdom born out of necessity, a combination of survival and art where every facade proudly carried the weight of history, weathered and worn, like the cariocas themselves.

The Portuguese may well have been the first European nation to *run* their luck to zero or to the full exhaustion of their imperial steam but the buildings they left behind were a testament to human resilience, to the ability to carve something lasting out of an unforgiving environment. They embodied robustness and serenity, both qualities that were shiningly absent from my architectural trajectory up to then, given that serenity was forbidden in France and robustness was unknown in my native Hole.

"Serenity was also clearly *verboten* in Germany, this is why I left", chipped in a serene and robust young lady while I was expounding to her French girlfriend my above theory about the ban on serenity in France. It was during the general consulate's Bastille Day reception (to this day, the only diplomatic reception that I ever attended). One could legitimately wonder what the duck I was doing there, given that I did not have and still do not have a French passport. I must have had a few empty illusions, a past *desire to belong* that some pitiless circumstances, or simply put *life,* have since put *hors de combat* for good.

"Conforming devoutly to the society's expectations is the only acceptable path to serenity in Germany and this, in my book, is a phony serenity; I'm too much of an *électron libre* to acquiesce to that", continued the young lady who turned out to be an *ethnic German*, as if to make an unintentional point that one doesn't need to be a born Holer to be unhappy where one came from.

Free Electron -I find *free spirit* as the English translation of *électron libre* not really to my taste so I shall not conform to *unorthodox translatory* expectations- had grown up sloshing between continents after her well-educated parents escaped the ridicule of the levelling-down experiments in East Germany. Then she had spent her soul-forming teenage years mostly in Ivory Coast, hence my calling her an *ethnic German* above.

Instead of taking the primrose path to one of her two mother tongues, Free Electron had ended up going to college between Toronto and Madrid, but a mother tongue never really abandons its speaker. She spoke a quaint and elegant French, the kind that seems to have vanished in the modern world and that pops up every now and then when you talk to some people from ex-colonies and protectorates. Her use of the language felt like a relic of a distant past, carefully preserved in the amber of history, untouched by the rush of progress that has diluted and simplified language. Each phrase she uttered carried the weight of having been plucked straight from the musty, yellowed pages of nineteenth-century novels, of times when sentences conveyed not just meaning, but depth, nuance, and texture. When she spoke, she seemed to be drawing from a deep well of cultural memory, using phrases that had been passed down through generations, uncorrupted by the flattening force of modernity. The *unburdensome* formality of her speech, that self-confident *deliberateness* made you pay attention to the cadence of her words, the way each syllable was pronounced with care. Her vocabulary belonged to an altogether different era, when people used to write letters by hand and conversations were as much about the art of language as they were about exchanging information.

And yet, as soon as she was not speaking French, the speed and voracity for life that she had adopted during her carioca years made her condense most of her thoughts to the incompressible bare minimum. A bottomless well of aphorisms is what she had become, in every language except the French of her childhood, many of those aphorisms quite obscure but nevertheless delightful.

"No self-respecting émigré should ever look back", she would nonchalantly state, talking of Germany. Thereby she wouldn't make the slightest effort to distinguish if she was referring to her parents' East Germany or the disappointing re-united Germany where she had previously tried to lead a second German life that had led to nothing. And after that single sentence of judgment, the subject was closed for her, without deserving further breath expenditure. Most émigrés that I met in life were not just looking back but were *continuing to live in that very back* and they were mostly pretty self-respecting folks... but I wouldn't argue over that subject with Free Electron.

How each drifting being handles rootlessness is not only a complicated but also very personal matter: some have illusions of belonging, for others that illusion *embers down* to a mere desire of acceptance by the *hosts*. Yet others will meander along that very large spectrum between invisibility and full integration where belonging is wished.

Free Electron had discovered the higher end of the spectrum, that *rage to belong* that she had felt for the first time in her life after ending up with her French girlfriend in Rio. Ever the resourceful survivor, never afraid of apparent contradictions, she had been living undocumented in the country for a year and a half when I met her. "Every now and then I have to go to Paraguay but without getting my passport stamped," she said, "thanks to some local *acquaintances of the nodding sort.*" And there was nothing else to the statement, as most of her stories were shrouded in that peculiar kind of unfathomable, floating ambiguity, crafted to deflect further questioning. Every tale kept hovering just out of reach, full of gaps and half-answers, existing in a foggy limbo, where certainty and clarity dissolved, us mere mortals left brushing against its surface. "A woman without enigmas is not that much of a woman" was one of her preferred aphorisms, which seemed to be tailor-made for herself.

In these years Paraguay was the South American capital of electronics that had fallen off the back of a truck and Free Electron was making a living by trafficking all sorts of gadgets from there into Brazil. This was a very honorable occupation, I find, for someone with advanced degrees in applied mathematics which she never applied to a formal job.

Her chosen profession required a certain level of street cred, the more so for a foreign woman, so she started to tackle the subject from the most street-cred-generating angle by acquiring the argot of the bunch of *malandros* with whom she was collaborating. That argot was light years away from her social status -whatever *that* may mean- but she seemed to have yearned for it during all her years and through every language she had previously learned.

One particular evening when we were sitting in a *botequim* close by my place in Copa, burying deep into our stomach some deep-fried cheap unidentified objects claiming to be food and drowning them in generous amounts of cachaça to kill the taste of the over-re-used frying oil, a sinewy, swarthy carioca came out of nowhere to pick up a fat brown envelope full of Benjamins from Free Electron. They had a fifteen, maybe twenty-second conversation that *I*, living with a Brazilian roomie and working all day in Portuguese, did not understand almost a word of. "Brazilian Portuguese", she reflected when I asked what the duck they talked about, "it turned out to be the first foreign language that I have learnt *naturally*. By "naturally" I don't mean without grammar, unfortunately too much psychological rigidity runs in my German veins to skip rules and order, but *way beyond grammar.*"

One should learn at least one language way beyond grammar, I still hope to get there one day in a language that deserves it.

For clarity's sake, by learning a language *way beyond grammar* I do not mean the cliché concepts of moving past the structured rules and vocabulary drills to reach a place where the language flows intuitively blah blah. I don't refer to rhythm, idioms, and quirks unique to its culture or any such connection either. Oh and *way beyond grammar* is not about the ability to pick up the subtle shades of meaning, the in-jokes, and the unspoken connections etc. It is about picking up a fat brown envelope full of Benjamins from a sinewy, swarthy carioca with whom you have a conversation that even the *natives* around you don't understand; this is proper *way beyond grammar.*

Happy they were, magnificently happy, those carioca years, but there came a moment where being stuck in the bubble started to run my happiness to the full exhaustion of its own, *tropical* steam. *Le temps d'apprendre à vivre, il est déjà trop tard*, Aragon was singing, you barely learn to live and it's already too late. I was afraid of being late, of discovering the *unliveability* of certain lives, of gates closing permanently without my *carioca self* realizing that those gates had ever existed. The problem was that like many happy-go-lucky people stuck in the tropics, I was unwilling to make the jump, because I was feeling at home in Rio, for duck's sake.

And there came Free Electron again for *guidance*, returning from another Paraguayan expedition, eyes glinting with mischief and cachaça, the pockets of her khaki cargo pants bulging with more wads of Benjamins that would let her survive some more months in the urban carioca jungle. "Go", she said, in almost instructing tones, somewhat reminiscent of my talk with Mom back in The Hole, "go, don't rust here and don't believe you cannot come back once you are gone. Go, move on and live, you don't need a homeland anyway and the homeland that you don't need is not here in Rio. And if it were, a worthy homeland would also be able to wait for you. Go, because there is no exile for a savant and no fatherland for an ignorant. Only by leaving here, will you be able to find out if you are a savant or an ignorant."

Badly harnessed horses, we had said, break free easily, so I started to look for a job, any job, somewhere else, anywhere else, as long as it wasn't an English-speaking country. I was still in my ignorant youth, before the age of discretion, and I used to feel more at ease in company of those who had lost with *us* in Trafalgar, either directly or by cultural alliance so an English-speaking place wasn't appealing for me. I now regret profusely this point of view because of the lost years it caused in my linguistic development, but what can I do...

And once I had found that job and packed my stuff, I tried not to look back, although I still had some scores to settle with Rio.

From then on, for me Brazil remained the country of the future forever, as that local joke goes in its various versions: *o eterno país do futuro, o país do futuro que nunca chega, o país do futuro para sempre.* And countless times, over and over again, I've found myself drawn back to Rio in my dreams, wandering along Copacabana, with the ocean breeze on my skin and that faint, familiar hum of the city filling the air. I see myself ambling lazily on Ipanema without the *garota,* the sun dipping low, casting long shadows and painting the sky in fiery hues as it descends behind the Dois Irmãos standing watch over the city.

Brazil is not for beginners, they say, *o Brasil não é para amadores.* So, you need to stay and invest time and effort and energy, move past the beginner stage, to make it there or to do *something meaningful* there. But it just so happens that I love being a beginner, remaining a beginner in different places. This place was not for me, but was another place going to be?

# Let this not be our day

"Thanks for *choosing* to fly with us" announced the pilot in that staccato way of speaking Portuguese that Angolans share with Portugal, as we started our descent to Luanda. "As if we had a real choice" grumbled a voice in my head, there is no alternative airline for this route anyway, duckers… Difficult to overstate how much I hate this kind of verbal vacuity imposed on us by any corporate bullsheeters, for duck's sake, be it in a plane or on a worksite.

I should start the chapter by thanking the field engineer whom I had to replace. Thanks to her, whom I never met, I ended up in that shaky TAAG plane from Brazil with a hefty salary increase compared to my job in Rio. When I talk about *replacing* her, it's not that she had resigned or was fired, the two most likely reasons for a replacement that could come to the clear-minded Anglo-Saxon reader's mind. And she wasn't pregnant either, which would have been an equally acceptable reason, if not more. Nope, it was just that the market was brisk and vigorous so she had decided to try her luck in a similar position for a better salary with a competing company in another country and to do that, she had just taken a sabbatical, without blushing. At the end of that year, depending on how much she would like the other job, she could resign from her sacrosanct French *contrat à durée indéterminée* and move to the competition for good. Alternatively, she could come back as she wished and continue with the company in her previous position, of course maintaining the same rights and privileges, meanwhile kicking me out of my position. Having your cake, selling it double the market price without delivering it, and then eating it while angrily demanding some extra icing from the buyer that you just swindled is your birthright as a French employee. Anyway, deep inside I didn't care, a full year of employment meant eleven months more stability than what I was used to.

"We cannot give you a local Angolan contract and we have exhausted our quota for a French contract", declared the not-so-charming HR lady, before adding that they also *needed some flexibility*, in case the person I was replacing decided to return to her position earlier than anticipated. This I already knew but she repeated it just for good measure. Never trust an HR person who talks about flexibility.

So, the contract of my semi-expendable self was signed in a jurisdiction that the map refuses to show if one doesn't zoom in with a vengeance. It is one of those minute island states from a bygone empire that nowadays honorable British taxpayers use to *optimize* the extent of their contribution to their own society, of course in a very honorable manner. Again, not that I really cared about the jurisdiction. A job was a job, and a contract was a contract. Retirement, if my generation ever has such a thing, seemed a million light years away back then.

Talking about perks and social benefits of a job, on the surface I may seem *well integrated* to France, yes, but scratch a bit and one always keeps the reptilian reflexes from one's childhood: in The Hole where I grew up, nobody is going to give you a second chance to decide what you want to do with your cake and there seldom is any kind of icing, so I just took the ducking contract. Such luxuries as the option of a *staggered resignation through a sabbatical,* a permanent contract with social security, full health insurance, job security etc, I can leave them to *real* first-world kids. There are already too many references to "security" in this sentence for my taste.

The Angola of the late 2000s, that distant chessboard, was a place that was still footing the bill for wars that others had lost. At the time not many nations seemed to have the guts to fight, let alone lose, their own wars for their own sakes. I had never heard of the concept *proxy war* until I went there and then I came to understand that the Angolan Civil War was a quarter century of proxy war par excellence.

Beyond the countless horror stories I heard, I still cannot get my head around the subject of a proxy war, regarding basic principles. In my book, if you have a problem with a guy, you go and have *a word* with him. You don't just send your little brother to punch that guy's little brother in the face- there is no decency in throwing *proxy punches*, you coward… Oh sorry, it is obviously much more digestible to send Angolans and Cubans to die well out of sight instead of your own kids, right?

When the Cold War came to an end, the horrendous Angolan conflict lost its very raison d'être, like many other proxy wars and dirty wars and countless other subtypes of wars that it had given birth to. A bunch of foreign mercs went to slaughter that charismatic polyglot sociopath Savimbi somewhere in the bush, as if it was required to eliminate the very physical presence of an opponent already bereft of all political presence. Then more money started flowing into the country in the form of different investments and I piggy-backed on the foreign workforce that came with the money.

The population I was interacted with in my day-to-day life in the office and on the field consisted of Western Europeans and Angolans, with a healthy dose of mistrust between both. This was no big deal for my sore brass that was in the habit of being eternally split between two chairs, as the French saying goes. I had *never* belonged to a tribe so far in my life, including in my home country, so I wasn't intent on starting to belong just then by some kind of *divine insufflation* or unsuspected inspiration that I would have found in Luanda. Tribes are for those who know where they come from and often for those who *must* come from somewhere.

"I'm happy to have you here in my team", said my direct boss at one of our first *safety meetings* -code for BBQ and beer- on a Friday afternoon, after having assessed my skills on the previous ones. The specific skills were exclusively related to my proficiency in cutting thin slices of ham, which I had honed during my student years in Spain. "You are French like us but you don't have the citizenship so it improves our diversity statistics without causing discomfort for us", he continued, swallowing three transparently thin slices of ibérico ham at once, thereby annihilating all benefits of me having burst my brass to cut them so thin.

If there ever was a corporate medal of ruthless honesty against corporate bullsheeting, thanks to that one sentence that son of a gun should be among the first recipients, with a bunch of other dinosaurs of his ilk who were also loitering around the office. And as much as I appreciate ruthless *honesties*, I never again cut any ham for that idiot who *mis-tribed* me.

The fact that not all corporate dinosaurs are despicable pieces of sheet was embodied in the person of a heavyset Angolan director who was the *capo dei capi* on our floor and a master of that very fine art called *management by fear*. No, fear is not enough, let's call it management by Terror. A Jewish mulatto with a rather dark complexion for a mulatto and darker competences for a "simple engineer", Terror was the bard of untellable stories about mass graves, minefields and the horror of field tent hospitals during the Angolan Civil War. When addressing most of his direct subordinates, he would lead his conversations mostly with a decibel level off the charts, but everything would be forgotten by the Friday safety meeting. And each and every one of our providers and service companies had heard at least once that magic sentence when he found their proposals too expensive or their business ethics not to his taste: "Boy, have you tried to cheat an African Jew before? Do you remember how badly you failed, if you ever tried it? And did you not learn from that occasion that it's not a good idea?" A cliché-loving Anglo-Saxon would have written that *guys like him, they don't make them anymore*, whereas the truth was that guys like Terror had *never* been mass produced.

Although he was the terror of the floor, I was one of the few youngsters who were exempted from his wrath, what I initially thought was due to me being too low on the food chain or simply lying too low overall. Then one day a clear-minded German colleague put a name to it, probably thanks to the functional mechanics of his mother tongue that not only allows but also encourages and proudly displays the results of structured concatenations of several words into a single one: "You guys have a Verlustgemeinschaft, a *commonality of losses,* that's why Terror likes you", he said, matter-of-factly.

That Verlustgemeinschaft observation made me realize that I had had to travel halfway around the planet to vaguely remember that in The Hole of my childhood, which we all remember pretty much as a *racially homogenous* society, there were indeed here and there some Africans adrift, leading hand-to-mouth existences, like Mountain. Although their presence was visually surprising, nobody, absolutely nobody treated them inappropriately or, dare I say, *differently*. Maybe because the Holers had in their DNA the inherent tolerance inherited from the multinational Empire they had descended from, despite not having lived them good old times. Maybe because every group of Holers had enough hatred for another group of fellow countrymen that they didn't have any hatred left for foreigners, even for those who were visually identifiable as strangers. Or maybe, definitely maybe, it was thanks to their large-heartedness towards those with whom they had a *commonality of losses* as struggling descendants of a defunct Empire. Whatever the reason was, no black person was treated differently from any other foreigner in The Hole, which is probably one of the very few things I can be proud of about the place.

"You will avoid second-hand SUVs and *mulattas*, young men, because both cost way too much to maintain in this country", was Terror's recommendation to young male engineers arriving in Angola and sexist as they were, these eternal words saved a few young kids' brass during my stint in the country. I did not need to put any kind of effort into heeding that advice, as cars have never appealed to me: I have never considered them as anything other than a set of wheels that would bring me from point A to point B and hence never understood the fascination they exert on people, which adds another layer of absurdity to that one day when an Angolan general decided to pilfer the car I was riding in. Oh and yes I do know the difference between pilfering and stealing, no need to throw me a dictionary, *thank you very much it.*

The managing director of a large foreign service company had invited us for lunch, as we were his clients, but at the end of the meal, Terror pulled out a fat wad of kwanzas, against the usual customs. He paid the check for the whole table muttering under his breath in rapid-fire Portuguese that if those duckers believed that by inviting us to lunch they would get more favorable terms on the next contract, they had never met an African Jew. A little bit at a loss for having his clients pay for a lunch that was meant to be his invitation, and then seeing Terror ostensibly tear the check into pieces to show that he wasn't going to stoop as low as to even expense that lunch to our employer, subject managing director had the laudable idea of driving us back to our office as a gesture of goodwill. A great many mishaps did those laudable ideas cause in human history, a great many train wrecks under the tropical sun and we were heading for one.

The car must have been *something,* I guess. It had not struck me as something special, other than being a pretty large SUV, as Terror, another colleague and I were all sitting on the back seat and nobody's legs were even touching. Nothing else I remember of that car, no, but for the benefit of better grasping what will follow, I should highlight that in these years new cars would come to Angola in batches, and one would wait a few weeks to a few months for the car that one had paid in advance. It also wasn't unheard of that the last batch of a specific car, say Toyota Fortuners, that came with one of those largebrass Grimaldi carrier ships turned out to be models from last year. If you were hellbent on having this year's model, you had to wait for the next delivery, maybe in a month, maybe in three.

The car must have been something, I was saying, because three blocks after the restaurant we were stopped by the police, in the plainclothes version. Actually military, in plainclothes. Not that the distinction matters, because regardless of how he was dressed or not dressed at all, most people who weren't visually impaired or from another planet would actually recognize the face of the general who got out of the car that stopped us. "*Me dê as chaves e saiam do carro, o carro é meu*", he said to the Scandinavian managing director, "give me the keys and you guys get out, the car is mine."

Needless to say, we all understood enough Portuguese and had honed enough survival instincts in Luanda to exit the car immediately, except for the managing director. He sat there behind the wheel, rigid, unable to process neither the meaning nor the urgency of the situation. Despite having driven through the city's potholed streets for over three years, he had somehow managed to keep himself cocooned, untouched by the tougher realities of the country. This big car, his prized possession, was fresh off the lot, barely two weeks registered under his name. It was a sleek, polished testament to his hard work and it constituted a personal investment so he clutched the steering wheel, resolute, not quite grasping what was unfolding.

"This is my car," he insisted, holding onto the idea of property rights as though it were armor, "I did pay for it. It's not even a company car, it's my personal property and I do intend to keep it." His face was flushed, eyes wide with indignation as he looked toward us for support, clearly believing that a suitable explanation and a calm word would settle things. "Whoever this gentleman is," he added, nodding toward the general still demanding that he get out of *his* car, "could you please translate? Tell him it's mine."

The general did not understand English. He had been trained in Russia like a lot of folks from the governing party and he had not had any particular interest in learning the language of the Cold War's victors beyond "In God We Trust". However, in all objectivity he did not need a translation of that sterile monologue either. Visibly ignoring the empty-suit managing director, he nevertheless turned his body sufficiently towards Terror for both Terror and the Scandinavian to have a clear view of the large grip on the handgun that his fingers were gently stroking.

"Tell your friend here," he articulated to Terror, fully ignoring the rest of us, "tell him that he will now get out of that car because I cannot allow anyone to run around this town in a better car than mine. If it does matter for his ego, tell him also that it's nothing personal but *I* did win the civil war, not this blond foreigner, not that bandit Savimbi, not the ducking president of the United States, *I* did win it. Therefore, this city is mine, so the car is mine."

Every now and then, disjoint universes come together, such as the claimed-to-be-merit-based Western corporate universe and the Darwinian African dictatorship universe. They may briefly intersect for a fleeting moment of seemingly improbable mutual understanding and continue their own ways but I insist, they do come together for a moment. In that precious instant, the walls of respective realities blur, and for a heartbeat, the inhabitants of those disjoint universes find common ground amid their vastly different paradigms. The Scandinavian indeed continued without understanding any Portuguese but he had enough common sense to know that there was no way out of the situation other than unclenching his hands from the wheel. The impression I was left with was that he didn't even shake his head too much as he got out of the car.

"In one of those brainless Hollywood movies", started Terror once the car was already gone and we were five loser pedestrians scratching our heads under the heavy sun, "there was a line about destiny looking for a hero and always ending up finding him, thanks to a bullet that looks for someone and always ends up finding him".

"It's a first-world luxury to have heroes", he continued, "the luxury of those people who have free press, national media and publishing houses".

"On this continent…at least in this land, our destiny is to die in anonymity", he finished, "let's not learn again today that there can be no heroes in this country. For duck's sake, folks, let this not be our day".

# OF COLONIAL MYTHOLOGIES

Probably one of the most characteristic words in Brazilian Portuguese is *jeitinho*, which means the little way, the manner: to arrange things, to get things done, to get stuff to move, often involving a small bribe but usually within a predefined, almost ritualistic framework. With a manner, with a way, a *jeitinho*. A *waylet*, if neologist translations into English by non-natives are allowed...

In Angola, the characteristic word in their version of Portuguese was *confusão* and it could mean anything from the real etymological meaning of confusion to problem, difficulty etc. Mostly it would be equivalent to *situation* as in the eternal American cop of the movies twisting his neck down to the mic of his walkie talkie clipped on his shoulder and saying "we got a situation here". In all cases, the embodiment of *confusão* on our floor was our good old director Terror, the bard of untellable stories, the *let-this-not-be-our-day* man.

One day I had just committed the impudence of entering Terror's office during lunch time, trying to get my operations program signed, rushing around like a headless chicken, which was our normal life down there in those booming times. I found him chewing on an inch-and-a-half thick stick of fresh sugar cane, sideways, from an übermenschlich angle. His molars were the size of fifty-cal bullets. His chewing made as much noise as a jackhammer, and half of the cane juice was drooling down his right cheek then onto his long goatee, and dripping on his Crocs. Yes, Crocs. He wore them every single day in the office, starting at four AM. It's just natural to wear slippers at home, isn't it?

A guy who had served under him in another life had told me that it was *an honor for any adjective* to be used to qualify this man *on which rust would never get its grip*. Legends about him had spread like wildfire, a blend of awe and war stories that painted him as the übermensch of übermenschen. In that particular moment though, looking at the cane juice drops, I was somehow failing to see the point of *inoxidability* or Übermenschlichkeit.

"Where do you come from exactly?" Terror asked me. "Which part of that Hole of yours? Not that I have ever been there, mind you, but I have a keen interest, no, not just an interest, I have an obsession with maps, a *mapssession* if you will". When I named my native city, he answered, "oh, this is the capital, right?", which was a common question from foreigners.

"It depends," I clarified. "It used to be the capital, but when the Empire fell, they decided to name another city, more inland, as the new capital. They argued that the new one was better protected by geography and easier to defend but we know they just needed to kill the father. Anyway, no offense, many foreigners continue to believe that my native city is the capital."

"Sic transit gloria mundi", came the murmur from deep within his extra-large carcass that had spent a few years as a bricklayer in Portugal in the nineties, *thus goes the glory of the world*. At some point during the phony war phase of the early nineties, when he was demobilized, Terror had gone to work on construction sites in Portugal. Needless to say, he received no extra pay for his knowledge of Latin or his ability to disassemble and reassemble an AK-47 in half a minute. And he was an undocumented immigrant at the time; undocumented, because he was *barely a bit* mulatto i.e. not white *enough* for the Portuguese passport and too far from his Jewish mother's ancestors, as a fifth generation descendant in Angola. Now two decades later, with the boom in Angola, it was the Portuguese who came to work on construction sites in Luanda. To me it proves the point that a change of capital is not compulsory for the glory of the world to pass.

"Youth has this eternal quest," he continued. "For cities and places about which one will be able to tell in ten years: 'At the time, in that distant city named X, I saw this and that, we went through things, we *lived*'. Youth wants to have lived.*" His "at the time" was "à l'époque" in the *original text* because we were speaking French, which obviously conveys much better that sense of epoch than a period of time, but I digress.

In recent years, with age looming in the horizon I have started to come to the same conclusion as Terror and even more: I now think that youth secretly aspires for the places and epochs that they live through to then actually come down to rubbles once they passed there. Youth wants to have *un-re-liveable* stories to tell once they are themselves past their prime. Youth craves destruction. There is an innate need for nostalgia, a need to snub the old cities, the has-beens of geography. That insolence of young age hit me between the eyes after Rio, after the *eternal* Rio, when I came to be in Luanda, a city where things were happening, where tomorrow would be, for good or for bad, far more different than today.

"We are both children of fallen Empires", Terror continued to reflect, "we have both been on the receiving end of our respective Empires. In the intrinsic injustice of its construction, an Empire at least has decency, decorum, something *civilizationally rewarding,* even if, obviously, it is strictly forbidden to make such a statement now. Look at our new masters from the Middle Empire, they are, shall I say, maybe *jealous* of their civilization, or they do not see us worthy of their sophistication, what do I know, in all cases they have nothing to share with us, nothing to teach us. Taking is all they do, giving is all we can. Future generations will not be able to be nostalgic about the post-colonial *epoch* the way we may have the nostalgia for the colonial one, because the post-colonial will have left nothing tangible beyond street and city names changed by force. Oh and let's not even mention the *neocolonial* new masters, not only will they have left nothing tangible, but simply their epoch will not have existed once we will be dead."

His raw kind of discourse was unacceptable to my young and somewhat still not fully world-weary ears, but who was I to decide if it was acceptable or not, given that it was his life, his history and his country. Most importantly, given that Terror was wrong on the basic premise, which, had it been true, could have led to me *understanding* him: we were on *different ends* of past Empires. My family had left an Empire when it was taken over by the people who were on the receiving end of it. Then the grandparents came to settle on the ashes of something that wasn't an Empire anymore by the time they arrived. Furthermore, The Hole where I grew up was skilled enough to become a Hole without needing any country to ever colonize it. So, to be frank, despite all my genuine interest in the subject, at most I could potentially claim to have taken a fictive *Colonial Injustice 101* as an elective class. I certainly have no claim to having lived that class in the flesh like Terror had. Therefore, I can neither understand nor judge Terror, that pretty-swarthy-but-still-somewhat-too-mulatto Angolan who did not have the benefit of a Portuguese passport as a safety device when the pressure on that country-vessel started to exceed the maximum design value. One should rarely try to deeply understand someone else's perspective on such delicate subjects anyway, because the ambition to understand is the beginning of judging: one should just listen, much easier said than done.

Besides, neither of the two empires that flogged my family had even a hint of an overseas nature so I certainly cannot talk about *colonial mythologies about wogs and darkies* the way a Vidiadhar Surajprasad Naipaul can, I lack that peculiar perspective. Back in The Hole, we all lack the outlandish intimacy that only comes from the sea routes carved by empires into unknown shores, yet we are too shy to admit it, even those of us who have made a living at sea. In a sense the world of our childhood was limited, because our ancestors had no proper seafarers, no fleets to speak of, no intrepid explorers. They simply did not have any intimacy with the spirit of the open ocean, which in my book means that they never had an empire in the proper sense. They had turned their back to the sea that was surrounding them and no empire without sea presence is a real empire, they may at best become sponsors of some Mediterranean pirates.

This is maybe the reason why my curiosity is aroused every time I hear the story of a person of improbable nationality in a third country of *improbables* separated by the sea, say a fourth-generation Indian in English Guyana or a Chinese shopkeeper who has just arrived in Jamaica. Those are the stories that you couldn't have had without the masters of the initial empire mastering the art of seagoing.

"Je passe ma vie à batailler contre mes conditions initiales et la *déboussolance* du siècle", Terror would repeat after a few beers, a possible translation being "I spend my life fighting against my initial conditions and the disorientation of the century". "Don't dare bullshit me", he would add in the contained rage of the ex-officer that he was, "don't even insinuate that *déboussolance* isn't a word and that the right one is *déboussolement*... Instead, just send me one of them *immortels* doddery walking dead men from the Académie Française and I will explain why *my* choice of the suffix is the right one. I have lost enough men to know that nobody is *immortel* and I have broken enough compasses to decide on the suffix that I shall put on the erratic behavior of my own compass."

My eternal gratitude to Terror lies in him being the one who forced me to recognize the reality I had tried so hard to sidestep: that I would spend my life battling against my own set of initial conditions, that my victories over these initial conditions would never be final, that even in triumph, I wouldn't be free from them. Instead,

I would reach a new place where I would revive those conditions, slap them awake only to refight them, as though drawn back into the fray by some twisted sense of duty or an unbreakable thread linking me to the past. This endless cycle of defiance, struggle, and renewal was not a defeat but the very essence of life for many of us stray humans. If there was any deeper reason, any design to my ending up in Luanda, it was precisely to come face to face with this truth, to spend a few extra years churning through that realization and coming out on the other side with some sense of clarity about that.

What's a couple of years in a life anyway? A good friend of mine from Blackdog spent a full twenty-three years in Luanda. I'm convinced he was unable to make a sentence in English without the c-word from the very day he was born, and he was even less able to say just a simple *bom dia* in Portuguese after all that time but this is not the main point. During the repetitive cycles of all these years he had been able to *shunt* the obsessions of elsewhere, that driver of perpetual dissatisfaction and I do respect the guy for that.

When nine-eleven happened, all the other *Anglo-Saxons* and the various culturally down-and-outs ended up blowing a fuse on the work site, because all the TV they had consisted of the local channels plus two French ones none of them understood... So they couldn't get the news, they couldn't know if there would still be a world, a country, somewhere, *something* to go back to when their hitch would come to an end. All the other *Anglo-Saxons* except the fellow from Blackdog, who just turned off the TV out of pure disinterest in the possibility that life, *some sort of life*, was continuing outside. "Terror gave a few phone calls around and got CNN for these crybabies so they understood there was still somewhere to go back to after the hitch", he told me nonchalantly, "I couldn't care less about going back or anywhere else".

They say you cannot translate *saudade* and that the only place where you can really understand what it means is Portugal, not any other Portuguese-speaking country. This might well be true, Brazilians use that word simply for a deformed kind of *missing*, more with people than with times and epochs, in an unrefined *tô-com-saudade-de-você* that can quite vulgarly be translated by a simplistic *I-miss-you* without any perceptible loss in the meaning. In the final analysis of my lusophone adventures, in Brazil there was too much happiness, too much happy-go-lucky, too much tomorrow-can-go-duck-itself and yesterday-didn't-exist-anyway attitude to understand real *saudade,* which is conceptually a nostalgia of the present with much deeper ramifications. In Angola, on the contrary, there was selective happiness and selective drama, stemming from too much trauma.

Being parachuted into the Angolans' new world without bearing any of their scars, without sharing even a sliver of their past trauma, I found myself, as if by some blessed accident, on the side of happiness in the equation. I would have lingered there quite a bit longer, had it not been for the French doctor. Perhaps I owe her my thanks for shattering a few stubborn illusions about belonging just when I needed it, peeling them away without ceremony, without indulgence, and without delay. In truth, I might owe gratitude to her and every person who has sparked the beginning of yet another leg of this journey, whether they did it well-meaningly or not.

"You lost weight since last year, I see in the *records*", she gravely declared, during my compulsory, detailed annual medical, which I was taking a bit later than the year before. "*The record shows, I took the blows*", should have been the answer but Sinatra and New York were still far away and honestly I didn't know much English by then, barely surviving professionally with a shaky Globish. And the doctor, that navel-gazing French specimen, certainly didn't know any English or any Sinatra. Anyway, I started my answer with an easy "It's because of the period of the year", which the ignorant pickhead precipitously completed with "oh of course, *that* period of the year, you don't eat during daytime this month". I do hereby solemnly declare that under the right circumstances it is allowed to qualify a doctor as a pickhead, it is a profession-neutral qualification. If you are a pickhead, you are a pickhead, period.

Talking about months where one eats less... Superfluous as it may be to indicate it at this point of the text, I obviously am one of them *unluckies*: my family name has a consonance that evokes worldviews and cultural assignments that are misaligned with my own. In many circumstances I just don't care about these things, like, I could not rent an apartment or two in Europe when I was a student because of that consonance and seriously who cares, I always ended up finding a roof over my head. But among other things of my existence up to that point, Strong's mom couldn't be buried as she wished because of *that supposed worldview* that the consonance of my family name evokes. A few other mishaps happened due to the same cause, such as, indirectly, me having to leave the place where I was born and where I could live the rest of my life eating what I grew up with. So it irritates me particularly that an ignorant *pickhead* with a medical degree, with any degree, or no degree at all, for that matter, takes the liberty of imagining that I belong to *those people* because of how my family name sounds. With all due respect for *those people*, for any people, needless to say or write. They were stronger and we had to leave, I bear no grudge but just don't put me in the same basket with them, you donkey piece of doctor.

And yes, I was quite skinny at that point of the year, with my ribs casually caressing my skin because I had spent the last few weeks, the only ones with a bit of visibility in them cursed waters off Angola, spearfishing over twenty hours a week, including every single ducking morning before going to the office. Spearfishing is a very calorie-demanding business; I would recommend it to anyone who needs to shed a few pounds. On top of it, shedding weight and being slim improves freediving performance, one needs to carry less meat around. On top of the top of it, I always believed in hunting hungry, it also improves spearfishing performance, at least in my book. And on the very last top of it, yes, the records are correct and yes the year before I had a bit more circumference because, oh, guess what, you doctor of my brass, I had taken last year's medical *before* the convenient spearfishing period, with the waters still murky as duck because of the Congo river, the Benguela current and whatever else. Duck them currents. Duck the French doctor.

With that doctor moctor lady we had the same mother tongue, even if mine was a fake mother tongue… She would be surprised, oh probably sickened by it but we actually had the same religion of a different confession, even if I did not practice it. And we had the same skin color, even if this does not mean anything at all in my book, I'm taking the totally unnecessary liberty of mentioning it because I just have a reasonable doubt that it does mean something for her. Actually, my complexion is a bit lighter than hers, given that, as opposed to that arrogant hexagonal product, I'm *truly* Caucasian thanks or, better said, due to my grandparents. Not that it matters, I was saying, just mentioning it for the donkey doctor.

"Fair-skinned doesn't mean *socially white*, kiddo, in case you had taken the liberty of forgetting that…" whispered my inner voice as I was listening to her meaningless word salad over the remaining twenty minutes of medical check. Yes, I know my blood pressure is high, doctor, it's because I'm forced to sit here, breathing the same air as you and enduring your presence.

Right after that visit I went home and started to pack my bags. To shed some decent weight without spearfishing, I sent my hundred seventy-eight books to Europe where my brother had moved in the meantime. This first batch was the beginning of that "reconstituted library of all my books" that would never ever get together in one place, the *promised library*, that land which I seemingly will never reach, given all the other batches that I left on the way.

I then gave my guns to João from Mussulo, the most talented spearfisher I met in Angola, necessarily a slim ducker with a thin set of ribs caressing his skin on each side of his torso. And once freed of all the weight of the books and the awkward length of the spears, I was once again a-bum-and-a-bag, pretty much ready to move on, as far away from condescending ignorant doctors as possible.

I was unsure how many distinctly different lives one could cram into a single existence or fit into a few bags, how many different selves representing a fragment of the self that had to be left behind. Yet, in my pursuit of liberation, the kind that comes from shedding expectations and assumptions, I resolved to head *up North*. The free spirit within me, desperate to breathe without the suffocating pressure of preconceived identities, longed to draw closer to a semblance of civilization. In that imagined paradise called Norway I hoped to discover a world where people existed as they truly were, unshackled by labels or histories, where the essence of one's being wasn't tied to societal expectations. Simply seeking a refuge of anonymity, a place where I could embrace the simplicity of being just another foreigner, free to explore and rediscover identities old and new.

Has any human lived a whole life without even once wishing to shed the burden of who they have been before?

# In the plastic domain above the fifty-seventh parallel

When I was at high school, Mom used to read books by a certain Ingvar Ambjørnsen who was an acclaimed Norwegian author with a cult following back in The Hole, a little bit à la Bukowski, writing about marginal lives enveloped in intensity and drinking and music. The books were too recent and there was no Amazon back then, so their French versions wouldn't make their way to The Hole for a longbrass time after their first publication. So, my brother and I had to read them in our first mother tongue, which slowed us down quite a bit given that we weren't schooled in that language. More importantly, it was an unpleasant experience, as for us every translation from a European language to a non-European language seemed to reek of, well, *translation*. Regardless, we both owed a lot to *Uncle Ingvar* who made us dream of long cold Scandinavian nights to be fought with cheap moonshine and *mutualized body heat*, our teenager minds being still too green to dream of their magnificent fjords and real-life seascapes.

The only other place where my imagination had come into contact with Norway was Violinist's *shop* where the old-timers would tell wartime stories of commercial diving, platforms and *bells*, with nine guys living twenty-eight days in a row inside a pressure chamber in *saturation* and working on gigantic subsea structures. That faraway land stuck up North in bumducknowhere on the top of the map smelled of underwater welding, of risk and reward, of the pleasure of playing craps with one's own life.

We were kids then, innocent and wide-eyed, blissfully unaware that nothing could be farther from the truth. In our youthful naivety, we painted grand images of what these places might hold, fueled by stories of *real existence* straight out of the books of Uncle Ingvar who, as legend had it, had sold the copyrights of the translation into Holish for a symbolic pint of beer. Yet, in stark contrast to our fantasies, contemporary Scandinavia has been transformed into a grotesque graveyard for dreams of adventure, a place where once vibrant hopes lie buried beneath layers of soul-destroying routine and monotony. The very cities of Bergen and Oslo that I had imagined as a playground of possibility have become a reflection of stifling conformity where most deviations from the normal are drowned out by the realities of modernity.

Norway, by virtue of its endless boredom-generating capacity, made me understand most -if not all- of the parallelisms between the human nature, continuum mechanics and strength of materials, as an unhappily lived stint of Scandinavian dullness is a good way to extend one's initially linear deformation into the irreversible, non-linear, plastic domain.

For a quick overview of the subject in non-technical language, the strain i.e. *deformation* of a material under stress is measured by applying a gradually increasing tension on a cylindrical specimen of the subject material, say a type of steel. Under that increasing tension and the resulting stress per unit area, the specimen will first get deformed, but it will remain in the elastic domain where the removal of subject tension would remove all deformation. This would result in the specimen returning to its original shape, its original length and, let's face it, this case wouldn't be really amusing. Therefore, in their quiet but eternal search for fun, engineers keep pulling on the specimen to first bring it to the point where it can no longer return to its original shape and they call that the *yield point*. They then continue pulling further on the specimen, until it comes apart at the *fracture point*, giving a characteristic curve of initial linearity between stress and strain that then gets shambolic.

Shambolic is a technical term, I can confirm, based on my marvelously empty claim of authority called Chartered Engineer. I am patiently waiting for the day I will run out of toilet paper so I can use that particular certificate, but I'm too much of a planner to ever find myself in that situation.

Getting back to metals and humans, well, the human psyche is but a matter of metallurgy, as we share most failure modes of materials. Within this short review I shall, however, leave aside a number of those failure modes that occur in the elastic domain, before the stress on the material gets too high, such as fatigue and creep. May Chekhov pardon me with his claim that any idiot can face a crisis and that it's this day-to-day living that wears one out, we will not go into the subject of fatigue.

The more interesting changes seem to happen when you apply enough tension on people to deform them in such a way that they will no longer be able to return to their initial shape or *state*. Indeed, it is only once people are beyond the delusional repairs of the temporary return to the beginnings, a luxury which the elastic domain confers, that they become a subject worthy of consideration: life does become much more *delectable* beyond there. Presumably this is not always the case for those who are being subjected to these stressors and constraints but certainly for the distant, external observer the adjective "delectable" remains fitting.

To simplify it vulgarly, the phenomena that appear once the deformation of the specimen has become irreversible can be split into two phases; the uniform plastic elongation and then the *necking* that leads to the fracture of the specimen.

The uniform plastic elongation is when the subject person we are pulling on can still manage to keep some semblance of normalcy for the external observer. In the metallic analogy, the specimen visibly maintains the same outside diameter and shape, it continues its deformation under tension but even the fact that it has already entered into the irreversible phase of the deformation is not perceivable as long as the tension is kept. Arguably the subject person isn't necessarily aware of the extent of their own deformation, until either the tension is removed and they realize that a residual strain is left or the tension is increased and visible necking starts to appear.

Necking is akin to the behavior of melted cheese when you pull on it or when you tear apart a baguette, although, admittedly a baguette does not strictly conform to the definition of continuum mechanics and most importantly the traditional rotational hand movement to break apart a baguette induces some flexing moments that distort our equation. Nevertheless, the idea is a clearly visual one, a "neck" starts to form, and the specimen starts to become significantly thinner at the spot where it will end up breaking.

Necking has two major implications for the person subjected to that increasing tension from both ends. First and foremost, the imminence of that looming fracture begins to take shape, for the observer and for the person, regardless of the latter's level of *ostrichism*; it is no longer possible to claim any semblance of normalcy. The second implication, more subtle and technical, is nevertheless extremely important, in particular for the external observer and any stakeholders that may need to interact with the person during these necking phases: the significant reduction in the person's cross section declines as significantly as our ability to understand their actual in-situ stress, i.e. what they are truly going through.

This very large inaccuracy is due to the following artifact of measurement: the stress on the person that is recorded -technically called the *engineering stress*- is not a direct measurement but a calculation. On a body being deformed, the only thing that is directly measured is the tension applied to the person and the stress is then calculated by simply dividing that tension by the cross-sectional area.

This first order engineering approach is fine as long as the cross-sectional area remains constant, but it is already erroneous at the beginning of the plastic domain and then becomes *horrendously wrong* once necking starts because of the gallopingly decreasing cross section. Treacherously, that phony, artificial, despicable thing called "engineering stress" indeed *decreases* once you *necked* the person. And this happens despite the fact that the actual, "true stress" keeps increasing under tension, giving the outsider the illusion that the worst is behind us. That the subject person has now *become somewhat accustomed* to their current condition, that all hope isn't lost.

All hope is always lost, let me tell you, as soon as you have *plastically deformed* someone… When, on top of all that initial torture, you neck the fellow, you have indeed just added some *superior-irreversible* to the *already-irreversible* on hand: that person is lost for humanity.

The personal conclusion I drew from this theory was that I really did not want to become a cog in a Norwegian wheel, even if it's a Ferris Wheel with miles and miles of fjords visible from its top. Easier said than done because, as we discussed, the in-situ stress is impossible to measure and our perception of the situation is biased because the tension sensor is far, far away from where the stress is at its maximum on the specimen. Sadly for me, the *human sensors* in my life who could be up to the monumental task of giving a fair assessment of my Norwegian situation at that time, whether Violinist, Strong or Free Electron, were all scattered around the world. They all had enough common sense, enough wit, enough *présence d'esprit* not to be freezing their brasses where I was.

Contrary to the poor metallic specimen though, I, as an *almost-human* subject getting pulled apart in life's testing bench, had enough free will to adapt myself to the constraints and "take action" despite my Mediterranean fatalism. So, I did the only thing I knew and jumped again on the very first job opportunity to go back to Africa. I never, ever set foot again anywhere North of a little Scottish fishermen's-town-turned-city by the fifty-seventh parallel, on any continent.

Some great thinker said that History was written between the parallels twenty and sixty, well, I would say that in his drive to round things up, he seems to have aimed three degrees too much. Here come both the declaration of this chapter and my promise that this will be the last one:

I do hereby solemnly declare that there is no History to be written above the parallel fifty-seven.

# A-BUM-AND-A-BAG

When I say "I jumped on the very first job opportunity to go back to Africa", out of boredom, I should have the decency to state that boredom prevailed over pride, as the opportunity came naturally through a former colleague and the job was with a bunch of Frenchies. There was quite a bit of humble-pie-eating involved, as I was still thinking every now and then about the French donkey doctor from Luanda in not particularly laudatory terms. A good memory is not a good thing when it comes to forgiveness.

Anyway, this is how I went back to the continent of countries *who* made a national sport of changing their cities' names, and within that continent to the country with probably the highest number of cities that changed their name. The country itself had changed its name: welcome to the place formerly known as the *Congo Belge*, that many people still call *Zaïre* and that anyone who respects the pages that a people has decided to turn should by now only call the Democratic Republic of Congo. It is shortened to DRC for the initiated, RDC for the froggishly initiated as the word order is different in French. Anyway, welcome to DRC, welcome back to Africa, oh boy did it feel good!

"All possible stances of *Man* facing the World find their least sublime but most relevant expression in Darwin", our chief engineer Merc was telling me as a welcome, while we were waiting for the little plane that would take us from Congo to the Democratic Republic of Congo. My linguistic conscience somewhat de-Frenchified by that stint in the Northern latitudes had started to think, *well, of course you talk about men; women are way too smart to stoop down to your Darwinism anyway.* But then I caught myself, realizing that in my fake mother tongue "L'Homme" still meant simply *mankind.* Does one ever get rid of one's fake mother tongue, I wondered. There goes two years of futile attempts to *civilize myself* there up North.

A tiny linguistic parenthesis, that little plane that I took about eighteen times over the next three years was flown, quite fittingly for a chapter where the main character's moniker is Merc, by a couple of South African *rustics.* Over the duration of the project, together we killed a generous number of beer bottles in the international airport of the other Congo on crew change days while waiting for a number of commercial flights, thankfully flown by pilots other than my drunken ones. Maybe it's because I have Van Gogh ears for phonetics but to this day, for me the most amazing and enriching tonality of the English language remains the *broad South African* spoken by native Afrikaans-speakers, with its rugged richness, like language carved from ducking granite. There's something intensely vivid in the way vowels are stretched and consonants sharpened, creating a rhythm that feels both grounded and unpredictable. It is also quite passing to have my type of ears listening to Afrikaners talking English: that Van Gogh guy was Dutch and his mother tongue was a cousin of Afrikaans.

Merc was the most *established* engineer I have ever met, due to his outstanding intellectual capabilities but especially for being the kind of *chief* who spends the minimum amount of time in his air-conditioned container and all the rest of his time outside, hardhat screwed on his head, taking on the mud, the noise and the vibrations with us *expendables.* I have learned a thing or two in this job about leading people and I came to the conclusion that for any boss worth their salt, playing craps with their own life as much as they do with the lives of their people is the only honorable way to be. There has never been another path that holds integrity. It's one thing to set the stakes for others, but to lead authentically means staking something real of your own: reputation, money and, if it must be, your own life. Only taking the same plunge into the high-risk game you ask of your people shows a commitment beyond words, that time-tested spirit of leadership that commands respect and earns real allegiance.

The job in the DRC was demanding, painfully demanding. This was partly due to the outdated equipment in dire need of maintenance, partly due to our understaffing and somewhat due to weather conditions on the site. But painfully demanding it was mostly, ducking-mostly due to Merc having negotiated a large performance bonus on behalf of that understaffed team with the contract owner. The concept of performance may throw some notion of complex metrics and DuckKinsey style *key performance indicators* of the postmodern variety. Well, it shouldn't. There and then, in our misery, performance was just about doing it *faster*. You could do the dirtiest job ever, you could *butcher things* and work like a ducking *açougueiro* i.e. butcher as a proper carioca would say, as long as the project was done x days faster, we would get a bonus proportional to x.

That bonus, he declared from the outset, was to be shared equally among every single team member. There would be no distinctions for rank, project seniority, or any other criteria that might place one person above another. Even Merc himself would not receive a higher bonus than the others. "Our salaries reflect what each of us has done so far in life, folks," he would explain to the group, his voice calm but resolute. "That pay is a measure of who we've become up to this point, and since we each have different journeys, naturally our salaries will differ. But the bonus," he emphasized, "that's something entirely different. It reflects what we're doing here and now, the *guts* we're putting into this project at this very moment. We're all sweating under the same sun, putting in the same grind, facing the same dirt day in and day out, so when it comes to the bonus, we'll all get the same reward. It's only fair."

"I cannot shout instructions to someone who will get less than me on the bonus", he concluded. And shout instructions he did, all day long, flogging every single one of us first to equal measure and then inversely proportionally to the guts we were putting in our work or proportionally to the cleanliness of our coveralls. It was Merc who taught me not to trust duckers with clean coveralls and not once in the rest of my working life did I feel that he was maybe wrong; clean coveralls *stink* much more than dirty ones. They stink almost like corporate suits- they stink of treason.

Merc was the grandson of a teacher whom the Vichy regime had "not even had the decency to execute themselves and had sold to *ze Germans*". And of the *travail-famille-patrie* trilogy of that abject regime's motto, he only had respect for Work, with a capital W. His real *patrie* -fatherland- was his bank account and for that I valued even more the man and his stance about the way our bonus was to be divvied up. *Family* he had none because he "knew how to put on a condom" and children were the only responsibility he had ever been *afraid* of in his life. *Work*, he believed in, hard, agonizing, backbreaking work he believed in, the kind that makes your muscles ache, your back strain, and your mind burn. In tormenting work as redemption, he believed, carving out his identity with each relentless hour.

In the DRC I completed, even perfected, my transition to being a long-term bum-and-a-bag. Or at least, I came to the potentially erroneous but certainly reassuring conclusion that if a sixty-four-year-old *mercenaire de l'improbable* could lead an apparently fulfilling existence being a man-and-a-bag of no fixed abode, then I shouldn't be much concerned about getting settled down, pulling myself together or something along those lines. Merc was on his way to becoming part of the best wrong examples I would have at that point in my life, and I was very grateful for that.

"One day, one day many springs ago, when I was roughly your age and I was pushing the tools in bumduck Colombia, a *Human Residue* told me at my then-employer's headquarter in a no-name Parisian suburb, hey Merc, we will not promote you this year either, because our consensus is that something is amiss in your attitude. You work hard, your crew likes you too but, how should I put it, you don't really have a sense of belonging, the *company doesn't feel it,* you are just not *staff*, you don't have a staff mentality.*"*

"I mean, the ducker didn't call me Merc, it wasn't yet my name, he used the one that my parents put on my papers at birth. *The company doesn't feel it,* huh, motherducker, what about you feel my ducking fist on your ducking face, I thought. I then *didn't feel* like getting my fist dirty on *that* particular face, for a brief moment. The residue's face looked like the result of a random transgenerational crossbreeding between a long and ignoble lineage of nasty ditches and their *managers,* so, nope, I really didn't feel like getting my fist dirty on it. Then, ashamed of having thought in such terms about them, I mentally apologized to all those honorable women who needed to sell their body to survive, every single one of them thousands of times more worthy than this piece of sheet. I slowly got up and aimed well on the cheekbone -much more of a pain to fix than the nose- but I missed it because of the ducker moving at the last moment. So I made him swallow three of his own teeth but it was unintentional, the cheek bone was the real prize I had in mind, teeth are too ducking easy to repair. Anyway, those Human Residues were right, after all, something was definitely amiss in my attitude so I got fired, quite unceremoniously, I must add."

"Once I packed my bag, I started to learn *not to care about not being cared about*", he said, with less abouts and more guts in the original text, "it makes you indestructible -*increvable,* unpuncturable- to truly come to terms with the fact that nobody cares about you".

So, the unpuncturable Merc went back to Africa where he had started his career, to that one continent where he knew belonging would never be an option for a foreigner, because not belonging was exactly what he was yearning for and he had internalized that yearning.

Those who think that a search for belonging and community is a common trait to all humans or a prerequisite for happiness should, for statistical completeness' sake, first go ask *all* humans what the definition of happiness for *each one* of them is, then we may discuss the subject from this exhaustive perspective. Not before.

There were some grey areas in his story of the decades in between but most importantly there were stories of unmatched absurdity in his grey areas. When he was being evacuated from Soyo in ninety-two (was it ninety-three?) with the town about to change ownership (re-change, maybe?), the *real* mercs that were coordinating the exfil refused to take Merc's right-hand guy into the chopper with him. "Only European passport holders", they told him, "These are our strict orders, your Angolan can't come". Ignore that the guy he was trying to take into the helicopter wasn't Angolan but Zairean. Ignore also that the Zairean had *done* Centrale Paris, one of the best French engineering schools.

There and then Merc pulled out his French passport and his Zippo. He lit a cigarette first, then his would-be life-saving passport in front of the soldier of fortune's incredulous eyes. Then he waited for them to close the doors of the chopper, went to pee on the bird's landing skid in front of the whole crowd that was being exfiltrated and he calmly got away before the pilot pulled on the collective for takeoff. Something was indeed amiss in our guy's attitude, no doubt about it.

"Even to end up on the wrong side in somebody else's war was more respectable than to end up without war but in the same chopper with that son-of-a-ditch", he concluded, with his very specific interpretation of *Schicksalsergebenheit*, of resignation to fate, of *self-delivery to fate*. For the external observer it could look like he sabotaged his own fate because he could have taken that chopper but given that his *Weltanschauung*, his worldview, did not allow him to leave his right-hand guy behind, the option simply did not exist: *fate* had put this absurd chopper on his path, a chopper he could not take with a clear conscience. And, in front of that soldier he felt more enamored with his fate than with his set of initial conditions, among which the passport that could have saved his brass.

"Savimbi's guys didn't treat us badly at all. All this evacuation business was such an unnecessary fuss anyway" he concluded, with the moral rectitude of the guy whose word is his bond.

Fast-forward two decades, Merc still hadn't come to terms with his fate-freewill yin-yang when he had gathered us for the kick-off speech of our project in the DRC. He had solemnly declared, "folks, for this project I was able to negotiate and obtain the largest variability of performance bonus I have ever seen in my lifetime so we have two options here: you can work like limping ducklings and continue to have the usual kind of intercourse with fate, and we'll all be on the receiving end. Or we can duck fate, fair and square, by grabbing this opportunity and changing our lives for good."

So, following his lead and bursting our brasses, big bucks we made, all seventy-six of us. It could quite legitimately be considered big bucks for us *first-worlders* but the proportional impact for the Congolese colleagues was on another level: these three years resulted in an early retirement for many of them.

Early or late, Merc was never going to retire, alive, that is. The last time I saw him was at the end of the project, at a no-name *international airport* somewhere along that tiny strip of coast that the DRC has remaining. I was leaving for pastures of whatever color that life could next throw at me, and he was staying behind, on the continent where he didn't belong.

On the continent where he felt *alive*.

# THAT FLEETING JAMBON-BEURRE
# OF THEM LAST ILLUSIONS

In my book, a decent *jambon-beurre* is one of the main indicators of an established civilization, somewhere along the lines of mastery of fire, invention of anesthesia for wisdom teeth extraction or the use of electricity for purposes other than ending someone's life. To be qualified as "decent", the subject *jambon-beurre* must consist of a fresh half-baguette baked by an *artisan boulanger* sliced open -the bread, not the baker- with some Norman *demi-sel* butter spread inside and two slices of *jambon de Paris* i.e. cooked ham.

The jambon-beurre, dear reader, is simple, solid and honest. The jambon-beurre is more than food, actually, it is a testimony to *our* superior civilizational model, the envy of the rest of nations. Tough luck, the wind was blowing from the wrong direction in Trafalgar, and we lost the World but our model *was and is* superior. In its pure simplicity, thanks to the quality of its ingredients, our jambon-beurre would eat for breakfast any Anglo-Saxon sandwich including the original roast-beef version invented by that gamble-addict Earl of Sandwich of my brass.

After the end of the project with Merc, I catapulted myself from the somewhat wrong side of the Congo River to the very clearly wrong side of the 17th arrondissement in Paris where a friend's apartment was empty for a month. The 17th is scarred in the middle of its face by the tracks leading to Gare Saint-Lazare and the English expression "on the wrong side of the tracks" may well have been invented two centuries ago by an Anglo-Saxon lost in the 17th, clearly ahead of his time.

The DRC was in the same time zone as Paris but social jetlags are the most difficult ones to recover from. On our worksite in Congo, I knew every single one of the folks, many of their families and the grocer in the village close by. The village had one single *sapeur* "self-sponsored by Armani" with whom I would play checkers on Sunday evenings in my contrastingly inelegant coveralls. Every Friday the same band of exceptionally talented kids would play jazzy tunes in the local bar that they modestly called *le kiosk*, which was a crossbreeding of a tropicalized Irish pub and an Ivorian *maquis*. In stark contrast to all that familiarity, back in Paris after nine years I was just another number in that grey anonymity of antidepressant-gobbling masses of frustrated ants. I had barely a few friends left in town, all of them as busy as any self-disrespecting Parisian.

Not having set foot in France for so long, one day when I did not have much time for lunch, between the appointment to close a long-dead bank account and meeting one überbusy Parisian friend, I had a craving for jambon-beurre. On the wrong side of the 17th again, as it so happens. In the first bakery, the friendly fellow behind the counter replied, "I have jambon-beurre, but with *jambon de dindé*", with turkey ham.

It just so happens that I have a profound, profound dislike for turkey, please refrain from asking why... but beyond that personal point, a jambon-beurre is simply *not* made with turkey ham. For the by-now-almost-fellow American reader, it feels like asking for a Big Mac in Ohio and getting the reply "I have, but with chicken". Not that I would know if they make chicken Big Macs nowadays, I haven't eaten fast-food for ages but the point should be clear, I hope.

Thinking naïvely that the first bakery must have been an exception, I walked down to the next *boulangerie* on Avenue Clichy, where I received the same answer, this time from a less friendly guy behind the counter. And after the third *turkey-mongering* bakery, I decided to let it go and went into a supermarket, where I finally found my jambon-beurre or, better said, something *claiming* to be it.

The criminal product was waiting for some desperate client who would stoop so low as to purchase it, certainly not me, in one of them open fridges that supermarket chains put at the entrance of the shop for the grab-and-go stuff. It was put between his distant cousins invented by the gambling-addict English earl of my brass and bottles of colored, sugared, carbonated liquids that should be illegal to sell. The stay in the fridge had softened and somewhat moistened the baguette that must have been a barely-comestable piece of bread to begin with. The piece of ham sticking from between the two halves of the would-be baguette was discolored like the bottom of my duffel bag. Based on what I was seeing from both the ham and the baguette, it wouldn't even surprise me if the third ingredient turned out to be margarine instead of Normand butter. That miserable, despondent would-be jambon-beurre, with its own type of resignation to fate that would rival Merc's, was the perfect depiction of contemporary France. That jambon-beurre was the very eyesore I had chosen to avoid when I had first left Europe for Brazil. That jambon-beurre was the end of a civilization.

It's with lost, nope, with *vanished* appetite despite an empty stomach that I met an old friend with emerald eyes half an hour later for a coffee. I hadn't seen her since we had studied together, she had been posted for several assignments in South-East Asia and she had come back only recently to take care of her widowed and ailing mother. The mother herself was by now extremely limited in her mobility and she was still residing in the same place, where Emerald had grown up on the other side of the *périph*, outside of Paris proper, in one of the then-average but now-practically-unlivable northern suburbs of the city in the *nine-three*.

The American reader, I must add, should refrain from imagining an analogy with the apple-pie concepts of their own suburbs, where well-meaning and hard-working folks mow their lawn on Saturday morning and throw BBQs for friends and family on Sunday after mass. That kind of mental image is just far, too far from what we have in the modern Parisian *banlieues,* period.

"Why cry over spilled *jambon-beurre?*", Emerald joyfully poked into my deep dismay about the local state of affairs, "you should've taken the first available sandwich of whatever kind and moved on. A real Parisian never dwells on such trivialities, a real Parisian knows how to move on. You will never *truly integrate* here and become a real Parisian, right?"

I did not know what to think about *my* integration - I was probably too French to integrate in France and I was trying to convince myself that I wasn't interested in living back there, that it was just a pit-stop for me while waiting for the next jump, the next mission. But putting aside the subject of an irrelevant integration joke, she knew as much as I did that for a real Parisian *absolutely everything* is about trivialities. They do not dwell on them, no, they ducking *live* in them, *ostrichism* being the way they seem to have chosen to cope with anything going *beyond* trivialities in their new century. But we were too good friends for me to point fingers at all of that.

She had not worked a single day of her professional life back home in France until then. Her mom was living in the very apartment where Emerald had grown up, on a meager pension and the money her daughter had been sending her from her expat salary. Despite everything, their lives had continued, marked by their respective rhythms, until she had to come back and discover *the new ways of the hood.*

"They don't burn cars just for New Year's Eve anymore", she sipped on the über-priced Parisian terrace-espresso. "It's not the best when you try to sell your apartment and the next potential client has to walk past the consumed carcass of an old two-oh-seven to get to your building but never mind, let's say it gives a truthful view of the place, you're not scamming the buyer."

With an admirable absence of emotions about the place where she grew up, her detached manners and equanimity, she continued "I just *so happened* to be born here and parts of the country just so happen to be changing ownership, so what? It's not as if the country was *mine* for the simple sake of being born here *of old stock*… This cursed place does not belong to me more than Vietnam or Bulgaria or Zimbabwe, now it's their turn, duck it, I'm not going to fight unnecessary fights beyond what my mom needs for the last years of her life."

"We cannot live here anymore, and I don't have enough money to buy enough square feet -she said square meters, obviously- for the two of us in Paris *intra-muros*, which is the real indicator that I'm not *Parisian enough*. So I'm not going to overthink it, we will sell this place and move to Lyon where I can afford something livable. I understand the State cannot take care of everything or sometimes even the basics, depending on the circumstances. They already have a lot on their plate; they cannot provide for our security in this part of town. It's fine. If I can't afford to bring my mom to a safe part of town, I will look for a job in Lyon, *terminé*. There is no such thing as a birthright. Maybe a decent baguette is my birthright as a French citizen, the jambon inside the baguette is already a luxury, my dear… it's a sociocultural luxury. I have no entitlements other than a decent baguette; I made peace with our destinies"

Looking at her empty espresso cup on the table, I couldn't help but remember Violinist's story about his people who left our Hole: They left in search of the most rightful existence, not necessarily the most meaningful and certainly not the most beautiful, but the most rightful existence. They had preferred to be free in a foreign land, dispersed in many different foreign lands rather than a serf at their would-be home, on their ancestral lands.

Just as we were saying goodbye to each other, Emerald's full equanimity of the full hour from before fully disappeared in a moment of coming to full terms with her upcoming exodus, dragging her old and ailing mother behind. "We are the rejects, the *left-behinds* of the Republic", she said, *les laissées pour compte de la République*, which made me think about that excellent formulation of the excellent Arturo Pérez-Reverte in Cape Trafalgar: Liberté, Egalité, *Etceteré*. "Put the r of Republic in lowercase if you ever write about this", she added, before turning around and leaving.

I still cannot put that R in lowercase; the French Republic made me who I am.

Many years later when I was already on the other side of the pond and they had invented videocalls, Dad asked me about the French flag hanging on the headboard of my bed. I had never ever set foot back in France after that last time I saw Emerald but the answer instinctively came out: "What flag do you want me to have hanging there, Dad? This is the only flag worth something in my book, the only one that my brother should defend with his blood if needed".

"One should not defend a flag with one's blood", replied Mom from his side, "because no flag will ever defend the blood you're ready to spill".

"But neither should one hang a flag that one isn't ready to defend with one's blood", started Dad, in one of his sinuous monologues, at the end of which I wasn't that sure what to do with the flag.

After leaving Emerald, I spent hours walking through the city, left bank, right bank, good neighborhoods, bad neighborhoods, killed-alive neighborhoods. It was a long walk, a désabusé, désenchanté, dés-whatever walk of unbelonging from the city and the country. While unbelonging from there, I started to realize that I probably had never belonged there in the first place and started to wonder if one could unbelong somewhere where one had never belonged. Or if, in that particular case, another neologism was needed, maybe *de-belong* or *ex-belong*. I had never liked Latin, and not being much of a linguist, I decided to stop the struggle with the burden of such subtleties. It was past midnight when I finally made it back to my matchbox in the 17th and the city looked gloomily, terribly, irreversibly ugly to my tired eyes.

"When small men begin to cast long shadows, it means the sun is about to set", wrote the great and overlooked Lin Yutang and the sun always ends up setting on a city. Did you somehow take the liberty to think that Paris was going to stand and be the exception, *oh là là, l'exception française*? Rome fell, Babylon fell, Alexandria fell without realizing it had fallen, Cusco fell, Constantinople fell and then fell again, why should Paris stand?

Are you really that exceptional, you delusional fellow countrymen of my heart with whom I share the love for jambon-beurre but no patronym? Admittedly, you are truly exceptional in that no other nation has had so many charlatans and geniuses side by side as you, but do you *deserve survival* for that singular exceptionality? Does any nation ever deserve survival? Is survival even *deservable*?

Anyway, some conclusions are easy to draw; I had already spent the first long twenty years of my life without access to a proper *jambon-beurre.* So, by then the collective human adventure seemed to have reached the point where it was clear for my good self that it was time to move on, instead of giving France a last chance. This sentence is too long and life is too short, period.

I certainly was not going to become a serf in my *adopted* homeland, so decision was made, nope, *taken*, to put an Ocean between the old continent and myself, again and for good.

But before I jump on that transatlantic flight, again: is survival even *deservable*?

# It is constructive to be bogged down

"The most beautiful stories always start with wreckage", Jack London is supposed to have said, a statement that I as a diver can only appreciate, despite its apocryphal nature. Nevertheless, a few *enragingly beautiful* stories that I have lived through and many others that I have heard of, all started far from any sizable body of water and without the slightest involvement of ships. Many of those stories began with a Latino friend saying "you can trust me, this is the opportunity of your life". An ostentatiously unreliable you-can-trust-me, evidently unreliable from the beginning, has more than once been a trigger for chasing rainbows. This time, thanks to the buffer I had made in DRC, the timing was right to go look for the inflexion points and rupture angles of the human soul on the other side of the Ocean.

"Farming," said Seeker, "farming is the future, plain and simple. Land is the ultimate safe bet, more reliable than gold, oil, or any stock market gamble. The number of people on Earth keeps increasing, year after year, while the amount of land we have remains exactly the same. No new land is going to magically appear out of thin air," he added, repeating his father's words. "This means there will be less and less land to go around, fewer square miles per person, and eventually, land scarcity will become a reality no one can ignore. Combine that with the ever-growing demand for food and resources, and you have a perfect storm. Whether it's grain, livestock, or renewable energy like biofuels, it all comes back to the land. It's not just about feeding people either; nations will fight over land, over who controls the water and the minerals beneath it. In financial terms, that's what you'd call a structurally robust metric."

Is it just human to feel a murderous impulse at the repeated and meaningless use of that *perfect storm* nonsense, or should I book a session with a therapist?

Seeker, like any self-bull-sheeting trader, was blissfully indifferent to the logical flaws lurking in the metrics he conjured up, twisting them to fit whatever narrative suited him at the moment. Numbers, trends and projections were simply tools to bolster his case *du jour*, rather than search for any inconvenient truth. Meanwhile, the land-centric wisdom that he claimed to have inherited from his father seemed to overlook a fundamental reality: our despicable species, with its endless appetite for expansion, was relentlessly carving new farmland out of forests. So, although no new land was created, the amount of *arable* land wasn't static; it actually did appear out of thin air as humans encroached upon every wild corner, voraciously gnawing at the trees and the wilderness that stood in their way, reshaping the planet without any second thought.

Seeker himself was no farmer. His grandpa had hailed from everywhere and ended up settling in Antioch. Not in Alexander the Great's Antioch but actually in Antioquia, the Colombian department whose East side is gently caressed by the legendary river Magdalena. The *hacienda* that he founded had somewhat survived under the second generation, until Seeker went to France and ricocheted from there to London. A clever kid he was, Seeker, very good in math, ruthless in that supreme exact science's application to the destruction of unknown destinies by transferring unknown *wealths* around, in plural please. A not so clever guy seems to have been Seeker's father because neither did he understand Seeker's wish to make a living in front of a screen, nor did he trust his only other child, "married to the wrong guy", to manage the farm.

"You should take over that operation", Seeker opined over mojitos, with that authoritative tone fitting for the great pathologist of fallen and yet-to-fall empires that he was. "Nobody seems to want to *come and get bogged down* somewhere anymore, in a given place, for the rest of their life, be it my grandpa's Antioquia or Mister No's Manaus. The concept of *bogged down* is anything but negative, by the way. So, I was saying, it has become *démodé* to fall in love with somewhere, people want to be on the move, whatever that may mean, they want to have their despicable country-counters running higher and higher. It's not fashionable anymore to know every patch of land or the humor of every little calf on your own piece of land. Nobody is interested in becoming the *terrateniente's* right-hand person in hopes of taking over the farm at some point. Yet, this is what makes the richness of an existence. This is what someone like you could do: go there, take over the operation from the current idiot, learn the ropes and be on your own at some point. Just shape your own destiny, fight the *great leveling* that they are imposing on all of us *ants*. You should fight it and realize the full potential of who you can be. You should be allowed to grab what you deem to be your legitimate chunk of life to be grabbed, it's not about a *better future*, it is about getting what you deserve. In order to do that, first you need to belong somewhere and our farm is an excellent place to belong." A whole program, Seeker was laying out there, somewhat excessive in its commitments, but a *little more belonging* was perhaps what I needed. I remembered Naipaul, that "annalist of the destinies of empires in the moral sense", as the useless Nobel committee had once called him. He had resentfully declared that History is built around achievement and creation; and that nothing was created in his native West Indies. But the mere fact that something, let's call it a farm, was or has been created somewhere doesn't mean that that particular something will thrive or age well. Creation, I'm reliably informed, does not confer any guarantee of survival.

Nevertheless, there is some honorability in knowingly accepting to be bullsheeted into a non-sense plan, especially if it involves yet another failed attempt by an umpteenth stranger to create his own Macondo in that great land of great passions that Colombia has always been. This honorability comes from the fact that before those incompetent engineers soiled its name in the Gulf of Mexico, Macondo wasn't just a village or the story of a family. It was a dream in its most alluringly frustrating form. Macondo had the incomparable appeal of all failed cosmogeneses since the dawn of time. There it was for all to feel, our good old friend Springsteen's dream that so much didn't come true that it became something worse than a lie.

Setting aside too much planning and pondering, I crossed the pond again looking for some *long unpromised* transatlantic happiness, this time on my own behalf, without a paycheck. I wasn't flanked by an up-and-running company or by any sort of previously acquired competency beyond the doggedness resulting from years of site work. To Violinist's concept of searching the most rightful existence, I was determined to add the most *intense* existence, in my new-found quality of *apprentice fate-forcer* who does not have the luxury of not crossing that Ocean again. If I hadn't crossed the pond again after Rio, I would be posthumously judged as not having lived life to the fullest.

An exact order of magnitude above the proverbial African tree and its twenty years, the best time to cross the Atlantic was two hundred years ago and the second-best time was now. Before making the decision, imagining the awe-and-fear-inspiring hacienda that Seeker described, I had a long hard think about the Big Reef back not-home where we had been diving since childhood.

When my arms were neither long enough to reach the rubber bands nor strong enough to pull sufficiently on them, Dad would load the speargun on the dinghy and give it to my nine-year-old self waiting in the water. The Big Reef was the one place that could have been my own *hacienda,* I knew every angle of every single stone and the humor of every single baby grouper on that reef. And despite all of that I wasn't lucky enough to get *blissfully bogged down* and keep diving there for the rest of my existence. As some sort of consequence, in order to deserve Seeker's legitimate chunk of life for myself, I convinced myself that I had no other option than crossing that Ocean and getting bogged down in that hacienda that his grandpa had founded. If I wouldn't do that, these two centuries of delay were going to come back to haunt me and kill my soul.

The dean of the sponge divers from past epochs back in The Hole, with his symbolic tombstone on the Big Reef, was called Giaour. As far as we know, he seemed to have been born around the turn of the previous century, when the civil registers and birth certificates on that land were somewhat wobbly. The Spaniards of the year nineteen hundred, on the other hand, had already mastered the *astounding feat* of associating a name, a place and a date of birth to a person, which they had then put down in black and white for the record in their *Registros Civiles*. We therefore know that Seeker's grandfather was born in the exact year nineteen hundred from a long lineage of sturdy Asturians and lived an exact four months short of becoming a centenarian. In contrast to Giaour, whose doddering body, consumed by soul-corroding saltwater, excessive sun and decades of unscientific decompression practices was a familiar sight in the harbor when we were kids, that Asturian grandfather had still not *expired* when he passed away. They said he had been a man of towering strength from his prime to old age, leaving behind the hacienda as an enduring legacy.

When I first laid eyes on Hacienda Nuevo Cartago in the middle of bumduck Antioquia, its magnificent solitude inspired me to think that there must have been a deep wound in a great man for him to choose to get bogged down, tangled up and then to end up lying flat horizontal on his face in a place like this. The kind of wound made by a broad blade that a ghost dagger-wielder keeps turning in there

A wound where each layer of tissue twists and warps in a different direction as it gets cut. And genuine, relentless grit that great man must have had. I may be without any competency in farming but am able to recognize hard field work when I see some; beyond his physical strength that kept coming back in every conversation, relentless grit that man must have had to build that kind of place from scratch in such inhospitable terrain.

The ghost dagger-wielder, as I learned from Seeker's father himself, had been a succession of older brothers who had been sent, as is the wont of poor families' kids in any country that goes through troubles, to some meaningless war that Spain was waging in Morocco. Some *compensatory* campaign, I understood, to create compensating myths for the losses of eighteen ninety-eight that deeply marked a whole generation of Spaniards. In order for him to escape conscription, the family sent the future grandfather at thirteen years old to some distant uncle in Cuba. There and then, his not yet fully formed bones and nascent muscles *started his life* as a stevedore, at that very age when most Western kids of our times throw fits about some electronic gadget of theirs not being the latest model. It is deplorable that sending our kids to get a taste of stevedores' life at age thirteen for a few months of mental re-education is no longer an option because there ain't no more stevedores in the monstrosity that our modern, mechanized ports have become.

When the grandfather finally landed in Colombia a decade later, with what I imagine was a then-comparable *buffer* in his pockets to what I had in mine a century later, the country was anything but trouble-free, with the international coffee prices in decline, the eternal divide of *liberales* vs *conservadores* and social tensions from labor movements. Sporadic and more and more wanton violence foreshadowed the broader conflicts that would plague the country in the decades to come and life in Colombia was a relentless series of hurdles, with hardships creeping in from every corner. In the middle of all this brainduck that gave its letters of nobility to the continent's most agonizingly creative culture, the grandfather bought that piece of land and spent half a century, half a ducking century, day in, day out, making a living for himself, his family and his workers, without spending a single minute in front of a *slide* about "value creation".

Then came the cataract and the failed operation, at the still early age of seventy-six, whereafter that rock of a man could no longer see. As if such a small inconvenience mattered. He just continued his life of back-breaking work, leading workers on the field, helped by his shadow of a little *india* girl, with her small frame juxtaposed against his weathered stature, who would be his eyes and give him directions. He continued burning down the years without getting old, the best gift one can yank away from life.

His daughters wanted to bring him to Spain one last time. They told him that the airplane had been invented since his departure from *home*, a marvel of modernity that promised swift passage across the vast Atlantic. They tried to convince him that he wasn't condemned to the previous generations' curse of crossing that Ocean only once in a lifetime, westbound, by boat, in a demanding journey. That he could go set foot on his native soil once again in this life and still come back to his adopted Colombia.

"No, no, you girls don't know a thing", he replied to them tall and fair-skinned *femmes fatales* of his Asturian blood in the Colombian jungle. "Many, many people crossed it back, *at least once* in their lifetime, at least a great many who had had enough luck with their adventures on this side of it. The Asturias of my childhood were already full of mansions that were called *las casas de los indianos* that the returnees built with fortunes made in the Americas. And even those who did not *make it,* the less lucky uncles from the Americas with pockets full of stories but not many coins, could mostly make a last voyage to come and rest in their native land when the soul was calling the body."

"But I won't be one of those people who will build yet another *casa de indiano* there. Nor will I leave your mother behind and travel on that flying mechanical animal that you are describing. To me, that flying machine seems like a contraption that no still-breathing Christian should embark on. And when my time comes, I will rest in this beloved and adopted Colombia of mine and be buried here in the hacienda that I built with my hands and back, this is where I belong, period."

And, yes, *anticipable* as the appearance of this sepulchral injustice was, through a combination of unfortunate circumstances, that rock of a man's remains ended up on a hillside cemetery in Bogotá, under the eternal caress of daily upslope breezes.

Never again did he feel the soothing rains of the forests surrounding his hacienda.

# What if Cavafy was right?

Cultural genocides, it seems, are gradual in nature. And disturbingly, short of a complete self-destruction, they tend to know no point of satisfactory ending, with their execution sometimes taking decades. Yet a slowly executed genocide will not necessarily be painless, especially if it's a cultural one. We can have legitimate questions and questionings about the distinction between the natural evolution of a culture and its transformation under a genocidal intent, but an unquestionable certainty of mine is that the subject is too relevant for the wider public to be left to social scientists.

"Oh, Giaour's tombstone on the Big Reef, that symbolic one made of imported Italian marble? They destroyed it, like five years ago. They said it was blasphemous to have a tombstone underwater." said Gambler. "I was abroad when it happened but one of the retired sponge divers posted a story about it. I thought by now you would've heard about it. I mean, *everybody* in the diving community knows about it. Like, if you weren't such a digital nobody, you surely would have heard about it by now"

Gambler was my primary school Benchfellow's great love story when we were teens, as big as love gets when you're a teenager. But as for many others, life after high school turned out to be too small for big love and Benchfellow left The Hole for good, going to some decent European country to study *something useful* and have a deterministic life in line with the parental guidelines laid out for him when we were primary school kids. Gambler, unmolested by the military service thanks to being a girl, was neither interested in moving abroad nor in studying. Conventionality never appealed to her so she started making a living by disc-jockeying and playing poker, at the whim of the opportunities that had the benevolence of presenting themselves.

During my university years, while I was *spending* money to learn about science, before even having the privilege of practicing my trade (simply *obtaining* those pieces of paper with the final purpose of convincing some manager that I could correctly perform a variety of calculations on a variety of topics) Gambler was *making* money on poker tables, first around the country, then around the world. When I had finally started to earn my life on a worksite with hardhat and associated personal protective equipment, cautiously defying statistics in order not to become one, she had already been *playing her own skin* for several years with an innate understanding of statistics and had come out victorious. One respectably possible and possibly respectable definition of victory is simply: to emerge and continue alive on one's chosen path.

I have immense respect for those who self-confidently blow off conventional success paths and even formal education to take their chosen risks and tick nobody else's boxes than their own, which is probably why I had answered the email she had sent me after the eternity that we hadn't seen each other.

After some absence from the land looking for fertile hunting grounds and suckers in the East, she had made a pitstop back in The Hole before continuing her trip, this time to the West. The pitstop proved the point that the returnee is bound to find out that things will necessarily have changed. Even more, it laid bare that in The Hole's case they had not just changed, they were so terribly destroyed, like Giaour's symbolic tombstone on the reef. Accessorily, the pitstop had also delivered fresh news to her about the place that I neither had nor ever intended to have, or maybe so I was trying to convince myself.

"Violinist is doing well, getting older and older but still doing well. When I told him I was going to see you, he told me to send you greetings and to tell you that the phone number of the shop is still the same, two four four, three four, three eight. Back home there is still nobody else who has travelled as much as him through the stories of others and yet he still doesn't have a passport. He still insists on seeing the World through others, well, now through me too. So, he's a bit pissed at you that you haven't been giving any news, because he gathers from your Dad that you have some of the most tearing and daring of them all stories."

Dad, I guess, was too proud not to talk about me and my *achievements,* whatever they may have been in his perception. Mom was the one with the wisdom to be proud of what I had *not* achieved and not talk about it.

With Gambler in the hacienda, we ended up giving one of *those wearing transatlantic calls* to Violinist. In a way it was a much more wearing phone call than the *ikona* call with my brother many years after, the one I referred to at the beginning of the book, because I could hear in the background the characteristic whirring of Violinist's lathe. I could almost tell how many tenths of a millimeter per revolution the lathe was shaving off from some guilt-free piece of low grade carbon steel that was weeping its soul out. Suddenly I tremendously missed that smell of long and curly blue steel shavings burnt by the cutting tool of the lathe, the smell that countless trains of my European years had imitated with the friction of their wheels on the rails while braking during the approach to a station, without ever equaling it. My olfactory environment in the hacienda was driven by the smell of freshly picked lemons under the tropical rain, as far as it could be from the workshop of my childhood.

I spent painful minutes trying to explain to Violinist the reasons and principles behind the absence of any phone call on my part during those years, going into unnecessary details about how I always knowingly avoided people from The Hole since I left. How in Europe I changed the sidewalk every time I heard people speak that first and painfully real mother tongue, how I was happy not to bump into anyone from The Hole in the Americas, given that they hadn't yet started to *invade* here. How the only people with whom I spoke in Holish since my departure were Mom, Dad and my brother, with the exception of a father in France whom I had helped to learn German many years ago and then finally Gambler who now had come to find me here in bumducknowhere of a farm. How so many words were now failing me in any attempt to homogeneously stick to that first language and how lucky I was that Violinist had the vocabulary of Lévi-Strauss in French so that we could express everything we needed in bilingual fashion. How during all these years I always had in my mind, in a guiding capacity, him and the other *anonymous giants* from the *shop*, on whose shoulders only a rare minority of *initiés -insider* is a bad translation, and there isn't any good one- could stand.

"Giaour was a good man", he started to answer from within the entrails of the *shop*, probably caressing the spindle of the lathe that had come to rest in the meantime as I was hearing no more steel being tortured. "He was too good a man to have his tombstone in *these waters,* with his body already condemned to rest in *these soils.* These soils where rationality will never flourish, as your Dad keeps saying, these soils you should be happy to have left for good, that your Dad at least is very happy that you have left for good. Giaour was too good a man for here."

"They have been systematically grinding down what defined *us,"* *he continued,* "but we are too old to care about it, we anonymous *non-victims* are also past the age of complaining that, as soon as we will be gone, they will *make sure that we will not have existed in the first place.* But painful as it is, to you and my Gambler girl there, these brassholes have also been grinding down what made you who you are. The real heartbreak is that you two are still just too tender and alive not to care about your past having been made not to exist, *condemned in absentia* not to exist. These idiots are now saying that after our supposed political and economic hegemony, it's the turn of our *cultural hegemony* to be annihilated… what is there to discuss with such resentful and ignorant donkeys?"

The Bakelite handset inherited from the Asturian grandfather who had built the farm, a heavy piece of kit even on the most joyful of days, was weighing a metric ton and a half in my hand by the time I hung up. Like most things in the hacienda, it was half a century old, if not more, an age and a weight in line with the gravity of that transatlantic conversation with the shop.

Beyond being simply old and clunky, most objects in the hacienda had that weight of legacy-building endeavors reflecting the grandfather's ambitions at his arrival to Colombia. The massive dining table where we sat after the call and the porcelain dinnerware we were having our lunch in, they had the same *anchoring* functions that I had previously observed at a French logger's house whose family had been in Congo for four generations. And the associated silver cutlery, that I still could not take the liberty of holding as unconventionally as Mountain, despite years of absence from parental scrutiny, the manufacturing of that cutlery alone seemed to have depleted half of Potosi's silver reserves in its heyday. "I'm vegetarian, my food doesn't need that much heavy cutting, can't you give me something smaller than this sword to eat, for duck's sake" was Gambler's view on the cutlery that I had inherited with the hacienda.

After lunch we spent a whole afternoon drinking black tea and playing backgammon, wondering if anybody had ever played backgammon in bumduck-Antioquia and cursing the absence of proper black tea abroad. Her wooden backgammon set, a *proper* one, was disproportionately sturdy for a backpacker and she had been schlepping it around for years. It was a means for her to spiritually disconnect from her continuous fight for survival, to play a game without having to gamble. On that afternoon, that set became for me the means to reconnect with The Hole's eternal art of leading an endless and beautifully random conversation about life, the cadence of which was set by the dice being thrown; the kind of conversation and backgammon playing that many unenlightened Westerners had dismissed as a local form of *killing time*.

"Going back to where one comes from, returning to one's own land, that hackneyed story…", Gambler started, "You and I will not be able to escape it either. Behind most hackneyed stories there is human experience *distilled* over many centuries, over tired generations. Mostly bad human experience, as good experience rarely gets properly distilled. You may be innocent enough to think that you are progressing by going somewhere else but any pro-gress, any move forward, on a spherical planet, is bound to bring you closer to the departing point. The zero-hour of the beginnings or at least *a zero-hour* of some sort will always loom above your head, your different heads."

"You see, me I could have continued fleecing our fellow countrymen back then and never left home but I believed I had to go searching for the legendary gambling scenes of South-East Asia that I had read about in the books from the last century: I wanted to find the Shanghai of the nineteen twenties, the Canidrome of Carlos Garcia and all those gutter hole casinos reeking of cheap alcohol and cheaper human existences. I wanted to indulge in both sensible gambling and reckless betting, but I wasn't looking for the game or the fame, all I was really looking for was the spirit of past times."

"And after years of Asia all I found close to that old Shanghai was modern Macao, which had all those big and shiny casinos full of lights but absolutely zero spirit. *Let it be told en passant,* Macao, my dear, is to proper gambling what Pizza Butt is to Italian cuisine. There at my zero hour I realized that the rage to live other people's lives from past times was the type of rage most bound to fail, in the same way as one's own rage to be living *several parallel existences* within the same one is bound to fail. You shall return, we all shall return, believe me, I don't see any other way. Whatever those idiots have destroyed, whatever will be left, we will return there to see all of that with our own eyes and settle down, sooner or later."

In the hacienda's monotony on that afternoon, Gambler's premonition and conjectures about destructions brought back memories of that mysterious map. One day back down South in The Hole, we were talking with an apprentice of Giaour, himself already of fully-white-hair age, *half prophet, half drunkard*, as Brel would sing. He showed me an old map with the wrecks from Ancient Greek times, wrecks where the wood had been eaten away by saltwater before they could tell their whole story. The very next day we had dived one of these wrecks with a few maverick friends, far from prying eyes, not anchoring on the spot in order to avoid detection by the coast guard or passing vessels of *concerned citizens*. What a sight it was, those amphoras, what a rare moment of bliss where we could for once feel privileged to be born where we were born, privileged to dive on History with a capital H that most kids our age would only see on television.

The millennia-old amphoras in their eternal sleep had the kind of historical beauty that would never exist on this side of the pond and like all beauty, they were copiously hated by them brassholes who took over the country. I was sure, by the time we were talking with Gambler, that those amphoras must have been either wantonly destroyed or greedily plundered, but I could still not shake off the clearly meaningless possibility that some, on a hidden wreck site, may have escaped the idiotic fury of humans and survived for a higher purpose.

On that hazy afternoon in that Colombian hacienda far from any sea I just terribly missed those amphoras, our amphoras. What if Cavafy was right?

What if I just haven't been able to find another shore, and the *city* -or simply the amphoras- has always pursued me?

# Blood is thicker than oil

To my great disgrace and dismay, in all my time in Colombia I just haven't been able to bring myself to get decently bogged down in the hacienda.

After the third harvest, my pride had come to terms with the fact that my grit didn't have in its spirit what it takes for my body to stay for another sixty-eight harvests until it would expire in that hacienda. Clearly too much of a Mediterranean runs in my soul for that, despite my lineage being from elsewhere. All children of the Med grow up with a variety of starters in small portions and depending on the country they will be called *tapas, antipasti or mezzes,* but none of these is designed to give you enough attention span to concentrate on a single, proper *main course.* Let alone spend the rest of your life in the same hacienda with the only *voyage* being the rotation of the crops. *Avec le fil des jours, pour unique voyage,* was singing Brel, with the passing of the days as the only voyage.

One must know how to admit when one isn't capable of such maturity. And so, I called Seeker's father to explain myself and smooth things over. Over a bottle of aguardiente, we settled the accounts of the year, each sip mellowing the sting of failure, and for the first time in months, I felt the tension ease. The next week I moved my meager belongings in the two duffel bags into a small, grimy rathole in Bogotá. It wasn't much, but I never liked comfortable hotel rooms anyway. I then started to look for a job that could patch together the wreckage of my agricultural plans.

Once I decided to go back to my good old profession from before trying to become a hacienda owner, a few possibilities quickly popped up for going back to Africa, but I had no more appetite for that. South America is closer to my heart than its former Siamese twin across the pond from before the Early Cretaceous. Here there are no disturbingly straight borders drawn with detached precision across cultures by them eminent Anglo-Saxon specialists using a theodolite and a ruler, in irreverent impunity. In my book, a few British civil servants of the last century could have been impaled on a theodolite with the corresponding level of impunity of the very reverent type and such an act wouldn't have hurt Humanity as we know it. Truly the world would have lost nothing if those who could cut through the tapestry of lives so ruthlessly had themselves been shown how sharp those lines could be. Anyway, it took a bit longer to find something in South America but still, professionally speaking I've been a non-choosing beggar all my life, so a job ended up coming my way, as comfortable as the average hotel room I normally take.

"Even to the layman's eye without any formal training in scatology, this equipment looks like a piece of sheet, its flange's never gonna hold the kind of pressures we are dealing with here." sentenced Foreman in these very convoluted ways of his to precision-strike micro nails on the head. Thereby he was conveniently forgetting that rather than the *equipment*, the company was paying *us* to hold those kinds of pressures, with bare hands if needed. It wasn't the equipment that earned the ultimate paycheck, it was our readiness to take on our face the blows that the equipment couldn't shield us from.

That company was the only kind of employer I had been able to find within a radius of five hundred miles, so on my end I wasn't going to complain just yet. On top of that, they had given me the *town* job where I had to go to the site only once a month, to ensure that I could still don a coverall and wear a hardhat with passable decorum, so in all honesty I also lacked the required legitimacy to complain.

The rest of the time I had the duty phone in the line of command for Foreman to call twenty-four-seven, and I had enough regard for that septuagenarian to refrain giving him orders even though in theory I was his boss.

Foreman hailed from the Dutch West Indies, where anonymous cargo ships kept running aground, in the company of equally anonymous crews, on perfidious reefs whose names elegantly evoked past desolations. His mother was the daughter of a Republican law professor who had ended up in Caracas when in nineteen thirty-nine the direction of the law decided to become aligned with the direction at which El Supremo Francisco Franco's decker was pointing. As if one fresh start per lifetime wasn't sufficient, after high school she had married Foreman's Dutch father and moved to Aruba, which Foreman then left two decades later, out of boredom, to move to her mother's not-adopted fatherland of Venezuela for a *stale* start. And there he learned his trade, our trade, and worked on all kinds of sites for over half a century, never ever going on any job abroad, quite the opposite of my wandering self. And there, talking to foreigners his path crossed with, he learned his impeccable English, full of the most colorful expressions he inherited and translated from his native Spanish with extra spice from his as native Papiamento.

The infamous flange, that proud cousin of Chekhov's rifle on our worksite, obviously did not withstand the pressure, resulting in a gas leak. In conjunction with the uninvited spark, that gas leak led to some fire, resulting in some pressure vessels meeting their makers - an unpleasant escalation scenario short of a full-fledged conflagration. After all the personnel had mustered and the toolpusher had somewhat mastered the situation, Foreman called me to ask for further firefighting and medical evacuation means to be deployed on site. It was not his first rodeo; his career had seen its fair share of accidents and he had been able to keep all his ten fingers intact, despite one of them being badly broken once and lopsidedly smiling in its irremediably crooked shape. He had been there, done that a few times before, and was *taking it easy,* he started to say on the phone, trying to keep his composure.

But having been there and done that before doesn't mean the next incident will be stress-free. Fire remains fire and the fact is, the older you get, the slower you can run away from fire. "I wonder if I should be here at my age, doing what I'm doing, boss", Foreman continued in a despondent sentence, with the connection crackling over the headset. But very quickly he recovered, as he wanted to show, to himself much more than to me, that he knew why he was there at his seventy-one: "Blood is thicker than oil, right, what can I do?" I never asked the details of his son's condition, but I knew he had a disabled son. And a failed state is no good place, if there ever was one, to have a disabled son. So, indeed there was nothing more he could do than keep working.

We recovered from that incident with three somewhat lightly injured people plus some asset damage, and life went on as before. Foreman continued working, I am told, for another eight years, until Covid brought him the final check at seventy-nine. Wherever you hail from or wherever you intend to go, under fire you belong to your next-in-line on the bloodline and all your rootlessness disappears into smoke-filled thick air. Because family is the ultimate remedy to rootlessness, to *Wurzellosigkeit,* the concept that once again lays bare how a poetic concatenation of words and morphemes is the essence of German.

Within weeks of that emergency, circumstances took it upon themselves to remind me that a dysfunctional family is a sort of belonging issue that can beset you at the most unexpected of times and I ended up on a transatlantic flight back to The Hole, wondering what volumetric concentration of red wine could actually be thicker than blood. In the middle of the flight, I decided to leave it at two bottles, in order for the returnee not to become a *revenant* on arrival, out of disrespect for etymology. It may have also been a wise decision to stop at that modest amount, as alcohol and jetlag *don't marry well.*

Once in The Hole, I spent long hours waiting in a hospital, waiting for news, waiting for results, waiting for meaning. May the reader forgive my discretion on the subject of that waiting and its outcome, suffice to state that the outcome was a partial contributor to the *ikona* ending up rootless and homeless many years later. Much more than the outcome, the very process of waiting was the main point worthy of note, however, because having forgotten in the hurry to bring a book with me and practically unable to read in that distant mother tongue of Holish, I ended up doing what waiting people do in this century and killed my due hours in front of a television screen.

In the news some journalists were talking to a father, whose son had been recently killed in an incident that seemed to have made the headlines, as I understood in the middle of the interview. The family was running a liquor store. The son was at the counter at some fateful midnight hour, with two innocent bystanders who also died at the end. Unquestionably, fate always needs innocent bystanders.

There came in four questionable fellows, clearly *unsavory types*, from what could be seen on the ample security footage that documented the scene and also recorded the sounds. I made a quick mental note to myself that liquor stores with security cameras from more than four angles did not constitute propitious environments for a peaceful shopping experience.

Them four questionable fellows had the ways and manners of people from the East. They talked just like Father back where I studied. Or like the father of the victim, now explaining his story on television. The questionable fellows asked the son where his father was and said they just needed to have a "quick chat" with him. East or West, doesn't matter, when somebody wants to have a quick chat with somebody else at midnight, it is rarely a well-meaning chat in The Hole. Or anywhere else, for that matter.

It turned out they had an on-going debt story, and the father had apparently shared something about that story on social media, which upset the fellows. I don't fully master these subjects as I have no social media, but I guess it must have been on a dedicated platform for those kinds of people, some FeudalBook of sorts, regardless of any East-West discussion and distinction.

One thing leading to the other, on the footage we move to an action-filled present tense and a scuffle ensues in that confined space behind the counter of the liquor shop. The son pulls out a handgun from below the counter but can't clear out enough space for making proper use of the gun in that hand-to-hand environment. He is prevented from shooting effectively by the guy next to him who has grabbed his wrists and is pointing the gun to the floor. The gun fires, by design or by accident, twice, without anybody getting touched. The son gets a whisky bottle smashed on his head by a second fellow. The bottle is indeed a meaningful improvised weapon, *arme par destination*. The shop is full of them; you could break at least two more dozen whisky bottles on two more dozen heads without significantly reducing the store's stocks. The impact of the full-liter bottle seems to be calming the son for a moment. It might be that he just needs another bottle to be fully calmed down, maybe even a smaller bottle would do. And honestly, to then break a third bottle would definitely be overkill in those circumstances as the first fellow is still grabbing the guy's wrists and things are somewhat under control. Still too naïve despite my first-hand experiences of wanton violence in Latin America, at that point of the fight I murmur to myself, *all of this should be over soon.*

Indeed, this just could have been over at that point but the third fellow that pops up from the right lower corner of the screen does not, dear reader, share my analysis on the subject. He comes slowly but with *solid determination* next to the son with whom his two fellows have been fighting. In all fairness they had pretty much immobilized the kid, holding him in the bent-over position that I described above, nothing more was really *needed*. Yet our third fellow pulls out his gun and puts eight bullets in the son's loin, in slow, pensive succession, plop, plop, plop again, well, let me not repeat the plop sound eight times.

An Anglo-Saxon would call that shooting *point-blank*, which again shows the intrinsic inferiority of their civilizational model compared to ours: in French we call this *à bout portant* or, even better, *à brûle-pourpoint*. The fire coming out of the nozzle, when the nozzle is in contact with the target person such as on this occasion, burns i.e. *brûle* the *pourpoint* of the victim*,* hence the name. *Pourpoint* is the kind of jacket that people used to wear in that distant past and that was called doublet in English. So, when you shoot someone *à brûle-pourpoint,* their jacket's fabric will be burnt as the nozzle will touch it. *Point-blank*, on the other hand, by most definitions has some empty space between the end of the nozzle and the target. Despite the undeniable closeness of the target, it doesn't touch it. Empty space is not good, nor suitable to describe our scene here.

"They dishonored our family by killing my son that violently," the father says to the journalist, his voice composed, bearing a dignity so resolute it seems überhuman and unbreakable. Not a single tear marks his face. His speech and reasoning are unnervingly structured, clear as water, as though crafted for the occasion, as if he were recounting someone else's tragedy, not his own. His thought process is disturbingly ordered, unflinchingly precise, almost clinical. He is from the East and yet - whatever the legitimacy of this *yet* could be in this sentence - his train of thought, I realize with growing unease, is *Cartesian...*

"Yes, we had some outstanding debt towards these people but over the years we had done different kinds of trade with them anyway. Sometimes they owed us money, sometimes we owed them money, it is trade, it is one's circumstances. One's circumstances are bound to evolve, I was gonna pay those guys. We had disagreements, we had fallings-out, and we later made up. A few months ago, one of these fellows came to our store and my other son had a *disagreement* with him so my son shot him in the leg. We then sent the guy to hospital and paid his medical bills. Then my son ended up in jail. *These are things that happen.* After that we spoke among the elders, and we made up again with that family. *These are things that happen.*"

"But now, they come in at midnight and kill my younger son, with such violence, so *cruelly,* for what? I'm not talking about the irreversibility of my son's death. Death is not what bothers me, *death is a thing that happens.* Two people might be having a discussion, I understand. Sometimes a gun may have to be pulled during the discussion, I understand. A bullet may ricochet from somewhere, I understand. It may accidentally touch a brain or a heart and the person who gets shot may die, I understand. I would accept such a death as divine judgment; *these are things that happen.* But to kill my son knowingly, to kill him that violently, that sadistically, because of such a small debt like that..."

"It's dishonoring for my family because now, whomever will see these images, what will they think of my family? They will say we must be such despicable people; we must have done such horrible things to these fellows that their revenge had to be *commensurately violent.* Because nobody would imagine that they killed my son that violently for some simple money issue, they will think we are bad people, we did bad things. This is so dishonoring for our family. If these people come to me and state, with *substantiated arguments,* that my family has indeed done x or y that deserved such a violent killing of my son in retaliation, if they are able to demonstrate to me that we have indeed deserved it, I promise on my honor that I will absolve them in the Almighty's regard for the killing of my son."

The father, one might say, was just searching for, *aspiring for* order within chaos, in his very own way. He couldn't have read that mighty sentence by Carlos Ashida, *toda sangre llega ai lugar de su quietud* - all blood ends up in its place of stillness. I only read that sentence much later in Mexico. The father was, it could certainly be argued, just searching for compliance with his own set of rules and rituals, within his own specific definition of ethics. The father was probably right, and it may simply be the case that we do not have the right set of tools to understand how right he was.

Whatever the case was, all of it felt like too much social jetlag crashing over me, too much Cartesian logic in The Hole that was impossible to absorb at once. Eventually, I had to turn off the television, feeling an odd mix of exhaustion and detachment. I closed my eyes, hoping to silence the lingering thoughts, and finally drifted into a hazy sleep, letting the remnants of the shooting scene and the father's discourse fade into some forced darkness.

"So, just like that you people will be part of my descendants' Union", was murmuring Herr Professor Immanuel Kant in my dream, watching the same interview from up there. I could hear him scratch his head almost as hard as I was over the meaning of the events. Pretty high he was, somewhere above Königsberg and he seemed still displeased with the city's new name of Kaliningrad. The very father of ethics, tired of scratching his head after a few minutes, decided, "I may need to go discuss it with Monsieur Descartes, at the end of the day our descendants are now in the same Union".

Somewhere on his flight to the Saint-Germain-des-Prés Abbey, he saw the Sartre guy on his left, wondered for a moment if that fellow knew how to spell "ethics" then decided to move on without so much as greeting the ignoramus. Obviously, Herr Professor Immanuel Kant had more urgent stuff to do than talk to that piece of sheet and Sartre was anyway too busy with a fifteen-year-old as was his custom.

"Blood is thicker than man-made unions", Herr Professor Immanuel Kant continued to think while starting his descent to the abbey.

# On Intangibles

My Dad's Jesuit teachers seem to have had a profound dislike for Victor Hugo, that giant of a man who set out to be Chateaubriand or nothing and ended up landing way beyond the stars. And as could be expected from most teenager-teacher relationships, my non-practicing and non-French Dad developed a true veneration for the forbidden French freethinker despised by his fellow French countrymen of the clerical variety. When we were growing up, he transmitted to us that veneration in an *optionally imperative* form: "If you don't read and understand *La Légende des siècles,* it's your choice and I'm not going to judge you. But just don't come back to me one day pretending you have understood the human soul. Nor to cry that you haven't understood the human soul in time and it's now too late."

While waiting in the hospital, apprehensive about yet another distorted feudal ethics story from a parallel universe on television befalling my vulnerable, now-foreign brain, I asked my brother to grab a book to relieve me. I had asked for *any* book from our childhood library at home. That the incipit of that random book mirrored my torments and soul-searching of the last twelve years was a tribute to randomness often not being that random.

"We have yet to *abdicate* one last selfishness: the homeland" Hugo had written, which had found its way into the book's incipit. The great man, the great European before the bureaucrats, had of course written *la patrie,* etymologically the *fatherland,* but it certainly was due to the absence of the equivalent concepts of *homeland* and *motherland* in his native French. To use the equivalent of *motherland,* 'la mère patrie", would have led to a clumsy two-word formulation, while still containing the fatherland concept. Languages, real ones at least, disdain top-down would-be-academic diktats as much as I disdain sterile discussions; *homeland* it is.

His ideas about the nation and the homeland, those ideas from beyond the grave for over a century now... well, modern times are proving to us again and again that they don't *yet* work, maybe because we humans have not been able to evolve to where that sentence would have been applicable. An objective observation is that most people and all peoples still belong and cling to a native tongue and to the soil where they have buried their elders, with some of us lost souls who are in an ever inquiring process of denial and experimentation.

For someone as conscious as me about the family tree and all the contributions of that tree to having become who I am, the contradiction of belonging to a small tribe of people who seem to hail from nowhere has been a burden for a while. This was because not only have I been selling to myself that idea that one could -that *I could* - hail from nowhere, but also because of the rather clearly observable fact that I don't seem to have gotten anywhere in the meantime. What my not very extraordinary self and most of them extraordinary rootless destinies that inhabit these pages have in common is that we haven't even reached the serenity of a ducking *tillandsia,* the vulgarly called *air plants* which share with us the remarkable quality of living and surviving without the need for any soil for nourishment. Let's be fair, the tillandsia, they at least do *settle* somewhere. Undeterred by their lack of roots, they seem to constitute their own, *ex nihilo*... and one might be tempted to add *ad nihilum,* towards nothing.

During the waiting days in the hospital I met another *eternal returnee,* a bit of a strange animal, an animal in his voraciousness and lust for life, almost exclusively material lust at that, who was attending to his duties as a grateful-child-turned-successful-adult. Successful is lacking as translation obviously, he would rather say that he had *made it to a good place* since leaving The Hole, roughly the same time as I. And most meaningfully, during the entire path of his, Animal had been *cudgeling his brains*, as elderly Brits would say, on the vulnerabilities that accompanied him, on what would remain, what he had acquired in an intrinsic fashion.

"It's the second time in three years that this place is tripping me up by bringing me back here, I'm sick of it. I have a lot, a lot to do *back home* in the US and I'm losing my time here, as if I hadn't lost enough of it here when I was a kid", started the rant. Irritation was tightening the lines of his face, a face that bore the depressing lack of tan, the paleness of someone who no longer belonged under this sun. His hands, thick and strong by birth but smooth enough to hint at his years now spent in boardrooms, clenched around his phone that I, in my profound ignorance of those gadgets, suspected was the last model. With fingers tapping impatiently against its case, "I'm sick of it," he continued, voice low but edged, bitterness like a tension building in his jaw. "Back home in the States, I've got work that matters, real work, not the… nonsense that runs through this place like a bad current. I've put in too many years building something there to be wasting my time here." He cast a narrow glance around, like the very city or the whole country was conspiring against him. "Enough of my youth slipped away in this place for me to be wasting even more time now," he repeated, half to himself. "Feels like every time I come back, I'm shedding skin, bleeding hours here and this place keeps taking more than it's ever given."

Somewhat legitimate, his rant, I would say. The Hole has rarely, if ever, given an adult person anything beyond losing their time. But to think that you have lost time *as a kid* is ambition without reason, leaning into absurdity, a pointless grudge. Does childhood owe anyone productivity? The *fight for net worth* can wait, Animal, relax…

"Truly I have progressed a lot, but I must admit that I lost a lot on the way and not just money. There is that intangible gain of the years, the one that will persist if every tangible thing that I own were to disappear today. The intangible is clearly not negligible, with everything I have achieved but it does not yet satisfy me. In a way this is rather comforting because... doomed to fail are those who are satisfied with the improvement of their intangible gain. I, this tangible thingy, these material assets, I will wipe my brass with this contemptible part of my life first thing tomorrow morning if my *shack* catches fire with everything I have in it. I will then go out in my boxers and live my life as well as I can. This is the only way I can eliminate any possible doubt about a possible return, to what is not there anymore".

His "shack", as Animal was quick to announce without even the practiced air of humility required in The Hole, was actually a sprawling four-bedroom apartment in Manhattan. And not any casual property, Upper East Side please, nestled among designer boutiques and within peeing distance of Central Park. He seemed to have long since perfected the art of dropping this tidbit into conversations, easing it in just when he knew it would hit the right note of envy or admiration. Becoming a piece of sheet who wears his address like a badge of honor showed some serious integration in the US. The guy made it and then necessarily had to rub it in everyone's face. Wealth *untalked about* doesn't exist...

The mention of his property taxes -it obviously had to come to that- turned a simple fact into an ode to his own achievements. "Parking in New York is such a joke," he'd lament, complaining about valet service for his Tesla here and there. He was the very picture of the guy that needs financial security to conceal all his remaining insecurities; wealth as demonstration, social spectacle, a necessary ritual where his peers were the unwitting audience.

Yet his talk about intangibles got me thinking about my own vulnerabilities which I had plenty of time to ponder while he went on bragging about his wealth. I tuned out the moment he started to dart higher than his brass and I started digging into the *invisibles* I had reached. Or achieved. Or *internalized*.

The current level of intangible gain, intangible assets, shortly put the *current intangible*, needed better definition and understanding. I would argue that *current* takes on its full meaning by requiring us to neglect experience because what you have built on previous experience also becomes irrelevant when the conditions enabling you to reuse that experience are irreversibly lost, say burnt down with your shack. What one may have experienced in Rio during a previous life does not enter into the calculation of one's personal intangible, strictly speaking. What does enter into that calculation is rather what one made oneself capable of experiencing in Rio *in a next life*, and also in another Rio. The definition keeps only the acquired reusable knowledge, including on the basis of previous experience but not the experience itself. The intangible is a toolbox that one can take anywhere one may or may not belong to.

These reflections on the intangible should help one to question the distance one could have covered under the most favorable set of circumstances, without being condescending towards the distance one has factually covered. Free will can only do so much against one's initial conditions, fate and natural selection. But true decency lies in the *ownership* of one's chosen path, of one's own battles and in the ultimate analysis of one's own *art* to shape one's own luck. I have also met many great folks over the years who haven't been able to shape their own luck, for a variety of reasons. I am yet to decide whether I should cry for them or rationalize their failure as mere pages turned, because the system needs someone to lose, period. The system, dear reader, is that ultimate ruthless son of a ditch…

A general in one of them not fully evolved countries had said, many decades before they killed that abject Prigojine piece of sheet, that "a coup plotter, from the very moment he has sat down to negotiate, has lost." Same applies to one's own battle with one's options. If you've decided to burn some bridges, if you have in a way decided to carry out a coup against yourself, you no longer have the luxury of sitting down at the negotiating table with yourself, because as soon as you sit there you have lost. Simply put, as far as "creating your luck" is concerned, when it's your own that you have created, even if she -yes, she, *la chance*- doesn't smile at you, you can't blame her. The moment you start to resent the luck you yourself sought out for not smiling at you, you're sitting at a negotiating table with yourself... you have lost.

Realizing that his wealth didn't impress me, Animal continued his rant, thereby pulling me away from past negotiation tables of improbable coups that I hadn't witnessed. "In my toolbox of intangibles... in that toolbox there is today less mathematical liveliness, I am no longer twenty, but there is a better mathematical understanding of the subsystems that constitute the world, my world. There is also a higher taste, higher but above all more conscious, better structured and less testosterone-intensive taste for risk-taking." Then he continued, apparently unable not to think about money for more than five minutes: "I now must transform my current set of intangibles into more tangible assets, meanwhile building more intangible wealth based on my current tangibles. And none of that is feasible here in The Hole. I first need to see the light at the end of this tunnel, bury my old man and go back home for that, because *home* isn't here. We used to have a country, we don't have it anymore, plain and simple, I have nothing to do here".

As a rule, I have sympathy... and understanding... and affinity, for... and with, the people who *used to have a country*. I just can't feel that sort of compassion with Animal, with his materialistic and *driven* manners. Having both been absent from The Hole for so long we both know the *shop is under new management now* and we are both similarly disconcerted by similar absurdities. Yes, we have both lost the same country, that much is undeniable, but clearly, we're experiencing that loss in profoundly different ways.

Animal feels trapped in The Hole during that short stay, suffering like a caged lion who is pacing back and forth, visibly tormented by both the memories of wasted times and the weight of his very present. Every corner he turns seems to remind him of what was lost in the past and what the present no longer offers and that unbearable misery radiates from him. Meanwhile, I at least try to force myself in a different headspace, trying to navigate this reality with as much equanimity as I can muster. I approach my time in The Hole with a sort of cautious curiosity, respecting the existential randomness of it all. Not that I dislike the place less than Animal but at least I try to have an element of peaceful resignation to it, a mix of nostalgia and acceptance, a willingness to confront whatever emotions arise during my stay. It's just a brief interlude in the grand tapestry of life and this too shall pass... As my friend Elia expressed it so elegantly way before me, *I don't have a homeland to say I live in exile...I live in postmortem.*

And with or without country, or *nation,* one just does not and cannot live as a caged lion in postmortem. Such a life, such a way of living, would have no dignity.

# A ROUNDED OFF HUMAN BEING

At times fate makes an exception to the rules, and distributes its constraints and whiplashes according to one's available resources and resilience; it adjusts everyone's burden to the width of their shoulders. Animal's troubles vicariously came to a quick end, coupled with the quick burial of his father, so he was able to go back to his beloved *home* without losing too much of his very precious time in our Hole.

On my side, I was obliged by the circumstances to stay in The Hole quite a bit longer until matters would settle down. It must have been fate's way of adjusting the burden to the non-physical realities of my shoulders that I never really measured in detail. My stay in The Hole, oscillating between our apartment and the hospital, ended up being more than a visit. I started languishing in that particular twilight generated by an adult's return to their teenage room.

Many unwanted thought processes those teenage rooms have been known to trigger in disoriented minds. In my case, after such meandering years since my departure, those ceiling-staring hours pushed me to reflect on what direction that meandering could take next. And that reflection, maybe by dint of the observation of a diminishing adaptation capacity that I didn't want to acknowledge, spurred me to better define my peers, i.e. those who I would like to be surrounded by going forward. That search for a better definition of my peers then brought me to dire conclusions on the nature of what makes a *completed* human being. One should better replace *completed* by *rounded off* or, if more German is allowed, by *vervollständigt. Ein vervollständigter Mensch,* a fully completed human is our subject here, whichever way someone may translate it.

The linguistic and cultural components of human beings constitute, in my couldn't-care-to-be-humble opinion, the most fundamentally indelible, defining and *irretrievable* aspect o f their existence. Those are aspects for which one cannot later *compensate*. And by cultural components I mean something very broad that encompasses more than traditions, customs, food, belief systems etc: my *cultural* extends to one's work, the way of approaching problems, the *grid* for reading life and the many ways we have to wrestle what life throws at us, in both its regular and exceptional components. *Cultural* goes as far as the vision of the world and beyond. *Weltanschauung* would stick out its inflexible nose if we hadn't banned German.

And by "the aspect of the existence that cannot be compensated for", I came to mean more and more the *unrecoverability* of childhood. For clarity, the subject childhood may go, under exceptional circumstances, until the end of higher education but no further. At twenty-three, say twenty-four years old, a human being is completed, rounded off, *constituted*. It will be able to evolve, it certainly *must* evolve further if it wants to survive but regarding the most indelible aspects as mentioned above, by that age of say twenty-four, a human being is constituted. And I daresay that from that moment onwards, our subject human being's evolutions will also tend more and more to follow that Persian proverb: from paradise to hell, one step can be enough, but from hell to heaven you have to walk a thousand miles.

So, on the *unrecoverable* side of a human existence, for me there is this devastating primacy of the mother tongue and the cultural universe that one builds around it, through it, thanks to it. There is, then, for those who are unlucky enough, a *fake* mother tongue piggybacked on the first one or floating around like a semi-evolved primate. That second language can constitute the comparative universe to better situate one's referential, *maternal* universe. Or the *paternal* universe, if one was lucky enough to spend more time with a father while growing up. There may even be more than one fake mother tongue for the truly unlucky people but none of this constitutes any particularity that requires distinguishing among cases. Obviously there are parallels and similarities or even repetitions.

And right after the mother tongue comes something almost as devastatingly important in defining and rounding off a human being: the primacy of the *functional system* that our subject human being has acquired in its prime years. My functional system, whether I can make peace with it or not and whether the word's connotations are liked by self-proclaimed sensitive souls of modern times or not, hails from the *West*. And this functional system is based on Cartesianism, on the Enlightenment, on the *marrow* of both the exact sciences and social sciences developed since the Renaissance. Therefore, my *congénère*, my peer in terms of the functional system as described above is alas, or fortunately, a product of the *West* i.e. someone who knows how to present a structured argument. The text of that *structured* argument may be called essay or *dissertation* depending on the nation but that, regardless of the appellation, it shall follow a logical path from exposing the subject to developing the matter and getting to a conclusion. More important than knowing how to write the essay in question, my functional peer is someone who, when considering how to tackle a certain problem, thinks along the lines of such an *unwritten* essay.

So, within the frame of this very personal definition, my closest friend on the worksite in the DRC years, a muscular, coal-black Cameroonian guy whose work ethics and moral values were as solid as his muscles, who speaks such refined French that I wish the average Frenchman had the command of half his vocabulary, is my *functional peer*. The fact that he had a *customary* marriage ceremony with another fellow Cameroonian -where, incidentally, I had a greatissimo time enjoying cheap booze and heart-warming local food- doesn't change anything on this state of affairs: that fellow is my functional brother because our brains are wired in the same way.

That basis of functional peerage strongly impacts my thinking about where I could go *chase existence* next. This also is a way of voting with my feet, in the choice of my fellow brethren. Simply stated, when I look at a map of the world, I see places where people are likely to be functionally wired like me and then the *other places*. Regardless of any idiotic constructs about colors, beliefs and the rest, in some places I have my *functional congeners* and regarding the others... Well, I could burst my brass in all the possible dimensions of a multidimensional space and yet I would not be able to become their functional peer in what remains of my life, because I am already a *rounded off* human being. Not old, just rounded off. One could qualify my approach as defeatist but in my book, I am simply being realistic with respect to my remaining potential for evolution.

Starting with the most extreme counterexample, I have a profound and sincere admiration for the Japanese people; by all accounts they are a nation of extremely sophisticated people. If I had taken the time to educate myself more on the subject and to gain an opinion with some level of legitimacy, I could probably say that no Western nation will ever reach the level of sophistication that the Japanese have- I do feel that in my guts. It simply is a fascinating people and a society admirable in its refinement, but the question is not whether that society is fascinating, whether it has such or such merit. The relevant question for my existence-chasing self is whether *I* could one day become *Japanese enough*, if I threw myself with heart and soul into it now, because of, say, a mad desire to go and live there.

I know for a fact that I cannot get there. I'm too old and any self-declared self-development guru who claims one is never too old does, in this particular case, simply not know what he or she is talking about. I could observe and read and ask all manner of questions to well-meaning and helpful Japanese people to eliminate my upcoming social blunders, which already seems to be quite some work in that highly codified society. At the cost of agonizing pain on my Indo-European-wired brain I could, over several years, hypothetically learn near-perfect Japanese, but the *near* will always remain. And more importantly than that residual "near", I will not be able, one day, to read a Japanese text while feeling it as much in my guts as a song by Brel or a poem by Hugo, those giants I met in my teens. Basic neuroscience has proven that I will never again have the malleable brain of a teenager, despite stubbornly keeping a teenager's thirst and lust for life. My *guts* are not fifteen anymore so it would be phony to expect that I would feel that hypothetical text in my guts one day: the discussion, ladies and gentlemen, is over.

Let's continue with another counterexample whose failure based on my pre-defined criteria could be disconcerting, because of the counterexample's proximity to Europe. After all, many have the feeling that the Russians are also somewhat European: their ruling classes of two centuries ago spoke French at home almost without exception. They most likely had no reason to envy their French, German or British counterparts in terms of culture or enlightenment. This is the nation that has generated the most solid literature of all nations and languages, for duck's sake and I haven't put the conventional "arguably" in this last statement because I just wouldn't argue about it. And yet, it is a shame but all that was two centuries ago, or even a little less. In the meantime they failed like sheet…and I should underline that these lines were written way before the meaningless bloodshed in Ukraine started.

I said *they failed like sheet,* mainly because later on they did not have the necessary understanding that freedom and equality were not just empty words that the French had sown in the declaration of human rights for enjoyment, and that *little difference* was enough to make Russia non-European. Beyond the "psychological warfare" aspect, there is a simple, non-conspiratorial reason for the designation *Free World* that the West used to define itself vis-à-vis the Soviet world and its allies during the *first* Cold War, that reason being that the designation was simply… true.

The Russians wanted to build their own model of civilization; this was in itself a commendable undertaking, and I respect the audacity of all dreamers, always. And for the sake of consistency, I will of course even go so far as to respect the audacity of those who, in their attempt to build their own model of civilization, chased my grandparents out from their land because *respect for audacity* does not equal endorsement of their actions. But the outcome of the attempt was clearly a non-Cartesian or, in my primary school Benchfellow's words, *indeterministic* model of civilization.

The people that *resulted* from this experiment can be observed to adopt this Slavic fatalism in life, devoid of analytical lucidity despite the more than respectable *scientific baggage* of this nation that trained some of the brightest mathematicians in history. The despondent souls that constitute that nation seem accustomed to injustices, undermined as a nation by the failure of a civilizational model based on a great amount of hypocrisy. Taste and sense of initiative have been confiscated from them by generations of freedom-killing brassholes and these traumas do not disappear in a generation or two. So, I cannot emphasize how much it kisses me off to say this, but the average European "peasant" is alas more, much more my congener and less a peasant than what may have remained of those Russian aristocrats there. And to come back to the original argument, learning Russian to a level sufficient to read Dostoyevsky in the original version -what a titanic task- will not fundamentally change this state of affairs in the near or medium future. Admittedly, I lost that option when my grandparents lost their land in nineteen seventeen.

A very important clarification is that my deeming someone a non-congener to my insignificant self does not in any way constitute a judgment on the value of that fellow human being. It just constitutes a judgment on those directions of the human experience that my development hasn't been able to encompass, it's as simple as that. It is just a personal recognition of the fact that I will not be able to establish the same affinities with all fellow humans on Earth and that a *commonality of functional systems* is non-negotiable in establishing these affinities, in particular for someone who is in the rounded off years of life.

Maybe The Hole had once been a place that one could reconcile with the Western functional system that our parents and teachers had inculcated in us but it wasn't the case anymore. And my simplification of the second law of thermodynamics may not be beyond reproach but it does clearly lead to the kind of irreversibility that is manifest when a cathedral is reduced to rubble. That specific pile of stones cannot, by miracle, rewind the tape to reconstitute a cathedral. Some re-evolutions are just not within the realm of possibilities.

After having understood and pondered all of that, of course my rounded off self of thirty-eight tender years escaped again, at the first professional opportunity. To Mexico this time.

# You can't have too many
## passports

In those years, Mexico was booming in my line of work, and two ex-colleagues of mine had already moved there. They easily convinced my mentally tired self of the Old World to partner with them and go see what extensive and enticing Eldorados -in plural please- were waiting for us in the New World. With five centuries of delay on that short-lived-but-long-dreamt Eldorado concept and totally oblivious to the absurdity of mentioning it in the plural, I made the jump from freelancer-with-a-duffel to would-be entrepreneur and moved to Mexico City. We were innocently hoping to get maybe not a share of the pie but at least a few crumbs that people with our technical background could legitimately aspire to.

"We'll get your residence permit arranged, that's easy" said the lawyer, "but you should already think about your naturalization in a few years as well. Look, here is the list of conditions you need to fulfill, all it takes is patience. You never know what can happen in life, you never know what can happen on a *continent*, you just can't have too many passports."

Lawyer, to whom a childhood friend had referred me, was himself a passport collector, born in the same Hole as me but also a naturalized Mexican citizen since he had been living there for over ten years. He had yet another passport or three in his back pocket, through genetically expandable *jus sanguinis* and geographically flexible *jus soli*.

He had achieved that within a convenient bandwidth of truth that allowed him to be born in different places, which he did not consider to be that much of a dilation of the facts.

"I need to find a rabbi in Bulgaria who can confirm our family tree', he complained to me one day when we were pigging out on small platters of nostalgia at Al Andalus in the city center, "They jailed the Portuguese rabbi I had found; it seems for corruption, you know, that story with the oligarch… so my naturalization case in Portugal has stalled. But my great-grandfather was born in Bulgaria, so if I find the birth records from there and have a rabbi to certify, I can get a Bulgarian passport. It's not a bad one, you know, it's also European after all. I'm lucky, you know, my great grandpa was born right after Bulgaria ceased to belong to *us* and the year after that they moved to The Hole."

I had never met Lawyer before Mexico but we were both kids in The Hole in the nineties. That decade has shaped the anxiety that most of us have since been trying to fight off in different ways. Our generation of kids has grown up witnessing the daily powerlessness of our parents' generation, that heartbreaking *impuissance* of honest people in dishonest countries that wear down their brightest. Those of us who then left The Hole did it with a burning thirst for the tools that could help us avoid that sort of impotence in our own futures: a residency in a country with the rule of law, some money in a non-toilet-paper currency or a passport from a so-called first world country. Nevertheless, Lawyer clearly was an extreme case of passport collector with acute anxiety disorder arising from the potential for simultaneous geographical implosions on several of *his* countries.

There was a bit of Stefan Zweig in Lawyer, both in their respective exiles, perpetual and rotating, a painful succession of exiles. "My inner crisis consists in that I am not able to identify myself with the me of passport, the self of exile", Herr Zweig had stated, while he was living his *posthumous existence*. Very few sentences hurt as much.

But thankfully for Lawyer, thankfully for me and many others, *our bunch of contemporaries* had been able to recognize the "early beginnings of the great movements which determine our times" and we had escaped in good time.

We will ping-pong across the pond back to The Hole for a moment but no worries, my eternal Mexico is waiting for us two paragraphs further down the road. Heavy years they were, the nineties in The Hole and also in many countries that I was *somelucky* to see afterwards, Colombia standing particularly out, the DRC faring not much better Somelucky, if you wonder, means *somewhere between lucky and unlucky.* the position of the cursor being circumstantially defined. Anyway, I was saying, heavy years they were and in The Hole they engendered the spatiotemporal concept of *being a child in the nineties,* which seems to be creating a flurry of nostalgia nowadays, as people tend to forget and rewrite the history of the bad old times.

So, many years later I came across the underwater video of an ex-diving buddy of mine who went diving to exactly ninety meters on air with three other kids of our generation. They baptized their *sortie* and the associated video "Being a Child in the Nineties", hoping for a good narcotic effect under pressure with nitrogen and to have a good time. They were all trained in gas diving but diving to reckless depths on air brought not only narcosis but most importantly the pleasure of danger, with the illusion of control. Alas we were no more in the nineties, those kids were no more kids and for lack of fitness or weight of fate, one of the guys didn't make it back. Heavy were the nineties, I told you, so this was a fitting finale, unfortunately. For the American reader, ninety meters is just shy of three hundred feet. You just don't dive that on air, there are better gas mixes for it. Or you just don't cry if you die doing it.

Escaping from our nineties, Lawyer had gone to the UK for work after having studied law at home and stayed there long enough to obtain the passport (the UK requires five years, I learned). He had then moved to Israel (there the passport is just a matter of months if you are Jewish, I already knew). And then he had launched a company in Cyprus that failed (failure can be a matter of months or decades, I presumed). Finally, he had then ricocheted from the *Canal* to land in Mexico where he had stayed and founded a family with a Mexican girl and all the rest.

Despite having grown up speaking Ladino with his parents, when I met him twenty years later, he seemed to have made zero effort to adapt his mother tongue to Mexican Spanish. For the record, akin to moving from Québécois to French, for anyone with a bit of a sense for sounds it should have been a matter of three months to switch from Ladino to Spanish. It should have been a matter of professional survival to switch from Ladino to Spanish for anyone practicing any language-dependent profession and he was a lawyer, for duck's sake. It should have been a matter of emotional survival when your wife and kids are Mexican, for ducking goose's sake.

"I don't understand, I was defending a client the other day at court, the judge asked me if I was Mexican, when I responded that I was a proud naturalized Mexican citizen, he asked me if I really studied law in this country. Is it written on my face that I *bought* my local law degrees?"

Maybe *that* wasn't written on his face, but a few other things were quite clearly and indelibly etched on his face. Among others the fact that he wasn't exercising his noble profession out of an unwavering belief in the power of law 'n order, I must say. There is that particular look on his kind of lawyer; once you have seen it you can't unsee it. And if you try to unsee it, he quickly brings you back to *hearing* it when he talks about some of his clients, in this case a bunch of assassins for *milk powder merchants* up North in Tamaulipas, much less romantic and cinematographic stuff than what they show you on Netflix.

"They're not bad kids, *you know*, their bosses just couldn't share the pie with the other guys so they sent these kids as *carne de cañon*. you know, as cannon fodder. The kids had a somewhat innocent or at least naïve approach to it, you know, it's like, their piece of land, they wanted to put their stamp on it, like, the good old ideals of. you know, fight for land, conquer and protect etc, you know, pretty much well-meaning and even heroic. They got really close to taking over the Tampico airport, like, the combats were raging, you know, a couple of miles from the airport."

Slight, very slight deformations there were, in his story, *you know*, with a soupçon of not-really-so-good faith. For starters, *you know*, *like*, his "kids" had an average age of thirty-two and almost all had previously served at the GAFE, *Grupo Aeromóvil de Fuerzas Especiales*, at least the Mexican ones. On top of it, some of those kids could *very difficultly* pretend to be fighting for *their* land as they were Guatemalan transplants, in the form of Kaibils, the most ferocious duckers the continent has ever seen, North and South. And also the statement that they "got really close to taking over the airport," does not really fly with the rest of the story about some innocent and heroic kids, does it?

*They got close to taking over the airport*, I murmur to myself. What for? What were they gonna do afterwards, if they had succeeded in taking it, *what was the final project?* Were they gonna plant a flag in the now-autonomous cartel-city of Tampico and declare it their own land? Never short of ambitions, were they gonna change the political map of the Western hemisphere?

Were they gonna issue their own ducking passports and apply to the UN for recognition, for ducking goosing pheasant's sake?

# THE TERRIFYING HOMOGENIZATION OF THE WORLD

"An American client of mine told me that civilization is when proper coffee comes to a neighborhood", Lawyer stated, looking down at the Starducks around the corner of his office on Reforma. "I beg to differ, you ignorant pigs", he continued, sipping on his *Eastern Mediterranean* coffee that the Mexican secretary had just prepared in a *cezve* as per his instructions, "real civilization is what was already there before you brought that unnecessary choice of thirty-nine coffee varieties to a neighborhood that had asked for nothing".

The *Avenue of the Empress* of two centuries ago certainly held more allure than modern day's Paseo de Reforma scarred by storefront signs from all kinds of international coffee chains, the same ones that you now find anywhere. There may be no justification to be upset about these coffee chains if one rightfully considers Mexico as one of the outposts of the original, *sinful* globalization. So maybe I'm overdoing it, nevertheless my sense of aesthetics is disturbed by these neon signs. Nothing healthy that was imported anywhere has ever needed so many neon storefront signs to attract mosquitoes, be it coffee chains that sell back überexpensive coffee in countries where it was originally grown or banks that bring back overvalued gold in countries where it was originally mined.

Pre-Columbian societies in the Americas had *mastered* the art of crafting gold and much ink has been spilled on the subject to make generations of adventurers and swashbucklers salivate. In my very humble opinion, those societies would have been far better off mastering steel instead of gold.

Had they mastered steel before the arrival of the Spaniards, they would have kicked brass or at least fought among equals, man-to-man, instead of steel-to-wood-then-thru-to-flesh. For my part, my curiosity would have found its way into that spellbinding country in all cases, on the shoulders of swashbucklers from obscure pasts. But if they had mastered steel -and what results from it- a century ago my Mexicans and I wouldn't be speaking that characterless corporate Globish. Cervantes is certainly tumbling in his tomb but I just can't imagine that Shakespeare is faring any better in his own grave, watching his tongue getting massacred by all of us ignorant simps, day in, day out.

Beyond language itself, the civilizational model that most easily exported itself also came from those who had mastered steel, or whatever relevant *techné* they had mastered, because once you know what kind of value you can create with your *techné* i.e. art, craft and skill set, you may as well dump the production of steel itself onto someone lower in the food chain. The *rope access* guys on my worksite in Mexico are called *alpinistas* and I bet my bottom dollar they will never have the means to see the Alps. Nor Aspen, for that matter, or Vail, which a local acquaintance of mine claims is the preferred skiing destination of Mexicans, without stopping for a moment to wonder *what kind of Mexicans*. On the contrary, for the foreseeable future no rope access guy in Europe will be called *sierramadrista* and they will have all the means to come and hike leisurely on the Sierra Madre Oriental -or, for that matter, Sierra Madre Occidental- during their well-deserved time-off after four weeks of monkeying on steel structures. And for the foreseeable future there will be a considerably higher risk of *unintended saturnism* on the Sierra Madre than in the Alps, which is understandable given that lead-free options such as non-toxic bullets or frangible bullets are a first world luxury. When you're poor you kill your neighbor with the means at hand. Anyway, that potential for unintended saturnism is why Gordito, my favorite rope access guy, had left his native Durango to come work with us on the Gulf coast.

Gordito is one of those people born to smile; he has major teeth and a happy-go-lucky approach to life. That his body has a certain circumference is obvious in his nickname and having such a heavyset guy work in the airs arouses in me a mixture of respect for the tenacity and talent of the guy as much as disgust for mister coca-ducking-cola. In this country, those drinks have destroyed more lives per year than the ducking cartels, without attracting one-tenth of the attention. Diabetes is just not as *netflixable* as optionless teenagers and their cynical bosses shooting at every single moving thing around them.

Gordito's nickname could also be interpreted as proof of the non-judgmental love of neighbor that the Mexicans have, possibly the least body shaming nation on Earth, but in this country, there is also a simply endearing side to the adjective *fat*. "*Gordo, pásame la llave de cadena*" is something you hear all the time on my site, *fatty, give me the chain tongue*. Often you turn around to see that the subject *gordo* is a skinny twenty-something year-old kid that must barely weigh hundred and twenty pounds before his toilet in the morning.

"I have two cousins in Arizona, hard-working guys who are living the American Dream or whatever is left of it", said Gordito, "and I even went there twice, crossing the desert on the way in, coming back like a gentleman by plane… twice I went there, but I didn't feel like *building* a life up there. Probably I'm biased for not having seen that many places and countries in my life but I feel that, for now, Mexico is the right place to escape that *terrifying homogenization of the World*, at least for me and my family. Here we are at least equipped to fight it and to carve out some protected niche where we can live our life in our own way."

"And for someone else if another place is the right one to escape it, I think they have the duty to go to that place, so that they too can escape that *maldita homogeneización* that is falling on us, without mercy. What's the point of crossing that river if on both sides of it we are all meant to eat different colors of the same sheet, watch the same stupidities on the same screens and be lulled by the same illusions. Most of my fellow countrymen say they cross the river for the future of their children, I had a hard think about giving a so-called head start to my kids too, such that they can be best equipped to avoid the *structural sadnesses* of our land... but does being a father allow me to make a judgment on what is an *acceptable sorrow there* compared to a *structural sadness here?* And who the heck decided that they will be sad by staying here, *carajo?* Me too I want my children to have a future but not just any future, mine shall have their *own future.*"

I admired Gordito's willpower and resolve to escape collective daydreams. The earlier before its eventual collapse one escapes a collective daydream, the more *moral value* one creates for one's beloved offspring. In the end, truth has no rush but it's just so much more *soothing* to grasp it before the others. And Gordito, who was listening to Celia Cruz seventy feet in the air while inspecting the bolts and checking that the vibration isolation washers had not loosened, his existence hanging on a rope, his balls hanging in between a harness, had come to the personal conclusion that Celia's *surviving, breaking barriers and crossing borders* may have belonged to the ethos of another epoch, despite everyone now crossing borders like *locos.* Maybe, just maybe, it was now passé, and people hadn't yet realized it.

That kind of doubt wasn't strong enough to stop me from crossing yet another frontier, the ultimate frontier, that same cursed river but in the legal fashion, two years down the road. However, the reflection had already started, with Celia singing in the background, *rompiendo barreras, voy sobreviviendo, cruzando fronteras, voy sobreviviendo...*

Back in Mexico City, I found Gordito's obsession with homogenization ambushing me in every neighborhood that was being invaded, around the corner of every Porfirian building in Roma transformed into a soulless stack of tourist apartments, on the sidewalk table of every hipster café in Condesa. Being another one of them brassholes parachuted into the city, I am myself part of the problem, but I just can't take that gentrification which de-souls our barrios. All the neighborhoods end up looking the same, which effectively means they all look like nothing.

Them de-souled and de-natured places resemble more and more the movie set of a fictional country where lives are too artificial even to be works of fiction. One evening when I was cooking for an American friend, he started streaming some show with successful and beautiful young people in a process of soul-searching between the urban jungle where I grew up and a nice seaside town in the *olive tropics*. "Look, this is a great show", he said, "it's your country, right?". The actors all spoke my first mother tongue and in my distant teenage years I had spent two summers in that same seaside town, drinking the same strong spirit of anise seed as them and eating the same veggies cooked with olive oil. Based on all of that one could -unconvincingly- argue that the show was made in my Hole... but it wasn't. It had been made in a dedicated digital utopia where nobody lived, which delusional first world spectators were pushed to believe that it existed.

"Well, it could have been made where I come from but it was not, I'm afraid. You see the *beau* with his guitar and the *belle* half-naked watching the sunrise on the beach after a night of *débaucherie*... I know that particular beach and I would strongly advise against emulating these youngsters if you ever went there with someone. A heterogenous army of frustrated love-haters would appear before you had any chance of finishing your first glass of wine, let alone go for the first kiss and they would first rape the girl and then you. Or maybe in the reverse order, but rape they would, on account of whatever worldview and excuses they can invent for the police later. With a little bit of luck, the police would in turn also rape you two, and in their case I couldn't guarantee in what order."

What to think of a World where the main *engine of history* has become the sale of illusions? Was it necessary to cross any river to fall on the same digital utopias on the other bank? In the following months, the *eldoradoless* Mexico went on to shape me from entrepreneur to observer and then to interpreter, of the monolinguistic variety who just tries to interpret and make sense of the surroundings. And when the carpenter shop of my semi-chic neighborhood turned into a *gelatteria* catering to hipster digital nomads, I told myself, here comes the awaited signal. If I stay in this city, those idiots are going to end up gentrifying my left arm. So I left for the coast where we had our operations.

# I KNEW YOU WOULD COME BACK

"It's because, you know, there is strong, real strong witchcraft in Comalcalco…He had no way to escape it," said Director. Actually, he wasn't a director or even officially employed; he had already retired from the *national mining company* without ever making it to Director, *Gerente*, *Subgerente* or anything of that sort. And probably that frustration was why he was insisting on everyone calling him *El Director*, as if a title could stick to that oily snakeskin of his.

He may not have made it to any significant echelon of the company before retiring but he had more street cred than the last CEO. You know, that heavyset guy with hidden bank accounts in Singapore that the president claimed was an honest civil servant. My Director had more street cred because his bank accounts, as Mexican as himself, were rightly *not hidden,* just like the cuts he was getting on different deals.

We were not close enough for that kind of statements, but he's supposed to have said "I get my cuts and yes, my dear, they are fat cuts, because I deserve them after a whole career of being on first name terms with the whole freaking misery of the world, plain and simple. Taking into consideration just the *succession of hells* I went through between the State of Tabasco and the State of Campeche, looking at the money I won and the money I lost, so far I have lived five different lives. And I have outlived myself in five different lives, *cabrones*. And I'm not even talking about my time in the glorious State of Veracruz, so duck off."

Some in the company, former colleagues turned rivals or newly minted enemies, told me that Director had compiled an extensive collection of tapes. This ghost archive of many legends allegedly featured both past and present directors of the company, caught in compromising situations with a variety of youthful and attractive companions, completely unclothed and in all manner of contorted positions. My take is, this must be nothing more than jealousy and malicious gossip because in all honesty, having physically met a few of these individuals as potential clients of our services, I just struggle to believe such stories for *purely physical* reasons. It's difficult to imagine these self-important scoundrels of mostly imposing circumference mustering the physical dexterity required to perform any acrobatic exploits. At least beyond the familiar territory of fiscal maneuvers and financial acrobatics, which they seamlessly performed for their own benefit.

In my eyes Director was that very guy who embodied the destiny shredder, the *triturador de destinos* that was Tabasco, the State where I had moved. To qualify him as a disgusting brasshole was a serious understatement: his massive debt collector's body was the kind that oozed corruption, unwelcome bodily fluids and street *tacos de chicharrón* of the soggiest type. And him being the guy who had invented true toxic masculinity way before it was a thing, a guy of questionable intellect, I hadn't expected him to go for such a deep personal dive into magical realism during an unnecessarily dangerous night ride we had together, the two of us and one of his mistresses, from *the city of three lies* to Campeche. And yet...

"I was on a worksite close to Comalcalco at the time. We were in our early twenties with my buddy, it was our second posting in the company. It was a carefree period of alcohol, money and love, all sloshing around in explosive mixtures in our lives. So many fiestas, so many girls -excuse me for my straight talk, *mi amor*- and so many adventures. Sheet was bound to happen at some point. It's just human nature, isn't it..."

Director's presence beside me was far from reassuring in that car on that night, and his endless stream of sleazy stories only added to my discomfort. But, in the end, work is work, and I knew I had to maintain a cordial relationship with the guy. It wasn't about liking him, it was a simple matter of practicality because in that particular environment, dealing with unavoidable cuts and middlemen was simply part of the job, an unspoken rule that everyone had to accept, so I kept listening…

"My buddy was not as careful as I was with precautions one should take with the girls. I was always protecting myself but he ended up getting a girl pregnant. Of all places in ducking Comalcalco. Bad luck, not Tampico, not Reynosa, or Poza Rica…of all places in Comalcalco it had to be, the epicenter of witchcraft in this region, for Christ's sake. And as soon as she told him that he was pregnant, he went to see his boss and asked for another posting. As if one could escape Comalcalco that easily. As if one wouldn't be chased and persecuted by Comalcalco for the rest of one's existence, for the rest of time."

The road to Campeche was as dark and ominous as any Mexican countryside road gets at night and that sinuous road through the lush jungle, insufficiently illuminated with our headlights, with Comalcalco gradually receding in the rearview mirror of our journey, brought again memories of Cavafis and Ithaca to me. Pretty certain, unjustifiably and unrightfully certain but nevertheless quite certain that Director and his mistress wouldn't have heard of Cavafis, I murmured only to myself, *wise as you will have become, so full of experience, you'll have understood by then what these Comalcalco: mean.*

"In the weeks following his departure, my friend started to feel sick and his balls, sorry *mi amor*, started to swell. It was gradual but constant and, as he was saying, they just kept swelling and swelling. *Se le hinchaban, y se le hinchaban, y se le hinchaban, y no paraban…*"

Meanwhile I was thinking, "that swelling has a name, man, it's called an STD, nothing to do with witchcraft" but I just didn't want to interrupt the social anthropology experiment in progress.

"First, he went to see a doctor, took some pills, to no avail. Then another doctor, more pills, to even less avail. Then, a few weeks later, when he was so swollen that he could only walk like a duck, that he couldn't get his feet one next to the other, he went to see another doctor from the *company,* one of them old dogs who have been everywhere and seen everything within the company. The doctor, upon the initial examination, stood up and asked the nurse to leave him alone with my buddy who was sitting still and waiting for the verdict. He then leaned close to his ears, put a fatherly hand on his shoulder and fired away, in a barely audible voice, the fateful question: son, tell me the truth, have you been to Comalcalco before coming here?"

"As most truthful answers come from the eyes rather than the mouth, the doctor didn't wait for him to utter a single word or for the uncomfortable silence to dissipate. He could see that after hearing the initial question my buddy had a lump the size of his bloated balls in the throat. Kindly but in a firm, fatherly demeanor, he followed up with the next stab, with the cold determination of a torero for whom the elegance of the *estocada* counts more than the efficiency of the blow: am I *smelling* that in Comalcalco you got a poor girl pregnant and then decided not to fulfil your manly duties?

"With that question, my buddy's eyes also swelled to the size of his balls, as he could feel the juggernaut of a verdict coming his way. Not the medical verdict he had been expecting but the *existential* verdict. By the end when the fateful diagnostic came to send shivers down my buddy's nonexistent spine, the fatherly hand of the doctor-priest on his shoulder was weighing a ton or two. Maybe ten, he couldn't say anymore: "There is nothing, absolutely nothing that modern medicine can do for you, son, you now belong to Comalcalco, because of your fertilization…you have to man up, go back and live there. The girl is waiting for the father of her child…"

"Shaken as he was by the verdict, he would still not man up and own his mistake and stayed a few more weeks up North in his posting, hoping to wake up from that nightmare one morning, back to normal with human-sized balls. Finally, one morning, in sheer desperation now with watermelons between his legs, unable to get out of the bed, with his last force he called his closest *compañero* who threw him on the back of one of the old pick-ups of the company. The guy then put his cleaning lady next to him in the capacity of an improvised nurse and started the long journey from Reynosa."

"In the shade of the makeshift tarpaulin that they had stretched out at the back of the pick-up, the lady kept wiping my delirious buddy's forehead with a wet towel, but the fever would just not relent. They then stopped at a roadside shop to put some ice into the water bucket where she was wetting her towel. And despite that his temperature was not going down, she decided, somewhere about Tampico, to wipe not only his forehead but also his balls with the wet towel. Alas this was also in vain; his fever wouldn't break. There is just nothing you can do against Comalcalco witchcraft, nothing."

"But as they arrived at Minatitlán at sunrise after a sleepless night on the bumpy road, my buddy finally opened his eyes for the first time since Reynosa. He couldn't have known his whereabouts, as he was lying in the truck bed, with the bedsides and the tailgate blocking his view, but he could feel that they were getting close to Comalcalco. His fever was receding and by the time they were in Cárdenas, his balls had seriously reduced in size such that he could, for the first time, move himself into an upright position."

"As the pick-up reached the church of San Isidro in the center of Comalcalco, now as a perfectly fit man, he didn't even lower the tailgate of the pick-up truck and he jumped over it, to find himself face to face with his wife of today, their month-old baby boy in her arms, looking at him from the sidewalk."

"I knew you would come back", she said, "you just had to realize that you belong here. But I knew you would come back."

# AIM WELL, MUCHACHOS, AIM RIGHT HERE

In the comics and westerns of our childhood, Mexico was the place to go after a last bank job, to any self-respecting American bandit looking for a tranquil retirement of tequilas and sunsets. Not really a place for starting a company from scratch and making decent bucks in an honest way, as I was finding out more and more through my entrepreneurial struggles and outstanding payments from clients who never answered the phone or whose grandmother died for the fourth time. Nor for building an empire, as poor Maximilian I of Mexico had found out during the short-lived imperial adventure of the country. For a real quick introduction, Maximilian was the kind of tragic figure who might have stepped out of a Shakespearean play, to wear a Mexican crown that didn't quite fit, after having been lured across the Atlantic by promises of glory whispered by European monarchs and the desperate pleas of Mexican conservatives.

"What do you think you are doing, guns in hand, in a country that isn't yours, surrounded by people who don't speak your language?" This simple question that carries the weight of centuries.. an outrageous number of people should have faced it at some point in their lives, from self-proclaimed honorable crusaders to outright despicable marauders. Of course most were never asked this question. Of course, even fewer possessed either the intellectual wherewithal to ponder its meaning or the moral clarity to reflect on it, until one day when history *demands* introspection. Often on the wrong side of a gun barrel.

In Maximilian's case, though, he was both asked the question and had the *bagage culturel* to reflect on its significance. Not that these points -nor the fact that his own hands probably hadn't touched many guns or at least spilled any blood- would change anything in the outcome. There can be a semblance of honor in fighting other people's wars but he found himself *not even fighting* other people's wars, as Merc would say. Fate tripped him up, would be my take on the matter.

Maybe Maximilian genuinely trusted Napoleon III who needed a client state in the Americas with a corresponding puppet at its head. Maybe it was a simple ego matter for the younger brother of Franz Joseph I who had a whole empire to himself. Where we come from, it has always been legitimate and customary for the ruler to kill all his younger brothers in order to preserve the integrity of the Empire, which, one could be forgiven to think, is a bit ducking extreme an interpretation of *primogeniture*. So, in comparison, our Maximilian at least had the chance to chase a separate imperial existence, as his older brother magnanimously *let him alive*. An enlightened guy he was, that Franz Joseph I...

Trust or ego, a bad idea it was in any case, to be parachuted as a foreign emperor to Mexico. A bad guy to trust he must have been, that Napoleon III guy, and not just because Hugo didn't like him. I for my part wouldn't trust my skin to a French ex-President-then-Emperor with a German accent who seemed not to have belonged anywhere after a wandering childhood, but then again, to each their own...and their down.

Rare are children who bear an imposing name with decency. Grandchildren seem to fare better, as both reason and happiness tend to skip one generation. I'm still cogitating on a fair verdict for the *nephew* that Nap the third was, as a nephew is some sort of bastard construct between a son and a grandson.

I like to imagine that after arriving to Mexico, Maximilian, now *Maximiliano*, was murmuring to himself, a good century and a half before me, *what a fresh feeling after my lost years living in Europe*, on that cursed continent where you must continuously justify your existence, your very existence, why you breathe. I like to imagine him believing in the possibility of robust and rewarding fresh starts, like many of us who crossed the Ocean, before and after him. I like to imagine him delusional enough to believe in it, eyes wide open and brain on standby.

Regardless of what Maximiliano may have believed, once the American Civil War ended and Uncle Sam was able to take a breather to look at what was happening down South, the *wider conjuncture* became rather unfavorable to monarchical pipe dreams of the transatlantic sort. I daresay Maximiliano was, way before Porfirio Diaz, the first Mexican head of state with the legitimacy to say: *Pobre México, tan lejos de Dios y tan cerca de Estados Unidos,* poor Mexico, so far away from God and so close the United States. And what does count is the *legitimacy*, not the authorship of the sentence -on which there are valid doubts as Porfirio Diaz was anything but an accomplished aphorist- because it was Maximiliano who would feel the consequences in his flesh. Feeling the consequences in one's own flesh indisputably constitutes the ultimate proof of legitimacy for one's statements.

Anyway, the conjuncture, I was saying, made Nap the third pull out of Mexico and pull the plug on Maximiliano, slowly but surely, cleaning the slate of state memory from the blood shed during the Second French Intervention in Mexico, including the legendary Battle of Camarone. A head of state, a *functional* one, the unwritten rule states, shall always *show* respect to spilled blood but never genuinely *feel* that respect. And Nap' the third was one of them *functional* brassholes. Furthermore, *that* particular blood spilled in Camarone was mostly not French anyways, it spilled from the veins of kids without past whose precise raison d'être was *not to be,* as the obedient and grateful subjects of *legio patria nostra* that they were.

Maximiliano met his Waterloo in the nondescript countryside by Querétaro where the republican forces caught him. Before the verdict of historians to come, Benito Juárez had already recognized the fellow liberal and humanist in his rival: under other circumstances, Maximiliano was the kind of guy Benito would happily sit down with to have some *aguardiente* and shoot the breeze. But, liked as he might have the man, Benito had to kill the parachuted monarch. And it was the giant Hugo, not that functional head of state Nap the third, who sent a last-minute appeal to his fellow liberals in Mexico pleading, to no avail, to spare Maximilian's life.

According to many accounts, while the firing squad was taking its position, Maximiliano went to give a gold coin bearing his effigy to each of the soldiers, then showed his chest and said, "aim well, muchachos, aim here". The squad commander looked hesitant and bewildered, so Maximiliano went to reassure him that a soldier's duty was to obey his orders. Taking his position, he showed his chest again and made his short last speech, wishing - in vain, as we now all know - that his blood would be the last to be spilled in that unhappy country.

In deference to his noble equanimity facing death, I like to imagine that in his short three Mexican years the thought crossed his mind, every now and then, that he could be buried in Mexico if he died there but that it didn't mean he could *belong enough to live there*. "I'm neither going to leave my men behind, nor shave my beard to avoid recognition in case they catch me. I will go down with dignity", Maximiliano is supposed to have answered to a Prussian officer of his men who, conscious that problems that cannot be solved with money can be solved with more money, wanted to bribe the Emperor's guardians out of his captivity and exfil him back to Europe. In the end, they didn't bury him there, but they honored his remains and sent them back to his native Austria.

Those honorable Mexicans had fought *for* their independence, not *against* a man, whose dignity they respected from beyond the grave, despite the unavoidable torments of a nascent nation. Roughly within ten years, on the other side of the pond, before The Hole came to life, in the long-standing and sophisticated Empire that a bunch of idiots wished eternal, they suicided the Emperor who had founded my French high school.

Had they barely suicided his body by cutting both his wrists, I wouldn't be honoring his memory here. Before suiciding him, they had to assail his dignity by having the court's official photographer come take his last known picture alive, in captivity, at some point during the four days between his dethroning and his "suicide".

Emperor was a man of the West with his roots in the East, who composed traditional and Western music, played several instruments to perfection, each note resonating with a discipline that spoke of years of dedication. His Empire sprawled across vast and varied lands, a patchwork of cultures, tongues, and histories stitched together under his reign. Millions called him their sovereign, from peasants tilling the earth in remote villages to merchants bustling in grand, labyrinthine cities. His power was immense, yet his greatest wish was not to rule over vast territories or command large armies; it was to be a humble shopkeeper, someone who would pull down the shutters at sunset, walking home to the warmth of his family with the evening call, his heart content with the simple rituals of daily life.

He was a man of imposing physical presence, built like a fortress, who found joy in testing his strength against professional wrestlers. They say he ate forty eggs and a kilo of pastrami in one sitting, I'm willing to excuse a little hyperbole. But none of this strength, none of this cultivated talent, could protect him from the final act of humiliation captured in that last, bitter photograph.

In the image, he sits in a battered chair, dressed in mismatched clothes that hang awkwardly on his imposing frame, far removed from the regal attire that once marked his status. His proud shoulders now bear the weight of mockery, as two half-pint *yavshaks,* whose mustaches have *barely started to perspire*, stand on either side of him. Their mere existence is a farce, their every gesture dripping with the arrogance of boys playing with power. Each rests an elbow on Emperor's shoulders, as if such pettiness would break his spirit. His eyes, sharp and burning with fury, cut through the lens, defying the mockery that surrounds him. It's a look that refuses to beg, that holds a silent contempt for his captors and the indignities they heap upon him. Even in the depths of degradation, the man within the ruined shell refuses to yield but the imbeciles keep their pose as though Emperor were no more than a defeated beast they had dragged back from the hunt.

I burnt through three dictionaries sideways trying to capture the precise posture of these two despicable sauceboxes with their smirking faces and infuriatingly casual slouches. Words like *insolent*, *impertinent*, and *fresh* seemed to barely skim the surface. *Churlish* and *high-handed* felt closer, hinting at the blend of crude arrogance and condescension they exuded, but even these lacked the strength I was searching for. My mind cycled through a litany of less printable concepts, of unholy combinations of profanity and invective but still, nothing seemed to fully pin them down. It was as if language itself recoiled from their particular brand of smugness, leaving me floundering in frustration, grasping at adjectives that slipped through my fingers like smoke. I am sure they even took the liberty of *speaking in first name terms* with the Emperor...*ces ordures l'ont tutoyé*, you can see it on their faces.

*Thus goes the glory of the world...* they suicided the Emperor and he was forgotten, as was and is and will be customary for fallen emperors. For no crown, my dears, no matter how resplendent, can shield a man from the cold indifference of the ages. The world moved on, as it always does, leaving behind only the faintest traces of those who once wielded power, now reduced to nothing more than footnotes in dusty annals. Forgotten not just in memory, but in the very fabric of history, with his deeds and failures dissolved into the fog of time. And this, too, was a custom as old as the Empire itself: the swift obliteration of those who fall, the erasure of their names from the scrolls of glory.

"May the great-grandchildren of these garbage bags one day acquire some crumbs of humanity from my beloved Mexicans", my inner voice said, boiling, looking at that picture.

# THE CAPITAL OF THE WORLD

A genuinely moving idea does, and not only *does* but most importantly *must*, transcend the mediocrity of whoever expressed it first. It must also go beyond the unavoidable hypocrisy that often clings to said idea when the originator is a politician. Ideas, when they are truly *weighty*, are not bound by the limitations of the individual mind that first brought them into being; they grow beyond their creators, taking root in the hearts of others, evolving, and resonating long after the flawed hands that first shaped them are gone.

"America lives in the heart of every man who wishes to find a region where he will be free to work out his destiny as he chooses.", said a former American president not worthy of note. When I first read the sentence, I had been working out my destiny as I had chosen for many years but my choices, shall we say, were not consistently appropriate.

I had been working my brass off in Mexico, pouring every ounce of energy into ventures that promised much but delivered little. The returns were moderate at best, the promises of clients as unreliable as the ticking of an old clock, with unpaid bills stacking up like dust on my desk and dodgy stories from clients accumulating beyond the point of being tenable. There's only so much one can endure the quiet erosion of their efforts without the comforting balm of results to show for their efforts, it's just a human need. People are not made to toil endlessly, like mules in a field, only to be met with empty hands at the end of the day.

This is, then, what made me move on, at least I would like to think. Not simply the disappointment in my present but the lack of faith in any variant of the possible *local futures*, which lead to a suffocating death of purpose. Without the satisfaction of seeing something take shape from my sweat, without the clear, tangible evidence that the hours spent at the grindstone have yielded something of value, my mind started to drift, unmoored in a sea of its own exertions. And so, I moved on, driven by the need for something more than the promise of work without reward, in search of the elusive confirmation that effort, at least in the right place, can still yield results worth having.

The other reason for leaving, a bit of an excuse, was that Mexicans are among the loveliest of all people I have met and so much kind company doesn't help to prepare you for the future... because the future will *by definition* be tough. Although I qualify it as an excuse, that one had more than some truth to it: in Mexico I found again the very same kindness and goodwill of my Congolese. They have the good-natured, conflict-avoiding civil way of co-existing that continued to impress me in that city of twenty something million people where you rarely hear someone raise their voice or honk in a traffic jam. But this also had only part of the truth.

The truth of the departure lay in the *albures,* these typically Mexican wordplays consisting of all kinds of innuendos and beyond. When I had finally reached a serious level in Mexican slang and an overall commendable integration in that country, *albures* helped me realize why I had left all my previous countries: I did not have enough stamina and doggedness to master the remaining *five percent* of adaptation that can make up *all* the difference.

Beyond the fundamentals of the art, that any self-respecting Hispanic can pick up quickly, the endeavor to *perfect* one's albures is just one terrifying story of diminishing returns on investment of effort and learning. The ducking spectrum of required learning covers slang, history, cooking, intercourse, politics and *whatnot*, all of that for that ducking final five percent of integration.

And yes, one might argue that many Mexicans themselves don't have such a good level of *albures* but given that such a level *did exist on the market,* my legitimate endeavor was to reach it. And from where I started, it was almost impossible to get there. The subject was a rounded-off being, again.

By that point in my life, I had already spent an unhealthy amount of time obsessively pondering how many identities one could *shed* in a given life, with a fully appropriated linguistic component. The conclusion I had reached was without appeal: one should, at least *I* should not dream to go beyond three, which meant that I had one single bullet left. And with all due respect and love for Mexico, I was not going to use that particular bullet for a language of eternally impenetrable *albures,* which was a confession that Mexico was *beyond me.*

That confession was a different return to an old subject. Brazil was not for beginners and Mexico was beyond me.

So, one thing leading to the other, first my professional life joyfully sabotaged my personal life, then my personal life pushed me to go up North... In the process, I came to judge that being reluctant to change *continents* for any reason could somewhat be acceptable. However, the very day one hesitates to simply change *countries* within the same continent for the sake of a personal story, one has really gotten old, and it would be indefensible. So, after crossing yet another border, that *holy grail of borders* -in the most legal fashion, I should add- I ended up having to reinvent myself in New York where my line of work didn't exist.

I knew it in advance: due to the vicissitudes of a wandering life my arrival in New York was delayed by two decades or at least one and a half, because I had to passably reinvent myself in the meantime. I nearly wrote "I was delayed" instead of "my arrival was delayed" but then revised it, based on the acceptability and legitimacy of different personal evolution scenarios that don't always shoot for the highest star. Yes, I knew it was getting late but given that I had one last emotional and cultural bullet left, I wanted to follow the French maxim that *it's better to have remorse than regrets.*

Leaving aside that I have yet to find a consistent and etymologically valid explanation of the maxim, my preference was to do something suboptimal rather than to not do anything at all. It came down to carrying the burden of not having taken Yogi Berra's fork, having been the victim of an invisible yellow light, amber for the Brits. I was not going to look back on my life and say to myself at dusk, "I could've gone to the US and I haven't done it". And as for the choice of the city in the US, I had a moral duty to choose the *current capital of the World* and nothing less, because two centuries ago an overzealous Frenchman with a Corsican accent had said of my native city that if the World was a country, she would be its capital. So, I ended up in New York, eyes aglow and expectations high…

"There is nothing to expect from this place", Irish was moaning, in an un-Irishly grumpy mood, "this country was supposed to be Darwinian and meritocratic, and I bought into that story. But now in this city I only see the Darwinian side of it."

Irish was the kind of guy sentenced to eternal returns that he couldn't understand. On my side, I had been in Brooklyn barely two months and with the metric system already a distant memory, we were both sipping on our respective *pints* of ale on a sunny afternoon in Williamsburg. The sun was setting behind the projects in the City, with the closest buildings at eleven hundred and fifty yards across the East River, as my new toy laser rangefinder was showing. Yard-to-meter conversions were easy. Something had to be easy in that new existence.

"It's just quite fitting," continued his tantrum, "that you came in late, that we both came in late, too late to this country, at its sunset as you see. We came late, running after past dreams of *even paster* generations, to *not make* it here in the West. That sun you see there is setting not on these projects but on this civilizational model, the whole freaking place is about to implode and here we came to, how do you always say it again, *chase existence?* I left the sacred land of my ancestors to come and struggle here, coding my life away on Python, day in day out, in this country of ignorant pigs who have neither history nor conscience and you call it *chasing existence?*"

"I descend from people who didn't have a *sacred* land", I replied, "I'm not equipped to understand your burden, just trying to make a living here".

Irish was in a particularly sullen mood since he had lost his main investor, business angel or whatever the duck it's called, the guy who put the money up for his company. His wasn't a company, it was a *start-up,* another distinction I wasn't equipped to understand. He was in *tech*... like myself, I thought with my engineering degrees and a pretty solid mechanical and operational existence in my wake, I am a *technical* person, but there was also a distinction there that I didn't necessarily grasp; I *wasn't* remotely in tech, I was just a technical monkey.

He seemed to have come to a forced reconciliation with the virtues of moderate and *uncannibalistic* capitalism when free money stopped sloshing around or at least stopped coming his way. "Listen up, this country has a major problem, I'm telling you, it is freedom. Or their wicked concept of it. You always need some sort of control, without necessarily being an interventionist. Too much freedom kills freedom, in a way. Where everything is allowed, what can you really achieve as self-surpassing? And what is then your *differentiator?* Life here is just too *unshackled*... When anybody can lie about anything in any way that doesn't need to be credible, seriously, what is my differentiator on the market? How am I to convince my next investor? Everybody puts *passionate about something* in their resumes, in this *lipserviceland* where nobody has any passion."

I felt for the guy, as he was being eaten away by the typical worries of the New Yorker who is afraid of *not having made it*. I observed the syndrome in several fellow New Yorkers in the following years - to me it's all the fault of the first guy who said, "if you make it in New York, you can make it anywhere". What about those who *didn't* make it there, huh? It's already a stress factor that most New Yorkers talk about their city as a living organism, which often exasperates me. "The city is very edgy right now. The city is tired. The city is angry. Etc." It's like they believe its veins hum beneath the asphalt. "The city is alive and plotting," they seem to be saying, as if it has a secret life that whispers in their ears.

OK I get it, if one city will be anthropomorphized, being the capital of the World, New York deserves it more than *anybody* else. But giving it living creature qualities just adds another dimension to the daily life there of fighting a living monster of sorts.

Fighting unexpected monsters seems legitimately to be a compulsory part of coming to try one's luck in the land of opportunities. Many of them monsters we bring with ourselves, Ithaca-style. Some we create on the spot and the Land of the Free has always been fertile ground for the creation of the most original monsters. So, I wasn't taking amiss the legitimacy of the requirement to fight more monsters there, but all sorts of ogres, beasts and brutes had already burdened my way until that point in life.

Therefore, that afternoon in Williamsburg, after the fifth pint, I still had no idea for how much longer I was going to have the necessary drive to keep doing it but I knew clearly that New York was to be the final stop: I might leave that city in a few months, in a few years or get buried there, that's not the point; the point is that there won't be a next set of unknown monsters to fight in bumducknowhere.

"It's useless to write about belonging", opined Irish, some months later, around another table of pints. "Look around you, those who really struggle with belonging don't *belong* to the reading class, your project is a waste of time, forget about it". A cynical curmudgeon he had become in the meantime, and I admired America also for that: it is no mean feat to transform your average happy-go-lucky Irish fellow with some perspectives into your average frustrated French *râleur* complaining about everything, it takes more than just removing the guy's perspectives and investors.

"It's a bit of a pity that you're not writing in the common educational vernacular of our respective childhoods", interjected a Lebanese acquaintance on the same table, while supplementing his pints with occasional shots of tequila. "Writing about a universal subject is clearly more meaningful in English than in French and certainly more reasonable in terms of the audience you can reach but something will always be missing. Any text written in a non-mother-tongue will contain many hidden desperations."

"Anyway", came his conclusion, "duck the idea of writing in French, we all need to kill the father at some point".

# INTO THIN AIR

Disappearing is the ultimate act of unbelonging.

Unless, of course, it is forced disappearing, the kind inflicted by regimes like those of Argentina or Chile in their darkest chapters, when disappearance was weaponized, a brutal erasure of existence. That kind of vanishing is an unspeakable violence, a silence that screams beneath the surface of history. It is a subject that neither my art nor my heart is able to write about.

But disappearing on one's own initiative is the strongest type of decision one can make to cease to belong. It is a severance, a conscious unraveling of the threads that once tied you to a place and its people, a quiet rebellion against the burden of belonging. Such a fierce act of autonomy is the ultimate declaration that one owes the world absolutely duck all: "I'm writing myself out of this narrative, folks, here is my middle finger, take it as a final assertion of self-sovereignty: you ain't having my presence or my participation in this story and I'll continue my life unchained by the gaze of *nuisances* of your ilk."

*Into-thin-air-matters* had become the obsession of a fellow New Yorker who hailed from Tokyo, let's call him Tokyoite so that at least *he* can belong somewhere, unlike his sister. It's a bit unfair to qualify him just as a fellow citizen, the guy moved from professional contact to work partner to my best friend in a stage-burning eight months. I guess he must have had the hidden mission of making me swallow my theory about rounded-off human beings and what I thought was the impossibility of one day having a Japanese *functional congener*. On the shared values side it may have helped that he was giving his seat to elderly people on the subway, which I rarely see happen in this transactional and individualistic society; and on the functional side it didn't hurt that he had gone to an American school and had a cartesian mind. The best of many worlds is what my Tokyoite is, a gem of a guy.

His sister had done *jouhatsu*, disappearing as tens of thousands of Japanese do every year, vanishing into thin air without ceremony, etymologically *evaporating*. She left no note, no trail, only the ghost of her presence lingering in the memories of those she left behind. Perhaps she had started anew in a distant city, or maybe she had simply folded herself into the labyrinthine sprawl of Tokyo, where one could easily dissolve into the teeming anonymity of its neon-lit streets.

"It's a common thing in our society," he explained, his voice heavy with resignation, "and mostly a taboo for families, like suicide." The word hung in the air, sharp and unforgiving. "It is, in its own way, a form of social suicide. And like any suicide you kill part of your family, whether you want it or not." He paused, his gaze fixed on some distant point, as though searching for her shadow in the cracks of the world. "The burden of her leaving us so abruptly lingers," he continued. "The not-knowing, the questions without answers. Did she find peace? Was it freedom she sought, or escape? Or did she simply tire of the weight of belonging?"

In *jouhatsu*, there is no finality, no grave to visit, no last words to hold onto. There is only an absence, a hollow space where a person once stood. Families are left to stitch together their lives around this emptiness, pretending it doesn't exist, because to speak of it would be to acknowledge a kind of death. And in Japan, where harmony and face-saving seem to be prized, in some ways similar to back in The Hole, even the pain of loss must be borne in silence. "We learn to live with ghosts," he said, "In our society, we have to."

Her disappearance had broken something in Tokyoite for they were close and he believed they understood each other. He searched for her, in and outside of Tokyo, used a sleuth, checked out many specialized online forums, to no avail. His sister's determination to vanish was as strong as Japanese privacy laws and his "happy, conventionally happy, traditional Japanese family" had to come to terms with their daughter's decision and respect it. So, after another year of reflection, Tokyoite decided to get as far away as he could from his native city and the vanished sister that he still believed was somewhere in that city, to come to New York. "If I knew for sure that she was in another city, maybe I could have stayed in Japan.", he reasoned, "but having the intuition that she was still in Tokyo and spending my days hoping to bump into her at some subway station was just wearing me down, so I had to leave and go far, far away".

A thought-provoking metric in defining what a *big city* is and how big it really is, would be to know not just how many inhabitants the subject city has, but how many it has had in its whole history, how many people it has *churned out*. Actually, it can be either over the whole duration of the city's existence or the *current churn rate* at some meaningful frequency, say yearly churn rate. If we are to continue the exercise of *anthropomorphizing* New York, or any other city, the yearly churn rate would be the metric with the most street cred, the one showing how destructive, how gluttonous and greedy a city is. A metric of broken souls spat out by a city, in a way. On top of that, if it was permissible or mathematically realizable, for New York I would add some specific metric to track the discrepancy between the expectation at arrival and the outcome at departure: regarding happiness, self-ducktualization, wealth, health, you name it.

Until I met Tokyoite, I was ready to think that New York would take the cake by miles for any *churn rate* metric but after learning about *jouhatsu*-plagued Tokyo, legitimate doubts came to haunt me about the subject. I had nightmares where my brother, as un-Japanese as one can get, was doing *jouhatsu*, but instead of vanishing into the maze-like alleys of Tokyo or the faceless towns of Hokkaido, he would disappear into thin Europe. I saw him in my dreams walking aimlessly through cobblestone streets, his silhouette dissolving into the fog of some foreign city, slipping beyond reach, beyond recognition. There, among centuries-old cathedrals and crowded train stations, he became one of the countless faces lost in the churn of humanity, an apparition in a place that neither knew him nor cared to remember.

It was a strange twist of the cultural narrative, but the underlying sorrow remained universal. The human sorrow, if it is to be human, must be equally penetrable for all of us and I am convinced it is. It creeps in through the same cracks, regardless of where we were born or what tongue we use to scream into the void. Pain doesn't care whether your childhood was filled with the smell of soy and miso or with mezzes and tapas. Loss just wraps itself around you in the same suffocating way, a reminder that beneath our curated identities, we are all equally human, equally breakable.

I had the honor of being the first foreigner Tokyoite ever spoke to about his sister's *jouhatsu* but nevertheless he did it, in an unexpectedly natural way, never doubting that I was going to be able to understand his story and feel his torments in my gut. So, I guess it gives me a definitive idea about where I can stick my *rounded-off human being theory*. Maybe it was the fault of Kerso, the French sailor who unintentionally inculcated in me the impenetrability of the Japanese *Weltanschauung* when he wrote that in Japan they don't let foreigners in the brothels: they think that without speaking the language, the foreigner would not be able to show the necessary respect to the women.

"A human being", Tokyoite reflected when I told him about all of this, my shared sorrows, my *jouhatsu* nightmares about my brother and Kerso's view on Japanese brothels, "a human being is entitled to a geography but also to an absence of geography".

The right to an absence of geography, however, comes at a heavy, heavy cost, is what I learned from him, the Japanese functional congener that I wasn't supposed to have.

# You can't take me with you
# to that harbor

*Polyglotitis* doesn't kill you, but it often makes you slow-minded and sometimes miserable. And it really is a problem, despite the fact that many, who are lucky enough not to have to grapple with *multiple mother tongues*, could consider it a rich people's problem, *un problème de riche.*

When one's thought process is enslaved by several languages that each proudly exhibit their own whims and vagaries, the resulting text leaves some whiffs of confusion in its wake. If the native English speaker who has followed my struggles up to this point has a different opinion despite the nature of my prose, I shall respect it. However, I can't help but observe that many polyglots end up fighting their mother tongue or tongues, and then the successive parasitic languages that build on them, the way one fights an ailment. Sometimes I catch my *unevolved self* wishing I hadn't learned any other language and that I had a virginal, unsoiled mother tongue.

My mind was filled with these kinds of thoughts, during an aggressive process of shedding off my first two mother tongues and embracing, no, not just embracing, *tattooing* inside my stomach the richness, functionality and practical strength of the English language, in the middle of the very New York winter, as Winter as it gets, as New York as it gets, when the phone rang. *Another one of them wearing transatlantic calls…*

Violinist was on the line, after an eternity, with another very respected *uncle* from the workshop. They had gotten my number from my brother, by then the only person in my life with whom I could technically speak Holish. With my brother I normally speak in a combination of our two mother tongues, but he had benevolently accepted, for two years by then, to switch to that *unnatural* English as part of my shedding off process. So, that call, at the re-zero hour, was the very first moment in a very long time that someone was talking to me in my first mother tongue and it made me reel for a second or two.

"Maestro's sister passed away", started Violinist, "she was the one keeping us posted about him. It's been a while and now we have no idea what he's doing there, so once we heard that you now live in the US, we thought you could get his whereabouts and news"

A little thought bubble popped into my mind… "Of course you thought of me to find him coz I live in the United States of America and it's well-known that this country is a three-donkey village of sorts where I just need to shout out his name in the town square and he'll pop up from somewhere, right?"

"If you could locate him, we have put some money together with the others from the shop for a plane ticket, we would like to help him come home…like, come home to die in peace, you know, he hasn't been back since nineteen seventy-two."

Next little thought bubble of mine… "Come *home* to die? The guy hasn't been there for half a century, and you call it home? Are you sure *he* calls it home?"

"He taught us so much, you know", continued the other *uncle* "he may be the best hydraulics guy to have ever walked this planet, he's a self-taught high school dropout but he could have invented every single law that Bernoulli invented. When he went to the US, he quickly ended up in the Coast Guard, responsible for maintenance programs, despite his lack of degrees, despite being a foreigner. Maestro is a genius, you know, we all owe him so much from our young years, we don't want to let him die alone there. Last we heard was that he had been made redundant and was at home, repairing fridges and washing machines, but this was already quite some time ago."

If this story is true… "Who the duck repairs fridges and washing machines today in our kind of first world, for duck's sake?"

Absurd as the mission was, I couldn't really refuse. Violinist is my childhood, the shop is what made me who I am and most importantly, these guys are legacies from Dad, I can't decline anything they ask for, within or beyond reason. What was it to track down someone in this century anyway, in the land of the free where everyone is tracked online, it would be a matter of a few days to find him and then I would go see him physically, why not.

Memories of The Buenos Aires Quintet come to revisit me, that formative book from the extraordinary, illustrious and mind-opening Manuel Vázquez Montalbán, may he rest in eternal peace. El *tío de América*, that *uncle from the Americas who used to exist in every single Spanish family* is no concept for our nation *who* has descended from non-sailors; we did not have a *tío de América* who would come back from across the pond, shrouded in immense riches and riveting stories. In a reversal of roles, fate has put me in a succession of planes instead of boats and the *uncles* have remained behind, but Uncles of the Old World are still uncles whose extraordinary stories one must respect and try to be part of, if one is given the opportunity.

Maestro was one of them historical anomalies. His parents were among the few human *crumbs* that had stayed behind after the genocide, some *remnants of the sword*, once the idiots had invented the nation-state. The only positive thing in that nation-state was that, if a digression on linguistics is allowed, the nation-state somewhat contributed to reducing the *visible symptoms of polyglotitis* by reducing the number of *involuntary polyglots* on whom the condition had been imposed by the imperial circumstances. Ethnolinguistic self-betrayals and imposed homogenizations culled a lot of people who had several languages playing musical chairs in their brain and many left without waiting for years like Maestro.

"He left, for reasons that we never fully understood, after the second coup", said Violinist on another occasion, when I had called him to report on the progress, as if that particularly stale information would help me understand where in the US he could be. "The second coup, you were not born, was in seventy-one", he continued, which I knew about since my parents' generation had their calendar punctuated by one coup per decade and they spoke a lot about it at home. "And Maestro left a year later but one should not try to look for any causality in that: the coups were internal affairs of the nation-state by then, so people like us and Maestro were normally not concerned in any meaningful way, being social, human and political non-entities in the *structurally lost battle* after the genocide."

To Violinist, descendent of other human crumbs, it came naturally to talk about *structurally lost battles*. To my family too, obviously, conceptually we grew up with it, even if until that moment I hadn't heard such a captivating way to formulate it. My biggest structurally lost battle of that time was the damned shedding process and I was waking up in sweats in the tendrils of Trafalgar, wondering if I were to *also* foot the linguistic bill for battles that *others* had lost two centuries ago.

My family has already been footing the bill for a revolution that others lost -yes, you can lose a revolution as much as a war- so am I, on top of that, also supposed to be accountable for the wind that was blowing from a direction unfavorable to the French and the Spanish armadas on that fateful day off cape Trafalgar? Oh, duck me, modern historians have already established that the wind direction had a minimal effect if any on the outcome, but regardless, why am I to re-change my mother tongue again and become *translingual*?

Anyhow, Maestro, I was saying, left after the second coup and came to the US. Thereafter, he either wanted to avoid being found by a not-yet-born *niece from America* like myself or, much more probably, he wanted to get better integrated and he started to go by an English-sounding modification of his *second,* Christian name. With no known family members left back *home* whom we could question, I could never have guessed that. In fact it's only after finding him online that I found out he was using his second name's anglicized version. Strange country, the US, where you can decide what your name can be.

After having waded through endless online garbage and fruitless phone calls to rightfully suspicious members of the various uniformed populations, I finally talked to a retired Coast Guard captain. He was the example *par excellence* of the decent, honest man serving with a sense of duty towards his men beyond their active years and took my story upon himself and tracked Maestro down to a no-name city on the East Coast thanks to a vets organization. No-name city where I ended up the very first weekend with a rental car and my own sense of duty towards the *uncles.*

Arriving at the address, I was greeted by a somewhat small version of the archetypal American one-family house in a small garden. As nobody answered the bell, I surprised myself by taking the liberty of heading towards a mellow grinding noise that was coming from the backyard. I didn't know the local gun ownership rate, but I was convinced deep down that someone called Maestro should not have become *integrated enough* in this country to put a bullet in the head of the first stranger walking on his "private property". There he was around the corner, all white hair and thick glasses, deburring the end of a quarter inch stainless steel pipe, with several carcasses of fridges and washing machines lying in the yard.

I didn't really need to ask for anything to confirm his identity, but formalities are formalities. The introductory question I asked in English, as a matter of good citizenship among integrated aliens, a soft sort of lead-in. Then I switched to the one common mother tongue we had, forgetting for a moment that he hadn't ever spoken it with his mother. "Violinist and the others from the shop sent me here to find you, Sir, they're worried about you as they haven't had any news since your sister passed away".

Maestro gently posed the grinder on the workbench and stood there in silence for a while. He looked more forlorn than the most disemboweled one of the fridge carcasses behind him while gathering the words and the power needed to mumble the beginning of an answer. Then, with intonations from past centuries and the pangs of a rebirth, he uttered his first and only sentence of that language after half a century, before kindly but firmly showing me the way out: "I do thank you for your efforts, young lady, but *you can't take me with you to that harbor*".

I am pretty sure these sophistications are lost forever by now, but before the gradual cultural genocide of the last two decades, anyone who was anyone used to know these lines by the *poet,* by The Hole's Neruda, who had ended up resting in the eternal colds of a foreign capital, without ever making it back to *any village* of his country, under any sycamore as was his wish.

*I'm very tired, don't wait for me, Captain, somebody else should keep the logbook. That blue harbor with domes and sycamores, you can't take me with you to that harbor.*

Where had I read the story of those anthropologists, or linguists, who were rushing to a village lost in Amazonia to record the last speaker of an indigenous language? The old lady had died the night before they made it to the village. She was literally the last of her tribe.

I called the shop after getting back to New York and told Violinist that Maestro wanted to die here, in the US, where he had made his life. That we can't *take him* to that harbor, make him *go up that harbor, jump ship* at that harbor, whatever an acceptable translation would be.

"Come back home, my girl", Violinist said, "come back home, you must be tired after all these years of chasing ghosts."

Back home was the one harbor where nobody was supposed to be able to take me back to, not even Violinist. And yet...

# THE *IKONA*, STATELESS BY BIRTH

If the uncles who return from the Americas are no longer the legendary anti-heroes full of stories and riches who they were once upon a time, then it becomes just another continent, nothing to write home about.

Consequently, the Americas were lost for humanity when *the uncle from the Americas who used to exist in every single Spanish family* became conceptually outdated. And regarding my little person, no abundance of adventure was waiting for me further West. Nature hadn't, alas, put a next continent offering that much opportunity and illusion in the middle of the Pacific, something like the next Americas, the *other* Americas. In my mind it's the end of that *inspiring unchartedness* that killed the Americas, as the realization kills any dream. Instead of passionate tangos with the uncharted, recurrent battles with *chartedness* have become the norm, which made us humans *lose our luster* by rendering the adventure obsolete.

If there had been another continent in the West, let's assume a continent called the Pizarras for the guy who *discovered* the Pacific, would I have continued the voyage, despite the lurking exhaustion? Despite the final realization and personal conviction that a large majority of people who try to really belong somewhere new are doomed to fail and that I haven't been able to become the exception that I hoped to be… would I have tried to continue? These by now are meaningless speculations, since no next continent was invented.

There was nowhere to jump to and the old continent was doing what it could to call me back.

It was indeed time to go back to The Hole or somewhere thereabout, despite abhorring that cliché of homecoming, after the long dance with the phantom pain of what that country had become for me. The kind of *Weltschmerz* that a phantom country can give you had ended up becoming a *phantom childhood pain* disconnected from every geography.

"Those good people mounted those beautiful horses and left for good", was etched into our collective memory by one of the best writers to ever come out of The Hole. I couldn't claim to know neither the specific people nor even the generation he was writing about, but I have met my decent share of *leavers* to understand that in many places, among which The Hole, it is a constant for good people to leave for good. If I ended up going back, would it mean that I haven't been good enough to leave for good?

Many of those who left took with them a whole cultural heritage of sophistication that was handed down through generations that I -should I return- would neither be able to find nor be witnessing anyone else restoring: in most cultural contexts loss is irreversible. The death of *any* human being is somewhat the death of a species in and of itself but seen from a higher level, it's only human that one mostly feels the pain of one's own species. And I do feel the pain resulting from the loss of my species' convoluted refinements that has by now been lost and will keep being lost under the masses and the *ignorantization*. The winners will keep re-writing History, even if the winners won by nothing but the sheer force of their numbers. One should reformulate this a bit more fairly, as I don't like that very American perspective of winners and losers so I shall call them the *stayers*, as they stayed, *thanks to the sheer force of their numbers.*

"A reasonable and realistic person should find a different objective, something less romantic, more meaningful, less cliché and more *productive for future generations* than aspiring to become the last of *a* species, the last of *something*", recommended my brother, the ultimate realistic and reasonable North Star that I am blessed to have. If you descend from two empires, it sounds crudely, childishly, better said, *un-adultishly* unsophisticated to aim for that cheap and corny Hollywood sentence *they don't make'em like her anymore.* And it's a sentence that I have already put into a dog's brass in a previous chapter about Terror.

My species has come so far and has contributed as much as it could for *future generations.* I do not expect any *independent third-party* approval of my final decision to spend what is left of my time on Earth back on a little island somewhere within the Empire, *à la recherche du temps perdu,* in search of lost time. I also do not expect any independent third-party approval of the validity and the not-so-apparent originality of this same decision to *return to the source* because the conclusion may be similar to what many other people have reached but it is the path-dependency, taken to the extreme, of this very conclusion that makes it noble. "What the duck am I doing here?" snuck into my life as the silent question of every morning of the last two decades over four continents to earn that legitimacy of giving the middle finger to them independent third-party legitimizations.

*Tout le malheur des hommes vient d'une seule chose, qui est de ne savoir pas demeurer en repos dans une chambre…* all of humanity's problems stem from man's inability to sit quietly in a room alone. Our French teacher Madame Nowaczyk had us read this well-known sentence by Pascal when we were eleven and I will not claim I had understood it then. Proof again, if it were needed, that one can read anything but understand only what one's experience allows.

"In final analysis, life isn't about what you are escaping from nor what are you hoping to find", suggested my brother, "it's about what is next when you realize that you haven't found *it?*".

This was one of the last conclusions he had after much drama about choosing his own destination, the island closest to his own heart, which ended up being re-defined as *closest to The Hole*. Two people unable to tear themselves away from a Hole, isn't it a bit too much for a family of four? But that very island he needed, this same sea, these same rocks, these same types of algae under the surface. The same groupers and snappers facing the same extinction as us... he needed them, to reduce the phantom childhood pain.

At first, he was just bickering about Northern European food and saying, "I want to go back to the Med, on one of those islands with whitewashed houses, where they cook real food, stuff that our grandma would identify as *fit for human consumption*". I idiotically recommended that he learns to *cook* Mediterranean style but of course this was beside the point.

Wary of getting too close too fast, he first wanted to look for an acceptable alternative solution and started scouting on the Western Med. One day he rented a sailboat on a Spanish island and he moored her to a rock that looked solid i.e. volcanic but that turned out to be sedimentary.

That my brother ain't no geologist is a fact but it's also a fact that those rocks are much more solid on our side of the Med. Or at least we can much better recognize the rocks of our childhood and their vulnerabilities... That sedimentary piece of sheet in Spain broke free a few hours after he moored because of a sideways gust loading on the boat, while my brother was having his *apéro*. And that sedimentary rock, unsolid under tension, was thankfully the end of his Western experiments and the beginning of the resignation to a move much, but much closer to the source.

By that point *we*, I mean the various versions of myself in my plural form, had come to terms with *our* quest for belonging having turned into a matter of ping pong between two sides of the Ocean... and I was willing, at least some of my versions were willing, to accept another ping pong existence of much smaller scale, between The

Hole of Violinist and one of them islands where fellow descendants of a same Empire sing the same songs and eat the same food. With the ping pong being, needless to say, solidly anchored to the island side, with the optionality to escape anything nefarious from the other side. Never forget to secure the optionality of escape, especially from a Hole...

The stone, our elders had said, is heavy at its own place, where it belongs. The weight of a thing, its meaning, its truth, is tied to the land and water it comes from; displaced, it loses its gravity and its purpose. So we moved back, drawn by some inevitable ancient tide, closer to the zero-hour of everything. To the same solid rocks by the same sea where I knew which ones to moor my boat on since before I had learned to read. We returned to those same solid rocks by the same sea, the unchanging witness to our lives. My brother, the knot freak with over seventy different ones in his memory, had learned to tie his first knot there long before he had learned to read, and the same rocks were waiting for him.

Dad isn't there anymore in our old orange dinghy, to load my speargun with his steady arms when mine were too short to reach the bands. Now my arms have grown long and strong enough to handle the speargun alone but there's a hollow truth I can't ignore: there's no need to load it anymore. The fish are gone. The vibrant, teeming life that once pulsed beneath the surface has dwindled, reduced to mere ghosts of what they were. In a collective effort of unconsciousness, we have bled the sea dry, leaving behind only memories of abundance and the quiet mourning of empty waters, so there is no real need to load any speargun on our part of the Med.

Speaking of returns, I must confess, with all due apologies to *our* church, that I *slipped my hand beneath the stone* and smuggled my family's ikona into the island. It wasn't an act of defiance, but rather of moral necessity. That ikona, born stateless, carried through storms of history, held the last fragments of who we were before the ground beneath us split open. It survived exile and erasure to come to the apartment where I grew up and now it sits here, in the only place that I can still hope to make feel like home. So, I don't need anyone's permission to keep my ikona close, to grow old with it, to let it remind me of who we were. This ikona doesn't ask for validation. Neither do my acts.

And yet, ikona with us or not, even here, under this familiar sky and next to these familiar olive trees, the salt wind carries whispers of old laments, with a weight that never lifts. Maybe that's what it means to belong to something broken, to keep trying to reattach yourself to a history that no longer exists. Since 1917, we've been clawing at the void, trying to fill it, to rebuild what was shattered. Trying to compensate for 1917. To undo it. To escape it. Just to realize that it's a scar that won't heal.

The truth? We have not been compensating for 1917. We have not been coming to terms with 1917. We have not been moving beyond 1917. We have just been fighting that cursed number. Every day. Every generation. Every soul that tries to live in its direct or indirect aftermath. We have been battling 1917, and not winning.

Some battles are just not meant to be won. Surviving them is good enough.